Kiss Me Katie

JENNIFER REDMILE

Prologue

Katie

There really should be some kind of early warning system that goes off when you wake up on what turns out to be the worst day of your life! I mean, how could my world go from DEFCON FIVE to ONE in the blink of an eye? But then, maybe it was just that my level of naïve stupidity was so high I failed to see the warning signs.

So... the end of my life as I knew it happened on a Wednesday. I had just delivered a message from my English teacher to the office and decided to swing past the music room on my way back to class. My gorgeous boyfriend, Mark Barnes, was the lead singer in an as-yet-undiscovered boyband, and I knew they'd be rehearsing. Okay, so maybe I shouldn't have detoured, but I loved watching him perform.

I reached the music room and hovered outside the open door, surprised by the lack of sound coming from the room. My heart skipped a beat as I caught sight of Mark on the other side of the room. *Damn, he was hot! And he was mine.*

Mark wore my favourite low-riding, faded jeans and a plain white t-shirt moulded to his perfect abs, his baby blue eyes sparkling with mischief as he stood huddled with his buddies, laughing over something on his phone. I totally had to fight the urge to run over, throw myself into his arms, and kiss his luscious lips.

I shivered as memories of making out in his room the previous night flooded in, tingles invading my nether regions. Why hadn't I let him go all the way? He loved me, and I loved him. After almost six months of dating, I should have been ready. So what was the problem? I was nearly seventeen, for God's sake. Most of the girls I knew had lost their V card ages ago.

Then, something one of the guys was saying pulled me from my happiness-bubble-of-memories.

"Holy shit Barnes, this is awesome, man. Having those ginormous puppies to play with has gotta make up for the uglies everywhere else. Hey, does she still not know why everyone calls her *Furby*?"

Mark barked out a laugh and slapped his friend's shoulder. "Nope... doesn't have a clue. Coming up with that name was total genius, if I do say so myself. Fat Ugly Rich Bitch Yuppy. And she still seriously believes I'm into her. God, if it weren't for the fame and fortune her Daddy's gonna bring us, I could get myself a *real* girlfriend. Anyway, she finally offered to ask her dad if he'd listen to our demo last night. I had to bite my tongue to stop myself from saying 'about bloody time.'"

OMG! What were they talking about? My heart now felt like it would jump out of my chest for an entirely different reason. Swallowing down the bile rising in my throat, I grabbed hold of the door frame before my trembling knees gave out. This couldn't be happening. Mark was talking crap about me? But... he said he loved me.

Even though my heart was breaking and my blood was boiling, I forced my reeling brain to process the reality of the situation.

Mark had been using me to get to my famous record-producing father all this time. And I'd never even suspected a thing. No wonder he said he wasn't into PDAs. What he *meant* was that he wasn't into PDAs with *me!* Maybe he should give up on his crappy boyband and try his luck as an actor. The creep was an Academy Award winner in the making.

Unable to hold back the tears pouring down my face, I stepped back out of the doorway. No way I'd give him the satisfaction of seeing me fall apart. I'd dump the jerk at lunchtime, and he'd never even know how he'd stuffed up.

Wait... so what were they *looking at* on his phone? My previously boiling blood turned to ice so fast it made my head spin. Something about *ginormous puppies*?

Oh please, no, he wouldn't...

Surely no one would be that cruel?

Well... only one way to find out! So much for waiting until lunchtime.

Wiping away the tears and sucking in a deep breath, I stormed across the room and snatched the phone out of Mark's hand before he knew what was happening.

Oh. My. God.

I almost vomited as I stared in horror at the video of Mark's hands fondling my breasts, with me whimpering beneath him. Without a word, I threw the phone against the wall as hard as I could, planted my size ten boot into Mark's family jewels, and stalked toward the girls' toilets with my head held high.

I found out later it had taken my best friend Annie over an hour to find me, still crumpled in a heap on the bathroom floor. Unable to make sense of anything I was saying, Annie called my mum and asked her to come pick me up. Of course, Mum was way too busy and sent her assistant, Pamela, to get me. By the time Pamela arrived, I'd lapsed into an almost catatonic state, and all Annie knew was that something had happened with Mark.

And that was the last time I ever set foot inside Northside Grammar School. I'd spent the rest of Year Ten studying online and hiding away from the world. Until the letter came from the Crescendo Academy of Performing Arts, announcing I'd been accepted into the prestigious inner-city boarding school for Years Eleven and Twelve.

This was my chance to start over, and it would be on my terms. No more Katie Simpson, daughter of millionaire record producer Reece Simpson. Meet the new and improved, plain old Katie Sims (at least that took care of the Rich Bitch Yuppie part). Pity the Fat Ugly part couldn't be erased so easily. But hey, this new Katie Sims was heaps tougher than that girl in the video.

No way would *she* ever fall for another hot guy.

What was that old saying?

Fool me once, shame on you. Fool me twice... yeah, let's not go there.

Chapter One

Katie

Oh. *My. God. It was finally happening.* It felt like a lifetime had passed since I'd received my invitation to attend *Crescendo*. After months of wallowing in lockdown, I was beyond ready to step back into the real world. Okay, so maybe it had started as a *self-imposed* lockdown, but had I known how bad being under my mum's watchful eye 24/7 would be, I'd never have even considered it.

By the time the car pulled up in front of Crescendo, I felt like my head would explode from the white noise throbbing in my ears. Okay, so I knew that noise was *technically* caused by my heart racing, and—added to the shaking knees —my reaction *might* be considered slightly over-the-top. But hey—when had my body *ever* listened to reason?

With every emotion I'd ever experienced—not to mention a few new ones—battling for supremacy inside my brain, I read the words engraved into the plaque affixed to the stonework over the entrance doors:

Crescendo

~Academy of Performing Arts~

Oh-my-god-oh-my-god-oh-my-god, I seriously needed to get my act together. I was determined to look cool, calm and collected when I stepped out of the car. So... hysteria, along with squealing and giggling, were *definitely* not on any of my meticulously compiled lists.

Yep, I was one of *those* girls. You know, those who can't function without the required list. I'd spent hours last night compiling the latest ones. *Recommended-Behaviours-For-Appearing-Cool-At-The-New-School* and *How-To-Keep-A-Low-Profile,* to name a few.

Dragging my eyes from the side window, I turned to share a goofy grin with the girl beside me—my best friend, Annie. I grabbed her hand and squeezed, relieved to find hers shaking as much as mine. Good to know I wasn't the only one struggling with normalcy.

"Oh my God, Katie—we're here. Like *really* here," Annie breathed in awe.

Annie and I had been best friends since our first day of kindergarten, our shared love of all things musical forging what had become an unbreakable bond. And now, eleven years later, it had brought us here... together. Years of planning... and dreaming... and wishing, had finally become a reality. Our senior years of high school would be spent in the hallowed halls of *Crescendo!* My chance to start fresh…

A soft chuckle from the front seat reminded me of my dad's presence in the car. "Ummm… girls. Are you planning on going in, or would you prefer to sit and stare at the place all day?"

And… hello, freakout 2.0. The earlier excitement morphed into absolute terror, and suddenly it felt like all the air had been sucked out of the car. Cold sweat trickled down my back just *thinking* about entering that building. No matter how many to-do lists or breathing exercises I'd prepared, it didn't change the fact that I had to walk in there and interact with people.

Did I even remember how to do that?

"Oh God, Dad, I think I'm gonna be sick. Maybe this wasn't such a good idea. What if…?"

"Kathleen Marie Simpson—oops, sorry, *Sims*—don't you dare start with the 'what-ifs' already. You have an amazing musical talent, and it's time for you to share it. And that goes for you, too, Annabel Keats. Get ready to take the world by storm, girls."

My thundering heart slowed as Annie squeezed my hand again. Her contagious grin and head bobbing up and down enthusiastically reminded me to release the breath I hadn't realised I'd been holding.

For the gazillionth time, I thanked my lucky stars for Annie. She was like my own personal little ray of sunshine on a cloudy day, always there to pick me up and put me back together when the world lost its perspective. If only I could carry her around in my pocket…

Right. Time to push all the stupid anxiety back into its box.

Sucking in a deep breath, I smiled at Annie. "Dad's right. Let's do this, girl."

I turned to open the door, hearing her do the same as Dad popped the boot lever.

"Hang on, I'll give you a hand." *No, no, no.* I watched in horror as Dad's door opened, the all too familiar heat flooding my face—*yeah, excessive blushing was another one of those stupid uncontrollable body parts.*

"No, Dad, it's fine." God, did my voice really just come out sounding like I'd been sucking on helium. Jumping out of the car, I waved his emerging body back into his seat. "We've got this."

Damnit, which part of this-is-not-the-first-day-of-kindergarten didn't he get?

Determined to ignore the disappointment on Dad's face, I hurried to help Annie lift our overstuffed suitcases out of the boot and roll them onto the footpath. Then, the guilt over refusing his offer of help wormed its way into my heart, and I rushed back to Dad's window, throwing my arms around his neck. "Thanks for being the best Dad in the world. Tell Mum I'll call her tonight after we're settled in."

Dad kissed my forehead, smiling as we each acknowledged the other's watery eyes. "I love you, sweetie. Try to have fun... but remember, if it gets too hard, I'm only a call away."

"I love you too. Now go before I start blubbering and make a complete idiot of myself."

Dad chuckled and shook his head. "Ditto."

"Bye, Mr. Simpson. Thanks for the ride," Annie called, and Dad stuck his arm out the window to wave before driving off.

My heart skipped a beat at Annie's slip-up. She'd called Dad Simpson. "Bloody hell, Annie... *Sims—not Simpson...* remember?" I hissed against her ear.

Annie's eyes widened as she slapped her forehead. "Oops... sorry, Katie. I keep forgetting."

Guilt swamped me at the worried look in her eyes. Damnit, I needed to calm down and stop acting like a chicken with its head cut off. Poor Annie had spent the last eleven years calling my dad by his real name. *Give the girl a break already.*

I sighed and reined in my frustration, rubbing her arm and throwing her a sheepish smile. "All good. Just *please* try not to slip-up again. I'm a big enough mess as it is."

"Hey, I'll try not to be such an airhead. I know how important this is to you."

Annie turned and lifted her head to stare up at the rows of windows overlooking the entrance to *Crescendo*. Following her line of vision, I squinted up at the students hanging out of their windows, blatantly checking out the new arrivals.

Well... that explained the overwhelming sensation of being watched. So much for blending into the scenery.

I swallowed down the anger trying to push its way to the surface, ignoring the urge to react to those staring eyes. I *so* wanted to do something to make them feel uncomfortable for gawking. *No!* I would *not* pull a face... or curtsy... or poke out my tongue...

Stop it, Katie. Just because they're watching doesn't mean they're judging.

Yeah, right, you just keep telling yourself that.

My face burned with the usual soul-crushing insecurity about my plus-sized, *oh-so-far-from-perfect* body. Okay, so I knew what people thought of me shouldn't matter. But it did... and it hurt, damnit. Was I just being paranoid again? Yeah... no. The memory of being called Furby was still too fresh. I knew *exactly* what they were thinking. So, what *I* needed to do was *stop* thinking and get on with it.

I turned away and looked at Annie. "You ready?" *'Cos I'm not even close.*

"Hell yeah. Let's do this."

I pasted on one of my *I-don't-give-a-shit* smiles, stuck out my chin, squared my shoulders, and linked arms with my best friend. Reefing out the long handle of my suitcase —yes, I *was* taking out my aggression on an inanimate object—I walked beside Annie toward the entrance.

Well... I could at least *look* tough. 'Cos I sure wasn't gonna give any of these people the power to hurt me. Been there, done that...

Go ahead and stare, or judge, or whatever the hell you want.

This is who I am... so deal with it.

Riley

So... the new batch had arrived...

Leaning on the windowsill in my third-floor room, I watched the new students stream toward the front entrance of *Crescendo*. Hard to believe that was me only a year ago. I still remembered the nausea churning in my gut as I looked around at all the rich, toffee-nosed students arriving in their designer clothing and wondering how the hell I would ever fit in. The whole thing had felt more like entering the gates of hell than a school.

As for my hope that no one would pick me as the poor scholarship student, that particular hope quickly melted into the concrete beneath my feet. My scruffy clothes, and the beat-up guitar case hanging over my shoulder, had worked like a flashing neon sign on my forehead. Basically, I'd stuck out like the proverbial sore thumb.

Still, I'd managed to hold my own—although it irked me to admit that my musical talent was *apparently* aided by my supposed 'smokin'-hot good looks'.

Yeah, 'cos that was something I had control over... not.

It never ceased to amaze me how acceptance into the world of the *beautiful people* could be achieved by nothing more than an anatomical fluke at birth. But hey... if my looks helped to convince them to *overlook* my lowly origins, and proved I deserved to be there just as much as the spoiled, over-privileged Kens and Barbies, who was I to complain?

So, while my financial status—or lack thereof—may not have qualified me as take-him-home-to-meet-Mummy-

and-Daddy material, my services for short-term-slumming-with-the-poor-hot-guy were always in high demand.

"Hey, Rye, checking out the new talent?" My roommate, Joel, interrupted my trip down memory lane as he jostled for space at the window.

"Yeah, right. Depends on what sort of 'talent' you're looking for. Bit hard to tell their *musical* ability from here."

Joel scoffed. "C'mon, man. Who cares about their *musical* talent?"

"Seriously, man? Can you not drag your mind out of the gutter for once? "

Joel spluttered and flipped me off. "You mean the same gutter you spent so much time in last year? People in glass houses, Stone…"

Yeah, whatever, Joel. Okay, so *maybe* I'd been guilty of acting just as shallow as Joel in my first year. But *this* year, I needed to focus. Make it all about the music… not just partying and hooking-up with random—

Whoa. I might need to make an exception…

A dazzling pair of emerald-green eyes, blazing a challenge to any and all takers, stared up at me. I mean, she probably wasn't staring at *me*, there were heaps of other students hanging out their windows, but it sure *felt* like she looked right at me. The eyes were framed by a head of unruly red hair, the morning sun turning it to molten lava. Goosebumps broke out all over my skin.

Holy shit. Intense or what?

A heartbeat later, before I could even process why the look in her eyes had such an impact on me, she linked arms with her friend, stuck out her chin, and disappeared into the entrance below.

Wow... the girl had some serious attitude.

Talk about eyes being the window to a person's soul. So many raw emotions exposed in one glance. Anger, fear, and sadness... vying with a bit of stubborn pride and hope?

O-kay. So that was why the look had shaken me. I saw it every time I stood in front of a mirror. Maybe we had some things in common...

"Hey... earth to Riley. Okay, stud... what's got your attention? Can't be their *musical*

talent..." Joel's voice in my ear pulled me back to earth with a thud.

I smiled and nudged Joel in the ribs. "Nope. I'm thinking it was more like a challenge."

"Riigghhtt. So... was the source of this 'challenge' hot or what?"

I shook my head—something I seemed to do a lot when around Joel—and moved away from the window. Flopping down on the end of my bed, I replayed the conflicting emotions in those fiery eyes.

Wait... was she hot? Wow, I hadn't even noticed.

I'd been so mesmerised by those incredible eyes I forgot to take in the rest of the package.

But one thing was certain: this girl was *not* just another Barbie.

Chapter Two

Katie

By the time we found our room, excitement had finally overcome my frayed nerves. Dropping my bags in the doorway, I threw myself down on the bed nearest the door and kicked my legs in the air, releasing the squeal I'd been holding back since we entered the building. *I mean, surely acting immature and breaking all my self-imposed rules should be allowed in the safety of my own room? Right?*

"Yeah, totally sophisticated, Katie. Can you at least move your crap out of the doorway so that I can get in?" I looked up to find Annie still standing outside the door, shaking her head and trying not to laugh.

"Oops, my bad." Suppressing a giggle— *'cos that would be sooo much less mature than the squealing and kicking legs* —I jumped up and dragged my suitcase over to the tiny cupboard next to my bed.

"Riiight," Annie drawled, taking in our shoebox of a room as she moved to the bed at the other end. "Guess we won't be throwing any wild parties in here. This room isn't much bigger than the walk-in wardrobe in your bedroom."

Unbelievable! She'd done it again! "*Annie!* That's twice, and we've only been here five minutes! You promised not to talk about—"

Annie waved her hand, frowning at my hands-on-hips stance. "Yeah, yeah... I know.

You don't want anyone knowing you're Reece Simpson's daughter and you've got money. But c'mon, Katie, who's going to hear us in here? I can't see them getting away with having the rooms bugged."

Okay... so maybe I'd overreacted... again.

I slumped back down on my bed. *Damnit... I really needed to chill.* Maybe Mum had been right, and I *wasn't* ready yet. If I couldn't even relax around Annie, what hope did I have of surviving life at *Crescendo?* But Mum's idea that I stick with the home-schooling for another year, until I was 'ready-to-face-the-world-again', had made me feel hopeless. What if I *never* felt ready? No, I needed to do this. No more hiding away.

I shrugged, playing with a loose thread on my jeans. "Sorry, I guess I'm still a bit freaked out. You're right. I know I sound paranoid, but this might be the only chance I'll ever get to find out what it's like to be *normal*. To find friends who like me for *me*, and not just for what my Daddy can do for their careers."

Annie's hands went to her hips, mirroring my stance perfectly. "Hey... what am I? Swiss cheese?"

That made me smile. "Nope. You're more like... ummm... cheddar?"

"Sorry?"

"Yeah. I've never really been a fan of Swiss cheese. It's so... flimsy—too many holes.

You're way more... solid."

I laughed as Annie's mouth opened and closed as if she were trying to say something. But all she managed to do was look like a fish out of water.

Wow. A rare moment. Annie Keats... speechless.

About to give her a hard time for not having her usual witty come-back, I jumped when Annie cracked up laughing.

"Interesting analogy," she spluttered. "Even if it *was* a bit 'cheesy'."

Riley

A COUPLE OF HOURS LATER, as Joel and I entered the auditorium for the first assembly of the year, I found myself scanning the newbies in the Year-Ten section for her fiery red hair and blazing emerald eyes. However, it didn't take long to realise *that* was an exercise in futility.

Damnit! Since when were there so many students in this place with red hair?

Slipping into a chair next to Joel in the back of the section reserved for Year-Eleven students, I pinched the bridge of my nose with my thumb and forefinger. The noise level created by the excited voices of over a hundred teenagers bouncing off the walls was starting to give me a headache. Well... *that*... and the image of the red-haired girl's challenging gaze tattooed on my brain.

Get a grip, man. You're acting like an obsessed idiot. What happened to the I'm-here- for-the-music-and-nothing-else mantra of a few hours ago? Time to start practising what you preach, moron!

I froze at the sound of a disturbingly familiar, high-pitched giggle, followed by the nostril-invading, over-powering scent of expensive perfume. The combination, or at least the person they identified, sent shivers up my spine.

Shit... Elise had found me.

"Oh, Riley. I missed you *so* much, baby." I bit back a groan. Just the sound of her whiney voice was enough to make me swear off alcohol for life. 'Cos I was pretty damn sure I'd never have hooked-up with Elise if I'd been sober.

I tried not to shudder as a pair of tanned arms slipped around my neck, Elise's groping hands worming their way down under the front of my t-shirt. "I can't wait to... catch up," she whispered into my ear.

Elise Dunn was a perfect example of what I called a *Barbie doll*. Long blonde hair framing a flawlessly beautiful face, her model-thin body toned to perfection. But after that drunken hook-up with her at the end of last year, I'd soon discovered she had way more money than talent, and her beauty was skin deep. Oh, and she did *not* handle rejection well, which was evident from the way she *still* refused to accept the fact that we were over.

Gently, but firmly, removing her tentacles—*okay, fine, so maybe they were arms*—I sucked in a deep breath and turned to face her. "Hey Elise... Sorry, but I – "

The microphone squealed with feedback, and I sagged with relief. The chatter in the room instantly ceased as all eyes turned toward the grey-haired man standing before a podium on the stage. At least now Elise would have to go back to her seat. Ignoring her hand trailing across my chest, not to mention the parting sultry grin, I turned my attention to Professor Hart's welcome speech.

"Okay, people, let's get started. I'm Professor Hart. Welcome, and congratulations, to our new Year-Ten and transfer students for making it into *Crescendo*. Oh, and well done to our returning students for surviving thus far and coming back for more." I smiled at the splattering of applause, whistles, and random sniggers.

"This year, the board has decided to introduce a 'buddy system' to help the new students settle in. This means that each new student will be paired with a Year-Eleven student for the first two weeks of the semester.

We tossed around the idea of pairing you according to your specific musical talent, but this proved to be a logistical nightmare. So... instead, you'll be paired in alphabetical order. Please stand up when your names are called, then move with your buddy to either one of the common rooms or the cafeteria."

Wait! Did he just say I'm gonna be stuck with a freakin' new kid for two whole weeks? Seriously? Oh God... please don't let me be paired with some vapid *Barbie*, or, worse still, one of those egocentric *Action Man* types. Then again, maybe it might be better if my buddy was a guy. Having to deal with some clingy, insecure girl on a daily basis would do my head in.

Well... unless she has red hair and green eyes...

Yeah right. As if, out of all the new students, that's gonna happen. Oh well, maybe a fellow guitarist would be cool. We could jam in our free—

"...and Joel Kenny." Hearing Joel's name called snapped me out of my musings. Well, that and Joel's elbow jabbing me in the ribs. Frowning, I followed the direction of his smiling face to a petite, blushing blonde standing in either the last row of the Year-Ten section or the first row of Year-Eleven. But it had to be the Year-Ten section if she was a newbie.

Before I could even comment, Joel sprung out of his seat, walking away backward while wiggling his eyebrows. "See you in our common room, Stone."

I shook my head—yeah again—but couldn't help smiling at the sight of my dorky friend moving toward his new buddy. Maybe if he lost the untucked plaid shirt, the baggy jeans and the old-fashioned, black-rimmed glasses, he might have a chance with a girl like that.

Wait... where had that come from? I sounded like a bloody girl. No way guys *ever* thought about giving other guys makeovers. Even if they were roommates.

Nope. Sorry, bud... you're on your own.

Right... back to focusing on my own life.

Whoa... the room was almost half empty already. How long had I been off in la-la-land? Still, it would be a while before they got to my surname, Stone. *Well, there's no point in sitting here stressing; it won't change who I end up with as a buddy.* Pulling out my phone, I opened my emails, the sound of Professor Hart calling out names receding into the background as I read and replied to a few. Slipping my phone back into my pocket when I was done, I looked up just as Professor Hart called out the name Katie Sims.

Getting close now.

I watched as a tall red-haired girl got to her feet, holding my breath as I waited for her to turn around. Did she have a pair of challenging, emerald-green eyes? But unlike most of the other new students, who'd immediately turned toward our section to check out their new buddy, the girl simply stood and continued to stare out in front of her, not even sneaking a peek.

Man... this girl was either terrified or she couldn't give a shit. And I still didn't know if—

"... and Riley Stone."

The girl... Katie... finally turned to look over as I got to my feet. But the smile on my face froze at her expression.

What the...?

Those blazing emerald eyes confirmed her as the girl from this morning, but now she was definitely glaring at *me* like she wanted to punch me in the face.

Ummm... sorry?

Did I miss something?

Tearing my eyes away from her intense glare, I took in the entire package. Okay, so she was a few sizes bigger than the girls I'd usually be attracted to, not to mention taller. But something about those fiery-eyes, set in a beautiful, rounded face and framed by long, riotous red hair, drew me in.

I tried to think of something cool to say, but the way she was glaring at me was so far from the usual reaction I got when first meeting a girl that my mind went blank. I watched in horror as her eyes flicked over me from head to foot, her lip curling in... *disgust?*

Seriously? What was her problem?

Was it the cheap department store clothes I was wearing?

Nope. Her jeans and shirt didn't really look any better than mine. So why...?

Then it clicked. *This was about bloody high school labels.* All those derogatory terms like 'fat-chick', 'pretty-boy', 'nerd' and 'jock'. She was expecting me to judge her on her looks. *And* she was judging me on mine!

Great... so now I was in trouble for being a 'pretty-boy'. Unbelievable!

I'd always hated the whole concept of 'labels' almost as much as the judgemental jerks who used them. And from Katie's look of disgust, and the anger blazing in her eyes, she was totally acting like one of *them*. She'd already pegged me as just another shallow 'pretty-boy-Ken-doll' type.

Well, no way I was giving her the satisfaction of showing a reaction. Sucking in a deep, calming breath, I stuffed my hands in my pockets and moved toward her. Time to prove her warped perception of *all* 'pretty-boys' was way off base.

Okay, so maybe I knew lots of guys who *did* deserve that label. But I was *not* one of them. Never *had* been, never *would* be.

Besides... wasn't she guilty of doing exactly what she obviously hated others doing to her? Judging a book by its cover? Well, she'd picked the wrong guy to slot-into-a-pigeonhole.

And don't you even start, I silently yelled at that tiny voice niggling in the back of my mind. The one asking why her opinion of me even mattered.

This has nothing to do with caring about her opinion. This is about proving a point!

Yep... sure it is. It's got nothing to do with the challenge in those gorgeous emerald eyes or—

Fantastic! Now I'm talking to myself.

Gritting my teeth, I shut the voice down and pushed it back into its box. Who cared *why*

it was important? It just was...

Besides... she'd started it...

Okay, Miss Fiery-eyes. Bring. It. On.

Chapter Three

Katie

My blood started to boil the minute I set eyes on the god-damned-pretty-boy-Ken-doll impersonator walking toward me. *Seriously?* Why couldn't he have been more like the guy Annie was buddied with, a slightly cute, glasses-wearing, nerdy type? No... I had to be stuck with this blonde-headed, blue-eyed Greek god. And what was with the smarmy smile?

Unbelievable! Obviously, some evil-minded deity had decided it would be entertaining to buddy me with exactly the type of guy I'd vowed to avoid like the plague. And, of course, my stupid brain was freaking out.

My freakin' buddy was totally hot! And I was stuck with him for two freakin' weeks!

Shit, shit, shit... Worst. Nightmare. Ever!

Just breathe, Katie. You can do this. It doesn't matter if the guy is the personification of sex-on-a-stick.

You're here to focus on music. Guys just aren't worth the effort.

Oh God, here he comes...

"Hey... Katie. Nice to meet you. I'm Riley." Still wearing the smarmy smile—*okay, so maybe smarmy was a slight exaggeration*—he stuck his hand out for me to shake. Well, at least he *seemed* friendly. And he didn't have that cocky *I'm-an-arrogant-jerk* look in his eyes. In fact, his eyes...

Wait... was that seriously a challenging look in his eyes? Was he challenging me? What the hell was that all about? Whatever. I could just ignore it and shake the stupid hand stuck out toward me.

But I knew I'd made a colossal mistake the minute his hand closed around mine. I swear a bolt of electricity jumped out of his palm, ran up my arm, and flooded my entire body. And, of course, my mouth turned to sandpaper.

Stop it, Katie. Don't you dare get all tongue-tied and gush like a mindless groupie. Oh, and remove your hand... idiot.

Right. Remove hand. Speak! Words, Katie. Now! "Yeah... ummm..." Throat clearing. "Nice to meet you, too. So... ummm... what do we do now?"

Hah! Was he starting to look uncomfortable, too? Good! "Well, I... ar... think the girl you were sitting with may have been buddied with my roommate, Joel. They'll be in the third-floor common room. That's where the Year-Eleven common room is. Wanna go find them and chat for a while?"

Wow... those perfect white teeth were blinding. In fact, the guy's smile should have come with a hazard warning. I needed to stop looking at him, before those big baby blue eyes, set into his perfect face, turned my legs to jelly.

An image of Mark-the-Betrayer-Barnes' smiling face flashed before my eyes, and that was all it took to break the spell. *Huge relief.* I dragged my eyes away from the perfect display of male beauty in front of me. Looking at the floor, I slammed the safe, protective walls in my mind back into place and pulled myself together.

No way would I *ever* allow myself to be sucked into making *that* mistake again. Hot guys

like Mark... and Riley... were *never* attracted to girls like me. *Ever.*

"Ummm, Katie? We could go to the Year-Ten common room if you'd be more comfortable...?" Was that a sigh? "Or, it's okay if you'd rather not hang out with me."

Oh shit. Riley was still waiting for an answer. Wait... had he really sounded disappointed? And was he seriously blushing? God, this whole situation was doing my head in. This totally hot guy was acting like he *cared* what I thought.

Yeah, right, Katie... stop being so delusional. As if!

Those ridiculous delusions were instantly shattered when he looked away, scratching his head and looking like he'd rather be anywhere but there.

Of course... that was more like it. Yeah, well, His Royal Hotness could suck it up. We were stuck with each other for two whole weeks.

"Oh... sorry. I... yeah, the common room sounds great.

Wait... why would I be more comfortable in the Year-Ten common room?

"Wait... you're not in Year Ten?"

"No. Annie and I transferred from another school. We're in Year-Eleven, too."

Riley raised his eyebrows and grinned, his eyes sparkling with mischief. The sudden change in his demeanour almost made me pass out.

Drowning here...

Everything inside me screamed not to believe the nice guy act he was trying to sell. Spending time with this guy would only make me want what I could never have. And I'd be right back where I started.

No, Katie. You are not that stupid, naïve girl any more.

Okay, time to apply the logical solution. Riley was just trying to do his job as my buddy, and I needed to do exactly the same.

And his grin was so *not* sexy! "Seriously? That's so cool. So I guess we'll be sharing a common room."

Bloody hell. The guy was making my head spin. Why was he being so friendly and pretending to be enjoying himself? Maybe he felt sorry for me.

Wait...

Oh. My. God...

Did he think I was being awkward because I was attracted to him? And, of course, that would be so entertaining... for someone like him. *Aargghh!*

My blood started to boil all over again. No way would I let this jerk think I was into him. Pasting what I hoped passed for a condescending smile on my face, I shrugged.

"Not that it matters. I doubt I'll be spending much time in the common room anyway. I'm not here for the whole *social* thing. I'm here to study, sing and write music."

Pretty-boy's eyes narrowed, his jaw tightening. "Last time I checked, that's what we were *all* here to do, Katie." *Oooh... it looked like I hit a nerve.* "But maybe, just for today, you could at least *pretend* to be nice?"

Riley

BULLSEYE!

Katie's face resembled a thundercloud. And yep, there was the lightning flashing from those incredible eyes. I couldn't hold back the satisfied smile as a blush crept up her neck and spread across her face.

Well, come on... it wasn't like she didn't deserve it. What gave her the right to think she was the only one here serious about music? She knew nothing about me... or how hard I'd worked to be here.

Then, a memory of the warring emotions in her eyes as she'd looked up at the building this morning flashed before me. That look had held some kind of painful memories. Damnit, now I felt guilty. This girl had my emotions jumping all over the place, and it was freaking me out.

"Look, I'm sorry..."

"Hey, sorry about..."

We'd both spoken at once, and I had no idea what to

do. Should I finish my apology or let her finish hers? Apparently, she was lost too, because we just stared at each other. And then we were both laughing, the tension finally draining away.

Which was about when I realised how much I enjoyed sparring with Katie. I felt more alive than I could ever remember. In fact, this whole scenario was amazing. I'd never spent time with a girl who wasn't either throwing herself at me or too tongue-tied to speak.

"Wow. That was intense," Katie said with a shy smile. But at least the smile appeared genuine, and the transformation was breathtaking. Her smile lit up the room. "Maybe we should start over? I think we might have got off on the wrong foot."

I returned her smile, hoping it didn't look as goofy as it felt. *And what was with the weird feeling in my stomach? Come to think of it, I'd felt that way ever since the... jolt-thing... when we shook hands.*

Must be gas...

Yep, had to be...

Breathe Riley. "Sounds good to me. So, how about we go catch up with Joel and... was it Annie? How cool that you both got accepted together."

Katie's smile became even more dazzling at the mention of her friend. "Yeah, Annie and I have been best friends since kindergarten. Getting into *Crescendo* has been our life-long goal since primary school."

"So why didn't you start here last year?"

Katie shrugged, a haunted expression flashing in her eyes. "If only. At the end of Year Nine, just before the auditions, Annie got really sick, and I refused to audition without her."

Okay, time to change the subject. "Oh, well. At least you're here now. So, is Annie a singer like you?"

Katie's smile returned as she giggled—*yep, definitely a giggle*—and it was kind of adorable. She really was cute.

Whoa... where did that come from?

Since when were words like cute and adorable even part of my vocabulary? Maybe it was time I got a puppy.

"Oh no, don't even *think* about asking Annie if she's a singer. She's a serious pianist and is convinced she sounds like a bullfrog when she sings."

"And does she? Sound like a bull-frog, I mean?"

"No way. Her harmonies are amazing. But for her, it's all about the piano or keyboards. She was one of those 'child-proteges'. She's incredibly talented."

"Well, now I *really* want to meet her. So... you ready to check out that *never-to-be-revisited*

common room."

"Just lead the way, smart-arse."

Chapter Four

Katie

Oh my God. How lame was I?

I'd actually giggled in front of Riley McHottie Stone.

I kept looking for the massive hole that was supposed to open up and swallow me whole. *No such luck.* This guy seemed to have the uncanny ability to bring out the worst in me. And okay, maybe he wasn't that bad... *for a pretty-boy.*

I followed Riley toward the common room, trying not to notice how gorgeous his incredibly toned butt looked in his snug jeans.

Katie!! What are you doing? It doesn't matter what he looks like. *Remember the mantra: Beneath the skin of every pretty-boy beats the heart of a true scumbag! Rinse and repeat. Now, just stop it!*

The flash of relief in Annie's eyes when we arrived in

the common room told me everything. She looked about as happy with her 'buddy-ship' as me. During some quick introductions, Annie's overly perceptive eyes flicked between Riley and me, the raised eyebrows telling me she'd picked up on the tension between us. "So, where've you been? I'd have thought the buddying finished ages ago?"

Oh God, Katie, don't blush! "Well... ummm... Riley and I were sort of just talking about... stuff."

Riley chuckled, dropping into one of the armchairs gathered around a coffee-table. "Yeah, Katie was having trouble deciding whether she could bring herself to speak to the

'pretty-boy'. That's *me*, by the way."

Wait... how did he know that's what I'd been thinking?

I folded my arms and threw Riley a filthy look. "Excuse me? More like you were pretending

to be nice to the fat-chick."

"Ahah! I knew it! And by the way, that was your interpretation... not mine! Bloody high school labels..."

I shrugged and glared at his muttering form. "Yeah, well, if the shoe fits..."

Annie and Joel's heads swung between us like they were watching a tennis match. Normally, I'd have laughed, but Riley's snarky comments had driven my sense of humour into hibernation.

The tension sizzled in the air until Joel slapped his leg and burst out laughing. "Holy shit, Stone. Never thought I'd see the day *you* met your match, pretty-boy. Hey Katie, I'm Joel, and I think I love you."

Annie tilted her head, squinting as if studying a pair of

rare specimens. "Wow. Sounds like you two totally succeeded in pissing each other off. Maybe we should swap buddies, Katie?"

I swallowed and flopped into the chair next to Annie. *Did I want to swap buddies? It might be better for everyone if –*

"No way," Riley growled—yes, that's right, he honest-to-god *growled*.

Wait... what? My eyes flew to Riley's in shock at his surly response.

But he just shrugged. "Sorry, Annie, but there's no way Katie's getting rid of me that easy. I intend to prove I'm more than just a Ken doll who's into Barbies."

What! How the hell did he know I'd compared him to a Ken doll as well? Huh, maybe he did have a brain under all that gorgeous, tousled blonde hair. But why hadn't he jumped at the chance to switch buddies?

Stop it, Katie! Right! Now!

Which is about when I noticed Joel literally glaring at Annie. "Sorry, Annie. Looks like you're stuck with *me* then."

Wow... so Riley and I weren't the only ones to get off to a rocky start. My head was seriously starting to hurt from drama overload. What the hell had happened between these two?

Only one way to find out. "So, ummm, Joel, what's your area of musical expertise?"

"Humph... I'm a drummer. You know, just a dumb Neanderthal noise-maker?"

Annie sucked in a breath and scowled. "Joel, I never said that."

"No, but you did a damn good job of implying it. Sorry, but we can't all be refined concert pianists like you, princess."

Annie's face was so red she looked ready to explode. "*Excuse me?* Who the hell do you think you are? As if I would *ever* belittle another person's musical talent. Not even a *drummer!*" Annie jumped up and marched out of the room before I could catch a breath.

Whoa... and I thought Riley and I were a mismatch. Maybe someone should inform the board about their epic failure with this whole buddy system.

I watched Annie storm out of the common-room with my mouth open. This was getting ridiculous. I really needed to have a *serious* talk with a certain evil-minded deity I was now *convinced* was causing all this.

I turned back to Joel and frowned. "Okaaay... that was weird. Looks like you and Annie have been pushing some buttons of your own. What happened?"

Joel rubbed the back of his neck, looking like I had earlier, as if he wished the floor would open up and swallow him. "Yeah, sorry about that. Maybe I kind of overreacted? But Annie wouldn't be the first person to think drummers are untalented douches. And when she turned up her nose and said she was a classically trained pianist, I *may* have... ummm... inferred she was a stuck-up snob?"

Unbelievable! No wonder Annie had stormed out. "Oh God, Joel, Annie is about as far from stuck-up as you'll ever meet. She's kind of shy when she first meets someone, but once she gets to know you, she's a total crack-up. *And*, she's been working really hard on the keyboard for the last year, hoping to avoid the label of being a boring pianist."

"Aww, man. Now I feel like a total dick."

Heaving a sigh, I stood and patted his slumped shoulder. "Hey, don't stress. Seems we might have all been a tad judgemental today. I'll talk to her, and I'm sure everything will be fine. And I'm thinking that talk might need to be sooner rather than later."

I turned and started to walk away, then changed my mind. Maybe it was time to put all this bullshit to rest. "Hey, you know what? Maybe this whole *buddy* thing isn't going to work for us. I'm sure we'll be fine on our own, and Professor Hart doesn't have to find out—"

"What?" Riley's unexpected outburst made me jump. "Are you seriously gonna throw in the towel before we've even started?"

A challenge, Riley? Seriously? Now my back was up again. "I'm not *throwing in the towel.*

I just think walking away might be the best option for all of us right now. I'm here to study, not to—"

"Oh, here we go again with the—"

Blood boiling... again. "Just shut it, okay? This is not all about you. I just watched my usually-even-tempered best friend race out of here like her pants were on fire. This..." I waved my hand around between us. "... is not worth it. So consider yourselves off the hook!"

I tried to ignore the shiver of excitement running down my spine when I locked eyes with Riley. That was when it hit me—I was enjoying myself. I couldn't remember *ever* feeling this wired. Arguing with Riley was exhilarating... it made me feel alive for the first time in a very long time.

"Twenty-four hours." *Okay, so maybe Riley's husky snarl did funny things to my stomach. I always did love a challenge.* "After that, if we all still feel the same way, we'll ditch the whole buddy thing. Joel, you in?" Riley's eyes never left mine.

"Ummm, yeah, sure. I think we all need to take a couple of deep breaths and start afresh."

There was no way *I* would be the one to look away first. "Fine. So what's the plan for tomorrow then? I haven't had a chance to go through my timetable yet."

Riley leaned forward in his chair, running his hands through his hair before resting his arms on his knees. *Far out,* this tension was killing me.

He blew out a slow breath, his eyes softening. "Yeah, me either. But classes start at nine, so how about we meet for breakfast in the cafeteria at about eight?"

"Fine, we'll be there. Well, I'm off to bandage some wounds. See you guys in the morning." But I couldn't help throwing out one more snarky remark in Riley's direction before I left. *Yeah, so sue me.* "Oh, and make sure you get lots of *beauty sleep.*"

Without waiting for a response, I turned and left the common room, my mind replaying the scowl on Riley's face at my parting shot.

He was sooo easy to rile.

Hah! His name was so appropriate.

Riley

I SCOWLED at Katie's back as she turned to leave the room. *Unbelievable!* She just *had* to throw in one last dig about the 'pretty boy' thing.

But what really blew my mind was how fast my scowl melted away. Watching her swing that beautiful big, sexy butt, encased in her tight-fitting jeans, *all* the way to the door, was just... wow.

Wait... since when did I find big butts sexy? I liked my women petite... didn't I?

And, of course, that stupid little voice in the back of my head *had* to throw its two cents worth in.

Yeah, but none of those 'petites' had Katie's fiery eyes, gorgeous face, and feisty attitude.

Shut. The. Hell. Up!

I knew I'd been busted when Joel cleared his throat. "Hey, Stone. Am I missing something here? What's with you eyeballing Katie all the way across the room? She is *so* not your type, man." Yep, he'd been watching me.

Okay, so I was a complete idiot. Just kill me now. "Huh... what? Get real, man. I wasn't

checking out Katie. I was thinking about this stupid buddy mess."

I must have been convincing because Joel blew out a relieved sigh. "Just as well. 'Cos that girl could chew-you-up-and-spit-you-out without breaking a sweat. Oh... and I gotta ask... how does it feel to meet a girl who's immune to your... *charms?*"

How did *it feel?* Well, apart from the dent to my ego, it felt... *exhilarating.* Being around Katie was like a breath of fresh air after being stuck in the desert. She challenged me to prove I was more than just what-you-see-is-what-you-get. Even if she did drive me crazy, and made me act like some form of soppy goofball.

Joel's foot tapping on the floor reminded me he was still waiting for an answer. *Pull yourself together, man.* "To be honest... it's kinda weird but in a good way. I might even give the whole friends-with-a-girl thing a go for the first time in my life."

Joel barked out a laugh. "Friends with a girl, huh? Now, *there's* an interesting concept. 'Specially for someone like you."

"What? You don't think I can do it? Look, Katie is cool, but there's no way I'd ever be interested in hooking up with her or anything. Besides, we kinda hate each other at the moment."

"You sure about that?"

"Yeah, I'm sure. And what's with the crappy attitude anyway? Did you wake up this morning and decide to piss the whole world off?"

Joel leaned forward, propping his elbows on his knees and dropping his face in his hands. "Yeah, about that. I've no idea where all the hostility is coming from. I just... aww hell. I acted like a complete jerk. Annie will probably never speak to me again, and I can't even blame her."

"... and that would be a huge deal because?" I couldn't

hold back the wicked smile creeping across my face. *No way.* Was Joel interested in Annie? If not, why would he care what some random new girl thought of him?

Same reason you were ticked-off about Katie having such a poor opinion of you, numb-nuts.

Where the hell was that crappy little voice coming from anyway? It was as if meeting Katie had created some smart-arsed cartoon character inside my head.

"Okay. Enough wallowing." I jumped off the lounge and tried to shake off all the negative energy. "Let's go do what we do best— make some music. All this talk about girls is seriously doing my head in."

"I'm with you, man. Thank God we don't have to think about them again until tomorrow morning."

Yeah, if only not *thinking about Katie would be so easy.*

Chapter Five

Katie

Eyeing Annie warily, I decided it might be best if I waited for her to stop fuming before I spoke. In all our years of friendship, I'd never seen her react like this—*ever*. 'Specially not over someone she'd just met. In fact, Annie was usually one of the calmest, most level-headed people I'd ever met.

So, you mean a bit like your overreaction to Riley?

Yeah, well, the guy was a master at pushing my buttons. Even after only knowing him for five freakin' minutes! God help me— every time he opened his mouth, I wanted to shoot him down.

Deep breaths. I just needed to shut my brain down and stop thinking about him. Only another twenty-four hours and I could start avoiding him like the plague as I should have done in the first place. So why did I feel like a deflated balloon just at the thought of doing that?

"Sorry about that..." Annie's quiet words pulled me back to reality. I sat down at the end of her bed in relief.

Yay... my Annie was back! "Okay, spill. What was with the big '*screw you*' grand exit?"

"Honestly? I've no idea. Something about Joel just makes me want to hit him!"

Sounded familiar. "Riiight... so that explains everything... *not!* Come on, Annie. You and I both know there's something weird about you having that kind of reaction to a complete stranger. What the hell happened before I got there?"

Annie groaned and threw her hands in the air. "I wish I knew! We were sitting there chatting about how awesome it was to be here, and I *may* have been thinking he was kinda... cute?" She cleared her throat, blushed, and waved her hand as if to dismiss the thought. "Anyway, he asked about my musical background, and I told him about my years playing classical piano. Before I could tell him how much I loved changing to the keyboard, he clammed up and gave me this funny look. Then, when I asked him what instrument he played, he got all weird. Why would he think I'd turn my nose up just because he's a drummer?"

"Oh, Annie, he was probably just feeling insecure. It's kind of a 'band thing'. People are always ragging on drummers, saying they're the apes of the music industry who only know how to make noise."

Annie groaned. "How was I supposed to know that? What did he expect me to do? Gush about how talented I thought drummers were? *Aargghh!* Anyway, that's about when you guys showed up. So, should I even ask what happened after I left?"

Now it was my turn to blush. "Yeah, about that. I may have just... ummm..."

"Oh, for God's sake, Katie. Please don't tell me you made things worse? Although, is that even possible at this stage?"

Aaannd that was it... Mount Vesuvius finally erupted. I jumped off the bed and started pacing the room. "Why is everyone acting like this is all my fault? This whole buddy thing is a freakin' mess. Riley and I haven't stopped arguing since we met, and then you run off like a screaming banshee! So... I told them we should forget being buddies, and Professor Hart didn't need to know about it."

"Right... and what did they say?"

"Riley got all shitty and said we had to give it twenty-four hours. Probably just worried

they'd get in trouble for shirking their duties. Anyway, I agreed to it."

Annie started to giggle. "Whoa girl... he really does get up your nose, eh? I'm kinda sorry I missed it."

At which point we both cracked up laughing. I fell back on my own bed, and we spent the next few minutes rolling around laughing until we cried while holding our aching stomachs. Every time one of us almost got it back under control, the other started all over again.

When we finally returned to the realms of sanity, Annie sat up, gasping and sniffing as she wiped the tears from her face. "Wow. Who'd have thought we'd have this much excitement on our first day? And here I was worried we'd be bored."

"Yeah, maybe we can blame all the other crap on first-day nerves, or PMS, or some other reason totally beyond our control. Well, I guess we'll just have to see how tomorrow goes. Worst case scenario: we only have to last another twenty-four hours."

Annie nodded, and I moved over to sit on the end of her bed. "Seriously though, Joel feels bad about what he said. Maybe tomorrow you can both just apologise... and *then* you can go back to focusing on how cute he is."

Annie smiled and gave me a searching look. "Speaking of cute, let's talk about the gorgeous specimen of manhood who seems to be able to get under your skin so easily. I thought you hated pretty boys?"

I did... didn't I? "Yeah, well, the jury is still out on this one. He's determined to prove his beauty isn't just skin deep."

Annie's eyes widened. "Is that what he was rabbiting on about with the whole *Ken-doll*

thing?"

The usual heat rose up my neck. "Well, I *might* have given him the impression I thought guys who looked like him were usually... shallow jerks...?"

Okay, so maybe I had been slightly judgemental... and acted like a mental case. But it was just my self-preservation kicking in. It always happened when I felt threatened or uncomfortable. And my *incoming-arsehole-radar* may have become a bit biased.

Annie actually snorted, followed by a groan as she

covered her face with her hands. "Wow... talk about totally stuffing up first impressions. So when do we have to see them again?"

"Ummm... breakfast, eight am, cafeteria."

Annie dropped her hands, her face pale. "Seriously? I don't suppose it would make a real good impression if we were sick on the first day of classes?"

"Come on, Annie. It'll be fine. We'll all have a civilised breakfast, and they can give us a quick tour. This time tomorrow, they'll be out of our hair. Let's just hope we don't have any classes together. I mean, it shouldn't be too hard to avoid them... right?"

Chapter Six

Riley

Okay, *I was officially screwed.* My sanity had up and left the building about the same time Katie had walked out of the common room the previous day. *Why the hell couldn't I stop thinking about the fiery redhead?*

Sitting in the cafeteria at breakfast the following morning, I replayed our first meeting in my head for the gazillionth time. Okay, so *maybe* I'd gone out of my way to piss her off, but she'd done the same thing. Seriously... it was like my head was gonna explode every time she opened her mouth.

But I knew I was way past screwed when I *also* couldn't stop my eyes from constantly wandering to the entrance to the cafeteria. It was five past eight, and there was no sign of the girls. Maybe they'd decided not to meet up after all.

What *I* couldn't decide, was whether that was a good or a bad thing.

I did feel *slightly* better when I caught sight of Joel's knee jiggling under the table. Yep, these girls had done a great job of putting the wind up both of us. I was starting to think Katie was right. This buddy thing wasn't working out for any of us.

"Riley, baby." *Oh, God... no.* "I was *so* disappointed you didn't come to visit me last night."

Damnit... Elise... again. Before I could react, she'd climbed onto my lap, wrapping her arms around my neck and planting her lips on mine. *Great... just what I didn't need. If Katie walked in now, she'd think—*

"Oh, *so* sorry to interrupt." *Of course,* Katie and Annie arrived at that exact moment. "I must have misunderstood. I was sure you said to meet you at breakfast. My bad."

Unbelievable! I seriously considered dropping Elise on her butt at the *I-told-you-so* look blazing from Katie's emerald eyes. But before I could move, or think of a reply, Katie and Annie turned and headed for the breakfast buffet.

Seriously? How was this my fault? Although I had to admit, the way Elise had draped herself all over me, I looked every bit the shallow, pretty-boy Katie had accused me of being the previous day.

"So who's the fat chick, baby, and what's *her* problem?" Elise asked with a pout.

Seething at the derogatory term Elise had used to describe Katie, I now wanted to *throw* Elise's skinny butt onto the floor. No wonder Katie expected that kind of reaction from people. But that didn't mean *I'd* ever condone it. It was time to deal with Elise once and for all.

With way more care than she deserved, I lifted her off my lap and propped her on her feet in front of me. "Don't be such a bitch, Elise. *Katie* and her friend Annie are our buddies. Weren't you teamed with someone?"

Elise waved her hand toward a guy sitting alone eating breakfast a couple of tables away. "Yeah, but he's a total nerd. Plays the cello or something equally boring. Still, at least he's not —"

"Enough, okay? Look, I'm sorry, but I don't have the time or the... desire to hook-up with you again, or anyone else at the moment. I want to concentrate on my studies this year. I wasted too much time partying last year, and I don't want to make the same mistakes again."

Elise scowled, smoothing down her barely-there skirt and tank top. "So you're saying I was just one of those mistakes?" She narrowed her eyes, pouting as she planted her hands on her hips. *Well, if the shoe fits...* I didn't say out loud. I shrugged and tried to look apologetic, mouthing the word *sorry*. "Fine. Your loss. There are plenty of other hotties around here who appreciate my talents."

I slumped back into my chair, sighing with relief when she finally turned and stormed off. But the damage had already been done. I couldn't even see Katie and Annie in the breakfast line.

Joel chuckled, and I looked over to find him rolling his eyes. "Well, *Princess Elise* seems to have got the message that time, unlike our 'buddies', who may have put their own spin on things. They've found a table on the other side of the room. What do we do now, Romeo?"

Rubbing the back of my neck, I tried to untangle my scrambled thoughts. So much for convincing Katie I wasn't a stereotypical 'pretty boy'...

Since when had my life become so freakin' complicated? Oh yeah... since a certain green-eyed fireball had come on the scene.

Well, no more. I needed to regain control of my life and stop overreacting to everything. This whole stressing about what Katie thought of me was doing my head in. Katie was just another girl—*who can't stand the sight of you*— so her opinion shouldn't even matter.

Yeah, but I'd seen the disgust—and maybe a little disappointment— mixed in with that look she threw at me, and it made me cringe. Damnit... I didn't know why, but I hated her thinking she'd been right about me.

Stuff it... time to fix this! "Grab your stuff. We're moving," I growled as I stood up, ignoring Joel's raised eyebrows as I turned toward the girls' table.

I stalked across the cafeteria, holding Katie's gaze the entire time, then pulling out the chair opposite and sitting down when I reached the table. "No misunderstanding," I said, as if there'd been no break in the conversation. "I did say to meet at breakfast. I just wasn't expecting an *uninvited* guest."

"Well, good morning to you too," Katie said in a fake, sing-song voice. "Please... feel free to join us now that you've wrapped up your... *other*... business." She tapped a piece of paper on the table beside her plate. "So, according to our timetable, *we* have music theory in room sixteen first. What do you guys have?"

Great... Katie wasn't going to make this easy. Not that I'd thought she would. I was seriously dreading having to tell her I'd checked the school website last night and discovered this buddy thing was mandatory. Especially the part about the "severe penalties imposed on students failing to adhere to the programme". So much for our proposed twenty-four-hour trial.

Hey, it was *only* for two weeks. I could do this... *we* could do this. "Yeah... ah... we're in that class too." I held up a hand to ward off the imminent explosion. Sucking in a deep breath, I tried to infuse a little enthusiasm into my voice. "Look, I know we're all struggling with this buddy thing. But before you blow a gasket, I checked the rules last night, and there's no way out of this without severe penalties. So... how about we call a truce and at least *try* to get along?"

Joel cleared his throat and rubbed the back of his neck, throwing Annie a sheepish smile. "Yeah, I'll go first. I'm really sorry about yesterday, Annie. I... ummm... I was a total dick."

Annie smiled and blushed. "Yeah, well, I'm sorry too. I *was* pretty rude... Truce?" She held her hand out across the table, and Joel reached out and shook it with a huge grin. Then Annie turned to Katie with raised eyebrows. "Okay, your turn."

A slow blush rose up Katie's neck and flooded her pretty face. *Wow. Was she seriously going to apologise?*

Looking directly into my eyes, she lifted her chin and

sucked in a breath. "Fine. I guess you're not as bad as I thought you'd be."

Wait... that was her idea of an apology?

I sat in stunned silence, digesting her words. She really was a piece of work. "Well, I don't know exactly *what* I'm apologising for, but if it helps... yeah... sorry... for whatever."

Katie's eyebrows went up, her lips twitching as if trying not to laugh. "Smooth..." she said and then burst out laughing. Which, of course, started me off, and soon we were all cracking up, the tension in the air melting away.

By the time we'd finished breakfast, it felt like our shaky truce had started to take root. Although, I was starting to realise being around Katie would always feel like being on an emotional roller-coaster. And the weirdest part? I was kind of enjoying the ride.

Katie

BY THE END of our first class of the day, I'd come to the conclusion that Riley Stone was the most annoyingly confusing guy I'd ever met. He was unbelievably gorgeous —*as in every girl's fantasy*—yet he acted like a *regular* guy. No, he acted like a *nice* guy, which was way out of character for a pretty-boy. At least, every pretty-boy I'd ever met, anyway.

Which meant he was *nothing* like Mark the douchebag,

or the other guys, who'd turned my Year-Ten into a living hell. As always, thoughts of the humiliation Mark had inflicted made my stomach churn and my face burn.

How had I given *anyone* the power to hurt me like that?

Oh yeah... because I was a gullible idiot who didn't realise how cruel people could be.

God, I'd been so naïve. All those months believing everyone called me Furby 'cos I was kinda cute, round, and fluffy.

I almost gagged at the memories of floating around in a blissful bubble of contentment. I'd been so thrilled and flattered to be with someone as *hot* as Mark. I had seriously believed he was all my dreams come true. But it had all been lies.

Scumbag!

The bell ringing for the end of class pulled me out of my maudlin thoughts. *Wow.* How long had I been sitting lost in thought? I hoped Annie had taken notes 'cos I had no idea what the lesson had been about.

I was packing away my folder and laptop when Annie nudged me, a worried frown on her face. "You okay?"

I shrugged, trying to pull myself back from the downward spiral that thoughts of Mark always brought on. "Yeah... just reminiscing."

"Well, that's *never* a good thing. Come on, best not keep our buddies waiting."

After declaring our *truce* at breakfast, we'd sat around laughing and chatting like old friends before walking together to class. Riley and Joel had grabbed seats up the back, but I'd deliberately walked to a couple of seats toward the front. We may have all been in the same class, but that didn't mean we had to sit near them.

We found the boys leaning against the wall outside the classroom, waiting to show us the way to the rehearsal studios. At least we weren't together in our next class.

Yep, that was a good thing. Right?

Which was why I was so surprised by how much my spirits lifted when I saw the cheeky grin on Riley's face. *Damnit... the guy was irresistible.* But the fact that he looked pleased to see *me* had me more confused than ever.

What was the deal with him? Why would he be happy to be hanging out with the fat-chick?

Maybe before Mark, I *might* have believed he could like me. But I'd stopped wearing those rose-coloured glasses a long time ago. In the *real* world, guys like Riley were *not* interested in overweight, red-headed freaks like me.

Unless, of course, said freak's father might be his ticket to a record deal.

So what *did* Riley want? There was no way he could know I had money. The week before I started at *Crescendo*, I'd gone shopping for 'regular' clothes so I could 'blend in' with the other students. The look of horror on my Mum's face when Annie and I came home loaded down with department store bags had been priceless. She did *not* get why I didn't want to hang out with the rich kids.

Maybe Riley was just a nice guy who felt sorry for the fat-chick? Or maybe he didn't even care what I looked like. I mean, *friends* didn't have to worry about that kind of stuff. Did they? Okay, I could be cool with the whole friends-with-the-hot-guy deal.

"Was it that bad?" Riley asked as we walked to class.

Of course, I blushed... "What?"

"The Music Theory class?"

"Oh no, it was fine. I just have a lot on my mind."

"Well, if you ever wanna share, I've been told I'm a good listener."

Okay, this was definitely weird. I stopped walking and studied Riley's big baby-blue eyes. "Why are you being so nice to me? I mean, I know you're stuck with me 'cos I'm your buddy, but you can stop pretending you're enjoying it."

Riley's eyes darkened, his jaw clenching. Ookaay... this was so not the reaction I'd expected. He didn't do the whole looking-anywhere-but-at-me thing or start shuffling his feet like he'd been caught out. He just stared at me and shook his head. "Wow. Why would you have so much trouble believing I might just enjoy your company?"

"Yeah, well, I'm the first to admit I have trust issues. But if someone is told something often enough, it becomes their truth. In my experience, people are only nice when they want something. And I cannot, for the life of me, work out what you think I can do for you."

"Bloody hell, Katie. That's a pretty cynical view for someone so young. I don't *want* anything from you, but I'd *like* us to be friends."

"Why? You don't even know me. And let's face it, I haven't exactly been the poster-girl for a successful friend-ship since we met."

Riley barked out a laugh. "See? *That's* one of the reasons I like you. You say it how it is. I am so over people who suck up and tell me what they think I want to hear. In a way, I get what you're saying about being used, but you and I don't have to worry about all that stuff. Neither of us is attracted to the other, so we're free to get on with being friends. Well... ummm... that's if you think you could stand me as a friend?"

My entire world tilted at his frankness. I'd never met another person who spoke as openly as me about the realities of life. Maybe I *could* look past his sexy smile, perfect body, and all-round awesomeness, and try being friends.

Fine. If he wanted to be friends *despite* our looks, then who was I to argue? "I guess we could give it a shot. It's not like I have people queueing up for the position."

Riley crossed his arms, his mouth curving into a smug smile. "I knew you'd see it my way... eventually."

Chapter Seven

Riley

"Okay, what's with the goofy grin?" Joel asked after we'd dropped the girls off and entered studio five. "I gather the deep and meaningful you and Katie were having ended well?"

"Yeah, we've agreed to be friends."

"Okaaay... and since when does the idea of being friends with a girl make you all goo-goo-eyed?"

Goo-goo-eyed? Seriously? Damnit, I was just happy. I *liked* being around Katie. She made me feel... *real.* I couldn't remember the last time I'd felt like that around a girl. Wait... I'd *never* felt that way. "Give it a rest, man. I just like the idea of being able to hang out with a girl without all the ballistic hormones getting in the way. You know?"

"Nope, can't say I do. Unlike you, I *crave* those ballistic hormones, especially if those feelings happen to be mutual."

I pulled my guitar strap over my shoulder and started tuning up. Joel's never-ending desire for meaningless hook-ups was a regular topic of conversation. Much to his disgust, Joel was the kind of guy girls only ever saw as a friend. When we'd first met as roommates at the beginning of Year-Ten, Joel had lived in the hope that what he called my 'chick-magnetness' would rub off on him. It hadn't taken long for us to realise we both wanted what the other had. Apparently, we were both victims of *the grass is always greener* syndrome.

Okay, it was time to deflect the conversation away from me and Katie. "So what's the go with you and Annie? Any sparks?"

"Nah. She's cute, but I get the feeling she's way outta my league. I reckon she comes from money."

"What makes you think that? I don't get that impression about Katie, and I gather they grew up together."

Joel shrugged, picking up his sticks and settling onto the stool behind his drum kit. "Well, she's been classically trained for one, and that takes money. And she's kind of refined. Ya know?"

"So you're not interested?"

"Well, I didn't say *that*. I just don't think *she'd* be interested in *me*."

"I don't know. She seemed pretty devastated when you had a go at her last night. Besides, Katie said Annie's been working on the keyboard for the last year or so. I can't see some snooty concert pianist doing that... can you?"

"Yeah, I suppose you're right. Still—"

"Look, I was thinking. Maybe we should ask the girls if

they're interested in booking a studio after classes today. Who knows? Annie might surprise you."

"Yeah, that'd be cool. Do you reckon they'll go for it?"

Huh. A jam session in a studio with other musos? Something told me they'd jump at the opportunity.

Aaand... just like that, the goofy grin was back.

Damn, life was good.

Katie

OKAY, I really needed to stop thinking about Riley's goofy grin when I agreed to be friends.

Friends Katie... nothing more.

I mean, the guy had made a point of saying there was no attraction between us. That was a good thing... right?

Yes, it was.

It meant there'd be no awkwardness about 'unrequited feelings'. Being friends was *much* better than being in a relationship. Friendships lasted... relationships didn't. Look at my friendship with Annie. We were still as close as we'd been in kindergarten. Yep, being friends was fantastic.

So why did I have that niggling feeling of disappointment in the pit of my stomach?

Get real, girl... why don't you just admit it?

Fine. Because deep down, I kinda wished he *was* attracted to me.

Seriously Katie? Did you even see the stunning girl on his lap at breakfast?

But he'd said she was an 'uninvited guest'. A past hook-up who couldn't let go, maybe? And suddenly I felt sorry for that girl. How hard would it be to *have* someone like Riley, even for a short time, and not be able to keep him? Nope. I was *way* better off having his friendship. At least I might have a chance of *keeping* that.

"Come on, Katie, you seriously need to get out of your own head," Annie called from where she sat on a piano stool. "What do you feel like singing?"

Annie was right... as usual. Time to shut the 'what-ifs' down. I sighed and moved over to sit beside her. "You suggest something."

Annie tilted her head and gave me a funny look as if assessing my current needs. "Hmmm... something upbeat, eh? How about a bit of Shania Twain? *That Don't Impress Me Much?* Seems appropriate, right?"

I laughed as Annie launched into the intro to one of our favourite songs. Annie knew me so well. This was *exactly* what I needed to put things back into perspective.

Life is what it is. Wallowing and wishing things were different wouldn't change the reality of a situation.

Pushing all thoughts of Riley aside, I jumped to my feet. This was *not* a song to be sung sitting down. *This* was what I was here for. To sing. Not to hanker after things I could never have. Besides, as my Aunt Suzie would say, *I'd rather shut-my-tit-in-a-car-door* than ever fall for another pretty-boy.

By the time I'd belted out the last few notes of the song, my *head* was back in the right place. My *heart* may not have quite caught up, but it could just get over itself.

Annie was grinning from ear to ear, relief in her eyes. "Now *that's* what I'm talking *'bout!* You nailed it, girl."

The grin was contagious. "Thanks, Annie. That was just what I needed to get my head out of my arse."

"So, is it safe to ask you yet? About the D&M you and Riley were having on the way here? What did he say? Do I need to go kick his incredibly gorgeous butt?"

I laughed and sat beside Annie at the keyboard, throwing my arm around her shoulder and pulling her in for a side-hug. "Nah. It's all good. In fact, everything's great. We sorted out a few issues and agreed to be friends. Apparently, he likes being around me for my 'incredible-wit-and-honesty'."

It was a shame he couldn't feel the same about what was on the outside.

Annie frowned. "Ookaay... so why did you look like you wanted to cut off his balls and shove them in a blender? Come on, Katie, this is me. You can't play the 'everything's-great' card after looking like your heart's been ripped out and stomped on. Spill."

I sighed and looked up at the ceiling. There was no use fighting it. Annie would dig around until she got to the 'heart' of things.

God, I was so over these stupid organs called hearts.

"Okay, so maybe I was a *tad* disappointed when he said we were free to be friends 'cos there was absolutely *no* attraction between us."

"Well, there's not... is there?" Annie's eyes widened at my silence. "Oh shit, Katie. Please don't tell me you're even the *slightest* bit attracted to him? He's a pretty-boy! We hate guys like him... remember? Heart of a scumbag?"

I groaned and covered my face, but the words bubbled to the surface no matter how hard I tried to stop them. This was Annie. She wouldn't judge me. "I know, I know. Why am I such a glutton for punishment? I mean, Riley doesn't even know about my dad or the money, so he must like me as a person enough to want to be my friend. But stupid me has to go and want more. *Aargghh!* And I can't even hide away and avoid him. These two weeks are going to be hell! I hate my life..."

The last thing I expected was my best friend's pensive silence. Annie frowned and started tinkling on the keyboard. I wanted to scream at her, tell her to give me all the answers, like she usually did. Why did she have to pick *now* to have nothing to say?

Without lifting her hands, or eyes, from the keyboard, Annie started to talk. "Katie. You are my best friend in the whole world, and it kills me to see what Mark Barnes did to you. But even more than what he did, it breaks my heart to see how much it *changed you*. You are beautiful, Katie, and special, loving, and caring. And any guy who can't see that doesn't deserve you. Mark and his cohorts were complete morons. But maybe it *is* time we stopped tarring all pretty-boys with the same brush. You want people to stop judging you on your looks? Well, you have to do the same thing."

I nudged Annie and winked. "Hang on... you lost me

back at the part where you said I was beautiful. Seriously...
are you blind?"

Annie's head whipped up, the look in her eyes warning
me to shut up before she even spoke. "Kaaatie... stop it!
Everyone is beautiful in their own way. *No-one* deserves
what Mark did to you."

I tried to ignore the tears building behind my eyelashes.
No way! I swore I'd never shed another tear over what that
dickwad did. But it was like the memory of that day was
tattooed on my brain in indelible ink. How did you erase
something like that? And then the dam burst, and the
memories flooded in. I was back in that classroom, staring
at the video on Mark's phone.

I jumped as Annie's arm slipped around my shoulders.
"Katie...? Katie, I'm so sorry. Please don't cry. I didn't mean
to bring it all back. I just miss the old Katie. It's like Mark
broke something inside you, and I just want to help fix it."

I wrapped my arms around myself and looked into my
best friend's tear-filled eyes. Annie was right. I *had* felt
broken ever since that horrific day. The months I'd spent
huddled in my room and avoiding the world had been like a
prison sentence. It wasn't until the day the letter arrived
from *Crescendo* that I'd felt like I was coming up for air after
nearly drowning.

Yep, I'd survived. And now I was exactly where I wanted
to be.

"You know what? You're right. Riley is nothing like
Mark and his boy-band wannabes, and Joel seems pretty
cool too. Let's just enjoy the next two weeks getting to
know our new friends and see what happens after that."

"That's my girl. Now, can we please get on with what we do best? Not that you could ever describe my backup vocals as 'best', but *meh*, we can only work with what we've got. Besides, I more than makeup for it with my sensational keyboard skills."

Chapter Eight

Riley

It felt good to be doing something normal again. The last twenty-four hours had been such a whirlwind that I didn't know whether I was coming or going. I strummed the last chord in the song we'd been playing, chuckling as Joel broke into a dramatic, unwritten riff. He always had to have the last word, even if it *was* just a drum beat.

Aaand, just like that, my brain was instantly back to thinking about Katie. Damnit, I couldn't get her out of my head. I wanted to hear her laugh, make her smile and forget whatever crap from her past haunted her.

All. The. Freakin'. Time.

But more than anything else, I wanted to hear her sing. No, I *needed* to hear her sing. And she was only two studios away, probably doing that right now. "Hey Joel, there's only, like, ten minutes left until the bell. How about we pack up and go see what the girls are up to?"

"Yeah, good idea. I'd rather find out if they're any good before we book the studio for this arvo. I mean... a concert pianist turned keyboard player? What if they're into church music or something?"

I chuckled as I packed up my guitar and leads and stashed them in my studio locker. It sounded like Joel was thinking along the same lines as me. I'd never even considered what *kind* of music Katie might be into. I couldn't decide whether it would be better or worse if she were into church music or heavy metal, or something equally distasteful.

Maybe better... at least for the sake of my sanity?

Well, whatever genre she was into, and even if she wasn't that good, I'd just have to prove I could be a good friend and offer lots of encouragement. *That's* what friends did. We'd dropped Katie and Annie off at Studio Three just under an hour and a half ago, promising to pick them back up on our way to lunch. So it wouldn't be weird if we just *happened* to get there a bit early and went in to wait for them... *would it?* The studios were all soundproofed, so we'd need to go inside if we wanted to hear the girls rehearsing.

Oh, stuff it. People were always popping into studios to check out the competition.

Besides, what performer didn't enjoy an audience?

MY HEART WAS HAMMERING in my chest as I quietly pushed the door open and slipped inside, Joel on my heels. Katie's back was to the door, but I was pretty sure Annie noticed us sneaking in before we moved over to the chairs just out of her line of vision.

I smiled when Annie didn't miss a beat. "Okay, we've got just enough time for one more song. How about some Alicia Keys to finish off?"

"Hell yeah. I love listening to you play that intro. Take it away, maestro."

Okay, so definitely not church music or heavy metal. I nudged Joel, and he grinned, wiping the back of his hand across his forehead and mouthing *'phew'*. When Annie started to play the introduction to *If I Ain't Got You*, Joel's eyes widened in appreciation. *Wow.* If Katie could pull this off, she had talent. And then she started to sing...

Some people live for the fortune...

I froze, goosebumps breaking out all over my skin as Katie's voice floated across the room.

Some people live for the fame...

Hot damn. Her voice was incredible. I could have sworn I was listening to a recording of Alicia Keys. No wait. She was putting her own spin on it. This wasn't just some karaoke performance. She *owned* the song and made it hers. Hiding in this corner where I couldn't watch her facial expressions was killing me. *Stuff it!* If she got mad at me for being there, I'd take it on the chin. I *needed* to see this!

Sucking in a deep breath, I stood and moved back to the doorway. Katie still had her back to the door, but when Annie smiled, raising her eyebrows and tilting her chin toward the door, Katie turned to see who was there. I smiled and held my breath, waiting for her reaction, praying she wouldn't go off at me.

Without missing a beat, Katie belted out the chorus, her eyes sparkling, her beautiful smile lighting up the room. *Wow.* This confident, passionate girl was nothing like the Katie I'd met the day before. *This* Katie shone with an inner light, captivating my soul and leaving me completely breathless. I stood mesmerised until the final note faded away, not wanting it to end.

Man... I needed to get a grip. I felt like I'd been sucker punched. My entire world had been tipped upside down, and I knew nothing would ever be the same again.

I watched in a daze as Joel strode across the studio and hugged first Katie and then

Annie. "Holy shit, you guys. That was incredible."

I was still standing there in stunned silence when Katie put her hands on her hips and stared at me. I tried to say something... *anything*... but words refused to come out.

Katie's face split into a cheeky grin, her eyes twinkling, as if she knew I was struggling to speak. "Well? Some *friend* you are. You're supposed to at least say it was okay."

Heat flooded my face—Jesus, I must look like a tongue-tied schoolboy.

Just tell her how brilliant she is, moron.

"Yeah, what Joel said." I finally muttered, shoving my hands in my pockets and looking down at my feet.

What the hell was wrong with me? Tell her she's amazing. That I couldn't take my eyes off her. That she's... beautiful.

Oh shit. *That* was the problem. The feelings flooding through me were way more than friendship. I wanted to pull her into my arms and kiss those soft, pink lips.

No matter how much I wanted to deny it, I was into Katie Sims.

Katie's grin turned to a frown, her eyes hurt and confused. Great, now I'd made her sad. Friends didn't do this to each other.

Fake it, man... do something to fix it...

I thanked God when the bell for the end of class rang. I needed time to sort out my stupid head—and heart.

Joel threw me a confused look and turned back to the girls. "So... me and Riley were

talking earlier, and we thought maybe—"

Nooo. Not today... "We'd... ummm... go to the coffee shop next door rather than have lunch in the cafeteria. You girls okay with that?" I glared at Joel, warning him not to argue, and he just shrugged and frowned.

Annie jumped up from her stool behind the keyboard, her eyes flicking from Joel, to me, and back to Joel. "Ummm... sure, sounds great, right Katie?"

"Yeah, whatever," Katie said, busying herself with packing away her microphone.

Rubbing the back of my neck, I mentally kicked myself for being such a jerk. Maybe aliens had taken over my brain? "Okay... cool." I still couldn't look at Katie. I seriously needed to get outta there. "So, we'll meet you out the front? I just need to grab something from my room. Let's go, Joel."

I winced as Katie slammed her studio locker shut and started rifling through her bag. "Hey, you know what? I think I'd rather grab something from the cafeteria and eat it in my room. You go if you want, Annie. I'm sure I can find my way to our next class."

Without another word, Katie picked up her bag and left the studio. After throwing me a filthy look, Annie apologised to Joel and went after her friend.

Wow! I'd totally screwed that up. How was it that I craved her company and then acted like a total jerk every time I was around her? And how the hell did I fix it?

Joel glared at me like I'd grown an extra head. "What the hell is going on with you, man? What happened to asking them about booking a studio for later and having a jam?"

"I changed my mind, okay?" *Whoa, had I seriously just growled?*

"That's total crap, Stone. You're acting like a moron, and I wanna know what's going on. This affects me too, remember. I was looking forward to the jam. Who died and made you God?"

Yeah... Joel was right. He at least deserved to know why I was acting like a basket case. The problem was that *I* had no idea why I was doing it. All I *did* know, was that I needed some time away from Katie to get my head back together. "Look, man, I'm really sorry I screwed everything up. I just... *oh God...* listening to Katie sing kind of scrambled my brain."

"Wait... what? Holy snapping duck shit! You're actually into her. Like, more than just the friends thing. I would *never* have picked you falling for someone like—"

"Just shut it, okay? I'm not *into* her." *Liar.* "I'm just sort of a bit overwhelmed by her talent. I mean, she's like... *amazing.* Why would she wanna hang out with someone like me?"

"Seriously? C'mon, Riley, you're every bit as good as her. But you need to stop acting like

a complete douchebag every time she's around. You're supposed to be friends, so start acting like one." A grin replaced the frown. "Hey, who'd have thought I'd ever be giving you advice about girls? Although, I think it might have more to do with the whole 'girls-as-friends' being my specialty. So, welcome to my world! Anyway, just snap out of it, okay? Maybe we can still catch up to them in the cafeteria if we hurry. But you need to play nice and eat some humble pie."

Shit. Joel was right. About everything. I was acting like a total tool. "Yeah... whatever," I mumbled, following Joel out the door.

Okay Stone. It's time to pull yourself together and sort out the mush you once called a brain.

Right. So why had I panicked when Joel tried to arrange the jam session?

Because I wanted some space from Katie.

Okay, so why did I suddenly need this space?

Because something weird happened while I was

listening to Katie sing. Like...me wanting to pull her into my arms and hold her. But maybe that was just how friends felt when they were impressed by something the other one did?

Yeah... but about the kissing part...

HAVE I mentioned that I might be at risk of falling for a certain green-eyed redhead? Yeah, well, I'm pretty sure it's no longer just a risk.

I groaned as an earthquake started playing havoc with my stomach when I spotted Katie and Annie at the front of the food line in the cafeteria.

Calm down, idiot. It's just because you feel guilty for not telling her what an amazing singer she is. Friends... remember?

Damnit, I could do this. I'd just apologise for being such a jerk earlier, and deal with the fallout. I stood with Joel next to the cashier and waited for the girls to pay for their lunch, trying to ignore Katie's what-the-hell-are-you-doing-here-jerk look.

Suck it up, arsehole, she has every right to be angry.

I held her gaze and shrugged, giving her a sheepish smile as she stepped away from the cashier. "Hey, Katie. Look, I'm sorry I was acting kinda weird before. I guess I was just stunned by how amazing your voice is. So, can you *please* just tell me I'm a jerk so we can all have lunch together?"

Katie's eyes widened at my apology, and then she softened, a smile tugging at the corners of her mouth. "Well, that was a backhanded compliment if ever I've heard one. What do you think, Annie? Can we stand their company for the whole of lunch?"

Annie just shook her head and looked between the two of us. "I don't know... I'm getting whiplash just from being around you two. But if you promise to play nice, I suppose I can suffer through it." She grinned and looked around for a table.

Joel chuckled and slapped me on the shoulder. "What she said." Then he looked over at the queue for lunch and groaned. "Damnit, I'm starving." His eyes flicked back to mine, his face breaking into a sly grin. "Hey Stone, grab me a ham and cheese sandwich and an orange juice, will ya mate? There's no point in us *both* standing in the queue. I'll help the girls find a table."

Seriously? So now I was his slave?

I opened my mouth to argue, but the look Joel threw me told me this was my punishment for being a jerk.

Fine, I'd get our damn lunch.

I shrugged and walked to the end of the line, standing behind a couple of what I would previously have considered 'hot' girls. I knew they were trying to flirt with me, but I was too busy watching Joel's hand resting on the small of Katie's back as he guided her towards a table. Okay, so his other hand was on Annie's back. But that didn't stop me being pissed by the sight of Joel's hand on Katie.

Okay, so maybe I was in even deeper shit than I thought. Jealousy was an entirely foreign emotion in my life, and I had no idea how to deal with it.

<h1 style="text-align:center">Chapter Nine</h1>

Katie

Did I mention that Riley Stone was the most annoyingly confusing guy I'd ever met? Yeah, well, those adjectives didn't even come close to explaining what he was doing to my head! Every time I thought I had Riley figured out, he did or said something so far out of left field I was left staggering.

I sat down at the table next to Annie as Joel slipped into the chair opposite. I seriously needed to claw my way back to some semblance of normality before I said or did something stupid. *Yeah right!* That would require me to stop thinking about *him*, something that had apparently become beyond the realms of possibility. Every time I was around him, it felt like all the air had been sucked out of the room, making it almost impossible to breathe.

Pretending to focus on unwrapping my sandwich, I snuck a glance toward where I knew Riley would be standing. *Of course,* he was looking this way, scowling, when his stormy blue eyes landed on mine. What was he scowling about now? And then the scowl lifted, and he smiled, turning my insides to mush.

How the hell did I end up a passenger on what could only end as an emotional train wreck? My brain was yelling *Stop—I wanna get off,* while my stupid heart refused to even acknowledge the possibility of the impending disaster.

And since when did I sprout all this philosophical bullshit?

I tore my eyes away and went back to unwrapping my sandwich, wanting to kick myself for my reaction to that smile.

Stop it! It's perfectly normal for friends to smile at each other.

So, even though I wanted to rip my hair out for doing it, I snuck another peek in his direction. The smile on my face froze. *Of course,* he was talking and laughing with the two 'hot chicks' in the queue in front of him. Why wouldn't he be? *Those girls* were potential hook-ups. I was just the friend.

So why did that thought hurt so much?

"What do you think, Katie? Sounds like fun, eh?" I looked up from my sandwich to find Annie and Joel both looking at me. Great, I had no idea what they'd been talking about, and now Annie was asking me to agree to whatever it was.

"Ummm... sorry, I was miles away. What did I miss?" *Well, not exactly miles. More like stalking the lunch queue on the other side of the room.*

Annie rolled her eyes and shook her head. "Joel was just saying they were thinking about booking a rehearsal studio for a jam after classes this afternoon. He asked if we'd come play. We'd love to... right?"

Seriously? More time around Riley? Just what I didn't need. But Annie's eyes were pleading with me to agree.

Stuff it, I could do this. Maybe if I spent some time around the guy while sharing our common interests, my *heart* might go back to listening to my *head*. "Yeah, sounds great. Time to see what you guys can do." I winked at Joel, smiling at Annie's noticeable relief.

Joel wore a huge grin. "Cool. We'll try to get the studio we were in earlier. Is that okay? There's a keyboard in there, and it's where all our gear is stored. You'd just need to grab your mic. from your locker if that's okay, Katie?"

"Sounds awesome," Annie said, her eyes shining with excitement.

"What sounds awesome?" Riley slid into the chair opposite mine, and butterflies swarmed in my stomach. *Why the hell wasn't it illegal to be that gorgeous?* He smiled and lifted an eyebrow, waiting for someone to answer his question.

Joel was still grinning. "We're on for that jam this afternoon. Now we just have to hope the studio's free."

Riley's smile faltered for just a second, his Adam's apple bobbing as he swallowed.

Wait... he looked nervous. Why would he...? No way. He *couldn't* be anxious about playing in front of me and Annie... could he?

Riley had seen us perform and seemed impressed. But

these guys would have to be just as talented, if not more, to get into *Crescendo*... right? Plus, they'd already had a whole extra year at the Academy to concentrate on their music.

But I did need to know one thing. "So... ah... I'm just going to assume you guys don't play church music or heavy metal or something equally obnoxious?"

Joel and Riley both burst out laughing. I looked at Annie to see if she knew what was so funny, but she just shrugged and shook her head. *Okay, so what did I say?*

"Sorry," Riley spluttered. "But that's *exactly* what Joel was worried you guys might be into before we snuck in to listen to you perform."

"Great minds think alike, huh?" Joel said, waggling his eyebrows.

I laughed and started to relax. These guys were *nothing* like the jerks I'd met in my old high school. Maybe it really didn't matter to them what I looked like. And the amazing part? For the first time in what felt like forever, I was actually having fun.

"So... Monday afternoons are usually when rehearsals for the end-of-semester musical happen. But seeing auditions aren't until Friday, there's a whole school meeting in the auditorium after lunch to discuss the upcoming production. It's not Joel's and my thing, but we thought we might audition for the orchestra."

A musical? Wow. I'd always wanted to try something like that. But my palms instantly got sweaty, my heart pounding at the thought of auditioning. Maybe it would be too much too soon... But the words burst out anyway.

"That sounds like fun. Any idea what the production might be?"

Riley raised his eyebrows. "Really? I wouldn't have thought you'd be into that kind of thing?"

As usual, I blushed. "Well, I've never tried it, but I'd love to give it a shot."

Before I'd even finished talking, reality raised its ugly head. In all the musicals I'd seen, the leading lady was always beautiful. So, even if I had the vocal ability to land a role, I'd never fulfil the right 'look' requirements. *Yeah, whatever.*

"Hey." Riley frowned. "What happened? You went from looking excited to depressed in less than a nanosecond. Cold feet about auditioning?"

Wow. He must have been watching me the whole time —*more of that stupid weirdness.*

I looked down at the table, running my nails along some random words carved into the table. There was no way I could tell Riley why I'd changed my mind. We'd already had the whole looks-don't-matter argument. Besides, I didn't want to ruin the relaxed atmosphere at the table.

"Yeah, something like that. Anyway, I think I'll pass. There's sure to be heaps of talented people auditioning with way more experience than me."

Riley tilted his head as if he knew that wasn't the real problem. "Are you serious? You'd be crazy not to audition. It wouldn't be the first time a new student got the lead. Besides, everyone is encouraged to audition, for the experience if nothing else. Auditions were a hoot last year. Some students dressed up in character and hammed it up, just for a laugh."

Annie nudged me, and I lifted my head to look at her. "How about we hold off making any decisions until after we find out what the show is? You never know…" She had that don't-you-dare-do-this look in her eyes, and I knew she'd figured out why I'd changed my mind. *Damn girl was always reading my mind.*

I was scrambling for something to say when the end of lunch bell rang. Avoiding Annie's eyes, I stood up and threw my bag over my shoulder. But when I absently reached behind me to grab my tray, my hand came into contact with something that sent tingles shooting up my arm. I looked back to find another hand under mine.

Yep, that would explain the tingles.

Time slowed down as my eyes followed the path up a muscular arm, a broad shoulder, a set of smiling lips, and finished at a pair of twinkling eyes.

Oh. My. God. I needed a damned fan. How was any girl with a pulse supposed to resist that?

Stop staring at him and say something!

"Ummm… that's okay, I've got it…"

"Yeah… I was just gonna…"

We both stuttered to an uncomfortable halt, my face feeling like it was on fire.

"Oh, for God's sake," Annie said, snatching the tray off the table. "Give me yours too, Riley, and I'll return them all."

"Hang on. I'll walk with you, Annie." Joel added,

jumping up to follow her to the rubbish bin and tray return. "We'll catch up with you guys in the auditorium."

"Look, Katie..."

"Look, Riley..."

Damnit, we'd both spoken at once... *again. Awkward or what?*

"Okay, me first." Riley rubbed the back of his neck and shuffled his feet. *Wow, this was so not how I'd ever expected a pretty-boy to act.* "As you can probably tell, I'm not used to 'hanging out' with girls. This might sound like I'm full of myself, but girls don't usually want me for my 'conversation skills'. Being judged on your looks works both ways... you know?"

My heart fluttered at his words. Who'd have thought I'd ever feel sorry for a guy like Riley? I'd spent my whole life wishing I was beautiful, never considering that there might be a downside to that, too. I guess you learn something new every day.

I smiled up at him, drowning in the depths of his beautiful blue eyes. "Well, I guess there's always a first time for everything. I'm not used to having a guy want to be around me... period. Anyway, how about you try to think of me as a mate, like Joel, and I'll try to treat you like I do Annie?"

Yeah, right... as if I'd ever want to kiss Annie.

Whoa... I did not *just think that. Shutting down all thought processes... now.*

Riley's shoulders relaxed, his smile lighting up his face. "Hmmm... not sure I'll ever be able to think of you like Joel. For a start, you have a much better voice..."

The giggle escaped— *damnit... no giggling. You sound like a ten-year-old with a crush!*—before my brain could kick into gear. "Okay, so maybe I could take up the drums?"

Riley shook his head and crooked his elbow. "No way. One noise-maker in this group is more than enough. Come on. Let's find out what amazing production we could be a part of this year."

A shiver ran up my spine as I wrapped my hand around Riley's offered forearm. I left the cafeteria arm-in-arm with my new *friend*, feeling like I was floating on a cloud. I couldn't help noticing some surprised—*oh yeah, and a few disgusted*—looks thrown my way by the girls we passed.

See? Being friends was heaps better than being in a relationship.

Yeah, you just keep telling yourself that, Katie.

Riley

MAYBE THIS WHOLE *just friends* thing might work after all. Having Katie sitting beside me in the auditorium made everything... well... just somehow better. Who'd have thought having a girl just as a friend could feel this good?

Okay, so it *might* have been a bit awkward when we'd first found Annie and Joel holding our seats in the auditorium. Katie had dropped into the closest seat, beside Annie, and I'd hesitated, just for a second. Should I push past all three of them and sit next to Joel, or take the closest seat, next to Katie? Stuff it. If I were supposed to think of Katie the same way as Joel, I would simply be choosing to sit beside my *new* friend rather than my *old* one. It had nothing to do with wanting to sit with Katie… it was just the closest seat.

Well, that's my story, and I'm sticking to it!

Professor Hart stood in front of the microphone, and when he cleared his throat and waved his hands, the noise level instantly dropped. "Good afternoon, ladies and gentlemen. I'm sure you're all eager to know what this semester's production will be, so I'll hand you over to our Musical Director, Professor Haines."

Okay, so I tried to focus on what the Professor was saying, but watching the emotions flitting across Katie's expressive face was way more interesting.

"…this year's production will be a little different. Rather than being limited to a few lead roles, I have put together a musical revue featuring excerpts from the music of Cole Porter's greatest musicals. I believe this will provide the greatest opportunity to showcase the talent of more students here at *Crescendo* while broadening the scope of the roles available.

A rundown of the excerpts, plus the relevant audition pieces, will be available on your way out. You may spend the afternoon working on your audition piece, and audition times will be announced later in the week. Please feel free to email me with any questions. Good luck, everyone."

Applause and excited chatter broke out as soon as Professor Haines left the stage. Katie hadn't stopped chewing on her thumbnail for the entire speech. She looked so... vulnerable... and I wanted to reach out and squeeze her hand.

What was it about her that made me feel this way? Katie was so far from my usual 'type' that it was ridiculous.

But then... did I really have a 'type'? Sure, I'd always *hooked-up* with 'hot chicks', but were they the type of girls I wanted a relationship with? Thoughts of Elise's stick-thin, grasping arms made me shudder. I couldn't think of anything *worse* than hanging out in one of the rehearsal studios with her after class. Apart from being a dancer who couldn't hold a tune, she was constantly gushing and fishing for compliments. *Ugh... no thanks.*

I snapped back to earth to find the auditorium emptying around me. Bloody hell, I'd been doing the brooding, silent weirdo thing again. Why couldn't I act normal around Katie? We'd already agreed we weren't attracted to each other, so I seriously needed to get over this... whatever *this* was.

I smiled when I realised Katie was in the same state as I'd been. At my gentle nudge, she stopped mauling her nails and looked up. *Damn, those eyes were beautiful.* "So, what do you think? Sounds a bit less intimidating than audi-tioning for a lead role."

"We'll see. I want to check out the audition pieces and what excerpts she's picked first. Hey, do you think we might be able to book a studio starting now, seeing we have the whole afternoon free?"

Of course. I should have thought of that the minute Professor Haines announced the free afternoon. Although... Studio Five was set up mainly for bands to practice, so maybe it wouldn't be booked yet. "Right. I'm on it. Give me five minutes."

Grinning, I jumped up and raced to the teachers' exit at the front of the hall. Relieved to see Professor Haines just stepping out the door, I jogged to catch up with her.

"Excuse me, Professor, do you have a minute?" I puffed from behind her.

Professor Haines turned, her eyebrows lifting in surprise, and then smiled. "Aah, Riley. It's lovely to see you. What can I do for you? I wouldn't have thought you'd be interested in a *Cole Porter* production. Not really your thing, is it?"

I shrugged and gave her a sheepish smile. Professor Haines knew my passion was more about putting a band together and eventually working toward getting a recording contract. "Actually, this is about my buddy. She has an amazing voice but not a lot of confidence. I was wondering if we could book a rehearsal studio for the afternoon and maybe work on an audition piece?"

Professor Haines' smile thinned, her eyes narrowing as she tilted her head. "So this is definitely about her 'vocal talent', right? Who is this amazing singer you're so enchanted with?"

Yeah. She was doing the judging thing too. Why did everyone always assume I was just some man-whore looking for a hook-up with a 'hot chick'?

Maybe because that's what you've always let the world believe, dufus.

"Ummm... her name's Katie Sims, and she really does—"

Professor Haines was looking at me as if I'd grown another head. Surely she couldn't know Katie already?

"So, you've been buddied with Katie Sims? I must say I'm impressed by your enthusiasm to help her out. Surprised but impressed."

"You know Katie? How—?"

"I was on the committee for acceptances last year and was fortunate enough to see Katie's audition. You seem to know a lot about her for such a short acquaintance. You're right; she does have an amazing voice but could definitely benefit from some positive input in the confidence department."

"Exactly. So... is Studio Five available?"

Professor Haines lifted the clipboard she carried and scanned the page. She smiled and nodded. "You're in luck. It's free all afternoon."

Yes! This day just kept getting better. "Thanks, Professor. I'll go let the others know."

"Others?"

"Yeah, my roommate Joel Kenny is buddied with Katie's best friend, Annie Keats. Annie plays—"

"Piano and keyboard. Yes, I'm well aware of Annie's ability as well. It seems you've teamed up with some very talented artists this year, Riley. Let's hope you *all* have a positive influence on each other. Enjoy your afternoon."

"Thanks, we will."

"Er... Mr Stone?" I'd only taken two steps when something in Professor Haines' tone made me stop and turn back. "Do *not* trifle with this girl's emotions. Are we clear?"

I swallowed and took in Professor Haines' stony-faced

demeanour. She knew something about Katie's past—maybe what had happened to make Katie hate pretty-boys and believe she was ugly? So, it had to be more than some trivial failed romance that had affected her so badly.

All the more reason she needs a friend, *Romeo.* "Crystal clear, Professor."

She seemed satisfied with whatever she read in my eyes because she nodded and headed back down the corridor. I turned and raced back to the auditorium. It was time to put a lid on whatever my *hormones* were feeling about Katie. This was about what *she* needed: a *friend* who didn't send mixed messages. Someone, or something, had tried to destroy this beautiful girl's soul, and I vowed to do everything in my power to repair the damage.

Even if it killed me...

Yeah... or it broke my heart.

Chapter Ten

Katie

"Hey, where was Riley off to like he had a firecracker up his arse?" Joel leaned over Annie to ask.

And, of course, I giggled—*yeah, I know, immature yada yada*—shaking my head as I turned to Annie and Joel. "He went to see if we could book the rehearsal studio earlier. Like, for the whole afternoon."

Annie clapped her hands, then winced like I'd done after the giggle. Okay, we really needed to work on squashing the over-excited-little-girl responses to things. It was time to start acting at least *slightly* mature.

Yeah, right, like that *was ever gonna happen*. A vision of a 'mature' conversation between Annie and me swam into my mind, posh voices included:

"Oh, Annie, I have such exciting news. Riley has managed to acquire access to the rehearsal studio for the entire afternoon."

"How lovely, Katie. I'm sure that will be a most enjoyable experience."

The added visual of the two of us sitting with demurely crossed ankles and hands folded in our laps brought me undone, and I cracked up laughing. The worried look I caught Annie and Joel sharing just made me laugh harder. They probably thought I'd lost the plot.

Which might not be too far from the truth.

"Ummm... Katie." Did Annie seriously sound nervous? I really must be acting like more of a nutter than usual. "Joel and I thought we might grab the programme and audition pieces while we wait for Riley. You wanna come, or are you happy to wait here?"

I wiped the tears from laughing away and smiled into Annie's worried face. "Nah. I'll wait here. I'd hate Riley to get back and think we ditched him." I reached out and rubbed Annie's arm. "I'm fine... really. Just a bit of sensory overload I think. It's been a long time since I've had this much excitement, or this many people, in my life. Ya know?"

Annie smiled, tears filling her eyes. "I know. Nice to have you back," she whispered, trying to blink the tears away before turning back to Joel. "Come on, Kenny. Time to brave the 'madding crowd'."

Joel threw me a wary nod, then grinned and walked beside Annie to the back of the auditorium. They certainly seemed awfully 'chummy' all of a sudden. Had I missed something there? Suddenly, I couldn't wait to get back to our room tonight. *So* much had happened in one day, and it was far from over. At this rate, we'd be talking half the night.

I looked back to see Riley entering through the same door he'd exited earlier. And just the sight of him had my heart doing that stupid gargantuan butterflies thing.

Okay, it's time to have some serious words with that particular organ. Which part of f.r.i.e.n.d.s didn't it get? All of it, obviously!

Being around Riley made me so wired I didn't know which way was up anymore. And it wasn't just about his hot body, ruggedly handsome face, and baby-blue eyes I could get lost in...

Okay... all that did *make him pretty irresistible.*

But it was more about the person he was on the inside. Even when we were sparring, and he wasn't acting like a surly weirdo, he made me feel good about who *I* was. And apart from Annie, no one else had *ever* made me feel that way.

Riley flopped back into his seat, grinning like the cat who swallowed the canary. "Hey. Mission accomplished. Studio Five is ours for the rest of the day. Where'd Annie and Joel get to?"

"Oh, they went to grab the audition stuff. I told them I'd wait here for you." *Seriously Katie? You sound like some puppy dog waiting for her master's return.* "I mean... we didn't want you thinking we'd ditched you or anything.

Besides, I was starting to feel a bit like the third wheel around Annie and Joel."

Riley's jaw dropped. "Wait... what? Annie and Joel? No way Joel would... I mean... nah, you must have imagined it."

Wait. Was he saying Annie wasn't good enough for Joel?

Right. Yet another blood-boiling episode coming right up. "Excuse me? Are you suggesting Joel couldn't possibly be interested in someone like Annie? What... he's only into hotties... like you are?" As soon as the words left my mouth, I wanted to take them back. Riley had been trying so hard to be my friend, and I'd attacked him... again. "Riley... I—"

Riley sighed and rubbed his hand through his hair. "Save it, Katie. I already know what you think of me. But that wasn't why I was surprised about Annie and Joel. What I *meant* was that Joel didn't think *Annie* would ever be interested in *him*. Look, just forget it, okay? I'm gonna see if I can find Annie and Joel and tell them the good news about the studio."

I watched him walk away and wanted to kick myself. *Why did I keep doing that?* Riley had been so excited about getting the studio, and I'd practically slapped him in the face.

Okay, Annie was right. I'd turned into a snarky bitch who didn't deserve to have friends. I needed to stop allowing what happened with Mark the scumbag to ruin any chance of future happiness.

Right! It was time to leave my past where it belonged... *in the past.* I was only sixteen, for God's sake. I had my entire life ahead of me. And unless I wanted to end up a lonely old lady with too many cats, I needed to pull my head in.

Starting. Right. Now.

Riley

UNBELIEVABLE! *What was that girl's problem?*

Sucking in a breath through gritted teeth, I tried to salvage the good mood I'd been in after talking to Professor Haines. No hope of that! Katie's words had gutted me like some freakin' weapon of mass destruction.

Maybe this whole friend thing was just a bad idea. Just because we were stuck together as buddies, it didn't mean we *had* to spend our free time together. I'd already gone way above and beyond the school's requirements. Maybe it was time to back off.

So why did that thought make me even angrier?

In her defence, Katie had looked like she wanted to apologise for what she'd said, but I'd been too angry to listen. Okay, so maybe what she'd said had hurt because it was *true*. But that was the person I *used* to be. Since meeting Katie, everything had changed. I didn't want to be *that* guy anymore. But I also didn't need someone throwing my past actions in my face every five minutes!

Damnit! Meeting Katie hadn't just changed who *I* wanted to be.

It had made me question everything I'd ever believed about myself.

It didn't help that Katie was like a powder keg, ready to explode at the slightest provocation. What if her snarkiness had nothing to do with whatever happened in her past? Maybe this was just who she was? And the last thing I needed was more of that kind of drama in my life. I'd thought I left all that behind when I left home.

No. Katie was nothing like my mother.

Damned if that thought didn't open the door to an entirely different can of worms. Being raised by a manic-depressive mother had almost destroyed me more times than I could count. Which was why winning the full scholarship to *Crescendo* had been a double-edged sword. It offered me a chance at a normal life, but it also came at a high price. The guilt of feeling like I was abandoning my family—*or at least my mother*—if I accepted it.

Hell, what if she stopped taking her medication?

Without me there to stop her, she might actually succeed in killing herself, something she'd tried before.

I'd been emotionally torn over the decision, watching my hopes and dreams gurgle sadly as they slipped down the plug hole. Until my older brother, Sean, finally agreed to step up and take some responsibility for the first time in his life. So I packed up and ran, terrified Sean would change his mind at the last minute. And *then* I'd almost thrown it all away, spending most of my first year at *Crescendo* partying and making out with any girl who was interested—anything to numb the guilt and worry.

Until I met Katie...

Joel's hand on my shoulder snapped me out of my internal spiral into depression. "So, how'd you go? Are we jammin'?" Annie stood beside him, her eyes sparkling with excitement.

Wow, I needed a bit of whatever these two were having. "Yep. Studio Five is ours for the rest of the afternoon. Did you get all the stuff we need?"

Annie nodded, tapping the folder she held against her chest and looking around with a frown. "Where's Katie?"

"Yeah, about that." I rubbed the back of my neck and blew out a breath. Maybe Annie could get her to chill out. "She's... ar... still over where we were sitting. We kinda had words... yeah, again. Look, how about Joel and I go set up, and you go with Katie to get her mic? We'll meet you there."

Annie sighed and threw me an apologetic look. "Another attack of the snarling bitch, huh?"

I shrugged and looked down at the floor. "Something like that."

"Hey, if it helps, she never used to be like this. Some shitty stuff happened last year that she's still dealing with. She just needs some time to get used to the whole... well, being here. Plus, I think *your* wanting to be friends has sort of thrown her for a loop. You being... well... you know." Annie blushed and tucked some hair behind her ears. "Anyway, we'll meet you in the studio."

I watched Annie walk away and scratched my head. Well, at least that answered one question. Katie's current behaviour wasn't the norm. So maybe I just needed to make a concerted effort to stop bringing out the snarling dragon.

Wow. Who knew that hanging around with girls could be so complicated?

"So, what happened this time?" Joel asked as we walked out of the auditorium.

I looked at Joel and shook my head. "Same ole, same ole. I'm a man-whore who's only interested in hot chicks." Okay, so maybe I couldn't resist adding the rest. "Oh, and you are too."

"*Excuse me?* Where did *that* come from?"

I laughed and told Joel about my conversation with Katie. By the time I'd finished, Joel had turned fire-engine red.

I nudged him and grinned. "So... was she right?"

"About which part exactly?" Joel growled.

"Well, we both know she's wrong about you being a man-whore. So what's the go with you and Annie?"

"We're just friends. I thought I'd follow in the master's footsteps and see what happens," Joel said, wiggling his eyebrows.

Me... a master? Yeah right. Master of stuffing-up, maybe.

We'd started walking toward the rehearsal studio when Joel grabbed my arm and pulled me to a stop, a frown on his face. "Hey, I just remembered something. I overheard the girls talking earlier, and Katie said something really weird. Something about her not being around people for a long time. What's with that?"

Okay, that *was* weird. Did she mean she hadn't been around people during the Christmas break? But that wasn't exactly a *long* time. What the hell had happened in her past?

Damn, my head hurt. "Who knows, man. But I'm not sure I have the energy to deal with whatever it is right now. I'm starting to think these two weeks can't go fast enough. Being around girls this much is seriously starting to do my head in."

Yeah, maybe walking away would be the best solution... for everyone.

Chapter Eleven

Katie

"Seriously, Katie, Riley is a pretty great guy. And you're doing everything you can to sabotage the friendship he's offering. What's going on?" Annie stood beside me with her hands on her hips and a scowl on her face.

I opened the locker in the studio, pulled my microphone out, and slammed the door closed, turning on Annie like this was all her fault. "I like him, okay? I mean, *like*, like, and it's driving me nuts! What is wrong with me? How could I develop feelings for someone like Riley after what Mark did?"

I slumped back against the wall and slid to the ground, wrapping my arms around my knees. "Oh, Annie, what am I gonna do? I *know* he's a nice guy. That's the problem. If he were just gorgeous on the outside, I wouldn't be having this problem. But he's *real*. And he wouldn't be attracted to me if I was the last girl on earth. He already said as much."

"Oh, Katie, I'm so sorry. Do you want me to go tell them you're not feeling well, and we'll cancel this afternoon? Maybe it's all been too much too soon. You've practically gone from hibernation to extreme exposure. Stepping away and giving yourself some time and distance from him might help you put stuff back into perspective."

I buried my head in my arms and let the dam burst, surprised by how therapeutic it felt to release the tears. Maybe I *did* need some time-out.

No. I couldn't do this to Annie. She'd been so excited about hanging out in the studio. Why should she have to miss out because I was a brainless sucker for punishment?

So much for my pep talk about not ending up the lonely old lady with too many cats.

Yeah, I was such an idiot!

When the tears finally slowed, I sucked in a deep breath, and couldn't help smiling when Annie handed me a box of tissues. Yeah, she was the best friend ever, and it was time I stepped up and acted like a friend should. I wasn't the first girl to develop a crush on a guy I couldn't have, and I wouldn't be the last. Wallowing in self-pity and lashing out at people who didn't deserve it was getting old—fast.

I could do this. "Nope. Riley went to a lot of trouble to arrange this, and I know you've been looking forward to it, too. I just need to put on my big-girl panties— which happen to be the only ones I own—and get on with it."

Annie laughed and held out a hand to pull me up. "You sure?"

"Positive. An afternoon of music with friends is just what I need. Just promise you'll kick me if I start with the snarly monster thing or making goo-goo eyes."

"You're on," Annie said with a wink as we headed out the door.

I pushed open the door to Studio Five, and I swear my heart stopped. Riley stood with his back to the door, singing and playing one of my favourite Keith Urban songs, *You Look Good in My Shirt.*

Hot damn. I had died and gone to heaven.

The butterflies in my stomach felt like they were on steroids. How could Riley possibly think I was anywhere *near* as talented as him?

Closing my eyes, I let his voice envelop me like a warm blanket, the emotion-laden lyrics bringing tears to my eyes.

What would it be like to have someone sing those words about me? Was Riley thinking about someone special as he sang?

I opened my eyes as the song finished to find him watching me. Without thinking, I crossed the room and threw my arms around his neck.

Damn, that felt good. "Oh my God, Riley... that was amazing."

I revelled in the feel of his heart thumping under my cheek, inhaling his masculine scent and wishing I could stay where I was forever. It wasn't until I became aware of the outline of his guitar trapped between us that reality rushed back in, and I realised what I'd done.

I just threw myself at Riley Stone. Somebody, please shoot me. I dropped my arms and backed away, my face on fire. "Sorry, I didn't mean to—

Riley's hand shot out and grabbed my wrist, sending shockwaves up my arm. "Don't you dare apologise. That's exactly what I should have done after listening to you sing. I was just too much of a wuss." He chuckled as he released my wrist and lifted his guitar strap over his head, propping the guitar against his amp. "So, I gather you're a fan of Keith Urban?"

"Yeah. But now I'm an even bigger fan of Riley Stone." I couldn't wipe the goofy grin off my face. "Seriously, Riley, that was... Oh God, I sound like a star-struck groupie. Maybe I need to start carrying around duct tape in my pocket."

"Hey, you might need to share that tape with me, Katie. 'Cos I'm about to start gushing too. Although, I might give the hug thing a miss." Annie still stood just inside the door with her arms folded. "That's some serious talent, Stone. And I may not know much about drummers, but you were rocking some serious beats there, too, Kenny."

We all burst out laughing, any tension from earlier disappearing. I sighed with relief. I'd been right. Music was the cure for everything.

Riley smiled at me, making my legs turn to jelly. It looked like my reaction to his singing had convinced him to forgive my earlier outburst. "So I guess we should check out the programme for the end-of-semester production. See if there's anything you're interested in?"

Annie had her head buried in the folder already, suddenly snorting as she looked up, her eyes sparkling. "You have *got* to be kidding me. Did you guys know Cole Porter wrote the music for a show called *Kiss Me Kate*? Is that a sign or what? Oh wait, it gets better. It's based on the Shakespeare play, *The Taming of the Shrew*, about a girl named Kate, a snarky redhead, who meets her match in a guy named Petruchio."

Riley must have seen the look on my face because he cracked up laughing.

A red-headed snarky bitch, eh? Hmmm..., it sounded way too close to home for me. "Can we at least listen to the audition song *before* we start type-casting?"

Annie grinned and pulled a thumb drive out of the folder, waving it around like she'd won a prize. "Is there somewhere in here we can play it?"

"Sure is," Joel said, swooping down and taking the USB stick from Annie like it was a baton in a relay race. They were all enjoying this way too much.

I breathed a huge sigh of relief as soon as the song started to play. It had been written for an operatic soprano, which definitely ruled me out. I sat with my arms folded, trying to hide the smirk on my face. But when a male baritone voice shouted, '*Kiss Me Kate*', and they broke into a duet to finish the song, I almost fell off my chair laughing.

"Oh, puh-lease. That was painful. I'd rather shut-my-tit-in-a-car-door than sing that drivel." I only realised I'd used my Aunt Suzie's favourite saying when I saw the horrified look on Riley and Joel's faces.

I shrugged and giggled—*yep, that's right... giggled—and was* shocked to discover I couldn't care less what I sounded like.

"Wait, I have an idea." Annie was studying the sheet music, chewing on her cheek, and flicking her pencil on the desk in front of her. "Riley, didn't you say some students dress up and like 'ham-up' their audition? What if we played with this and did a modern version of the song?"

No way! "Are you serious, Annie? It's not even in my key. And besides, it's a duet. I'd need a guy who knew the *new* version to sing it..."

Annie was staring at Riley, one eyebrow raised and her eyes twinkling. "Gee, I wonder who we could —"

"Don't look at me. I'm a guitarist, and I *don't* do musicals. As if I'm going to—"

Yes! Escape route right here. I held up a hand and tilted my head, pinning him down with a challenging stare. "*Excuse me?* What was it you said to me earlier, Riley? Oh yeah. *All* students are encouraged to audition because it's *good experience.* Maybe it's time you stepped out of the box and took a risk? I'll tell you what. If Annie can come up with a decent arrangement, I'll do it... but only if you do it with me. Isn't that what *friends* are supposed to do for each other?"

Riley continued to stare at me, his eyes blazing with an emotion I didn't recognise. It felt like everyone in the room was holding their breath.

I grinned, knowing this would get me off the hook. No way he'd say yes—

"Fine", he growled, his face turning red at the look of total shock on Joel's face. "But only if Annie can come up with a killer arrangement by tomorrow. We'll need time to rehearse."

"Ho-ly shit," Joel crooned. "This is going to be a hoot. Annie, if you can pull this off, you're a genius."

All I could do was stand there with my mouth open, gobsmacked that Riley was prepared to go along with this crap. I'd only challenged him because I was *sure* he'd say no. Damn him, he was supposed to be my out. I was seriously going to *kill* Annie when we got back to our room.

As if she knew what I was thinking, Annie looked at me with an angelic smile. "Great, then it's all sorted. I'm going to sit and tinkle at the piano in the corner for a while. Why don't you guys find some songs you all know and have that jam?"

I hadn't noticed how close Riley was standing until I felt his warm breath against my ear, his soft, husky voice making my blood pressure skyrocket. "Wow, she's good. Do you feel anywhere near as manipulated as I do right now?"

I turned and almost melted on the spot, his handsome face with its sexy five-o'clock shadow so close we were almost touching. "Y-yeah, she's a master manipulator, all right." I stepped back, sucking air into my deprived lungs. "But trust me, she *will* pay. And what about you? You weren't supposed to fold. I was counting on you to be my get-out-of-jail-free card."

The mischievous twinkle in his eye was mesmerising.

"Whadya mean? You were throwing me that fiery, challenging look of yours. No way I was backing down from that!"

I laughed and shook my head. "She played us both. I get that she knows how my mind works, but how the hell did she know you'd react that way?"

Riley looked over to where Annie sat, huddled in front of the piano. "Lucky guess? Either that, or she's been stalking me and taking notes."

"Hey... are we gonna jam or just stand around gasbaggin' all afternoon?" Joel was back on his stool behind his drum-kit, fiddling with his sticks and looking bored.

"Yeah, yeah. Keep your shirt on, Tarzan," Riley said, smiling down at me. "So, you ready to find something we can sing together?"

"Absolutely. Although I'm happy to sit and listen to you guys while Annie works on the song."

"Don't even think about it. I really wanna hear you sing again. Besides, we need to practice singing together. I'm sure we can find a duet we both know." He winked, and I gave up the battle.

It didn't matter how he felt about me. I was falling—*yep, hook-line-and-sinker*—for Riley freakin' Stone.

<h1 style="text-align:center">Chapter Twelve</h1>

Riley

"I still can't believe you agreed to this audition thing. What is going on with you, man?" Joel lay sprawled on his bed, playing a game on his phone.

"Oh, come on. There is no way Annie can come up with a new arrangement by tomorrow. Besides, I couldn't back down and let Katie win. She was trying to use me as her out." I laid back on my bed and put my hands behind my head, grinning at the memory of Katie's shocked face when I'd taken up her challenge.

"And if she does...?"

"Did you not hear that song? Never. Gonna. Happen."

"I d'know. Annie is pretty good. I get the feeling she's a bit of a musical genius."

Oh shit. Joel was right. What if Annie did come up with something good? I groaned as the reality of performing something like that hit me. Me? Riley Stone. The guy who'd spent the last year establishing himself as the cool guitarist/rock singer, performing a song from a Cole Porter musical in front of everyone?

"So... like I said before... if she does?" Joel had stopped playing his game and sat watching me.

Well... what would I do? "Ah, hell. If, by some miracle, Annie comes up with a show-stopper, I guess I'll just have to suck it up and go through with it for Katie. It's not like it'd be a serious audition. We'd just be hamming it up."

Joel stared at me with his mouth open, then shook his head. "Well I'll be damned. She really has you twisted outta shape. Why would you do that for someone you just met?"

I closed my eyes and rolled Joel's question around in my head. If anyone had told me a month ago I'd be considering doing something like this, I'd have laughed my head off. So... *why* was a pretty damned good question.

"Look. I get that you think I've lost my marbles, but I kinda feel like I *need* to do this. Whatever shitty thing happened in Katie's past seems to have destroyed her faith in the human race. I don't wanna back out and be just another person who's let her down. Friends don't do that kinda thing. So sue me..."

I opened my eyes and looked over to find Joel grinning like a loon. "Whoa, man, that was deep. You are *so* not the same guy I roomed with last year. But to be honest, he was a bit of a cocky bastard... so no great loss."

"Wow... don't hold back or anything." I threw the pillow from behind me at Joel's smug face and we both cracked up laughing. Joel was right; I had been a selfish arsehole. I'd totally lost sight of what mattered, drained from having the responsibility of looking after my sick mother for so many years. Katie made me feel empathy for the first time in as long as I could remember.

Something told me that Katie hadn't been first in anyone's life in just as long. Trust had become a dirty word in her vocabulary, and I intended to do everything I could to change that!

Katie

"OH GOD, was today the longest day in the history of the world or what?" I dropped down on my bed face first, emotionally wrung out from the never-ending roller-coaster ride.

Annie groaned, and I smiled into the bedcovers at the sound of her hitting her bed, too. "Understatement of the year!"

I turned my head to face Annie's bed and burst out laughing at seeing her in the same position as me. What a pair! Anyone'd think we'd never had any excitement in our lives. Wait... maybe they'd be right.

Annie's head turned, so she was looking at me, too. I moaned at the wicked sparkle in her eyes. "So... please tell me you weren't serious about this audition crap. 'Cos there is no way I'm singing *any version* of that bloody song onstage with Riley."

"Are you kidding me right now? *Of course* you're gonna

do it. Just wait until you hear it." She scrambled back up into a sitting position and dug her laptop out of her bag.

"Wait... you've finished it already? How the hell...?"

Annie giggled as her fingers flew over the keyboard. "Well, it's not quite finished yet. But I can give you a preview of what it'll sound like. You ready?"

I turned my face back into the bedcovers and groaned. "Fine. But I'm not—"

Annie must have heard my muffled words because her laptop blasted a slow, raunchy beat. What the...?

I pushed myself up off the bed and stood staring at my amazingly talented friend. Annie started to sing the lyrics, and my jaw dropped. Whoa, this was so far from the original version it was almost unrecognisable. The song had been rewritten to suit a sultry alto voice —mine, to be exact.

"See? I knew you'd like it. I'm almost done, so we can play it for the boys in the morning. Oh, and you really need to see what else I found." Annie stopped the song and hit a few more keys. The soprano version of *I Hate Men* replaced the new raunchy one.

I cringed, but Annie waved me over. "Quick, come have a look at what Kate and Petruchio are wearing. It's a crack-up."

I shook my head and moved over to sit beside Annie on her bed. "If you think there'll be costumes involved— "

I stared at the screen and burst out laughing. Kate wore a low-cut wench-style dress, while Petruchio pranced around in tights and a tunic. The thought of Riley in such a ridiculous get-up had us both laughing until we cried.

I almost choked on my laughter, all colour draining

from my face, as I watched Petruchio pull Kate into his arms at the end of the song and give her a toe-curling kiss. A stunned silence filled the room as Annie and I continued to stare at the blank screen. *How had I failed to consider that a song from a show called Kiss Me Kate would end in a kiss?*

Okay, this was not happening. I turned to Annie and opened my mouth but was cut off by her hand in front of my face.

"Wait! Before you lose your shit, just think about it for a minute."

"Think about what, exactly? There is no way I would *ever* expect Riley to agree to this. He'll be horrified at the thought of kissing me. We're friends, god-damnit, and something like this would ruin everything."

"Fine, so we don't mention the kiss to Riley and just leave it out then. What about the costumes?"

My head felt ready to explode. I just wanted to go to sleep and not think about any of it —ever again. "Oh, God, this is a complete nightmare. Can't we just forget the whole thing? Tell the boys you couldn't come up with a good enough arrangement?"

Annie's face fell. Damnit, now I'd upset her. *Of course,* she didn't want the boys to think she wasn't good enough to do this. She sighed and closed up her laptop. "Yeah, if that's what you want. But I still think it could have been awesome."

Guilt gnawed at my stomach. It wasn't fair to make this out to be Annie's failure. I needed to either suck it up and do the damn audition, or admit to Riley I was chickening out.

I put my hand over Annie's, where it sat on top of the laptop, and squeezed. "Okay, how about this? We'll play the new arrangement for the boys tomorrow, and I'll pray that Riley pulls the pin. But you have to promise not to mention the kiss or the costumes."

Annie squeezed my hand back and broke into a grin. "Deal. Now, go away so I can finish it already. Another hour and I should be done."

Chapter Thirteen

Riley

"So... how's the new arrangement for the audition song going?" I asked Annie as she and Katie slid into their chairs at breakfast the following morning. I knew my smile looked smug, but I was pretty confident Annie wouldn't be able to pull this off. "Think you might have bitten off a little more than you can chew, Annie?"

Annie just raised her eyebrows and lifted her coffee cup to her mouth, her own smug smile shooting me down in flames. "Oh, that? Yeah, it's ready whenever you want to hear it."

Katie grinned at the stunned look on my face and chuckled. "Did you seriously think she'd let us off the hook that easy? She's worked like a mad-woman to get it finished."

"Cool," Joel said, his eyes sparkling as they flicked

around the faces of everyone at the table. "If we eat fast, we should be able to sneak into one of the studios and have a listen before our first lesson."

Un-freakin-believable. Somebody just shoot me now!

I was seriously regretting not folding to the challenge in Katie's fiery eyes the day before. But there was no way I'd back out now. This was my big chance to show Katie what I was made of. Although, I admit I *was* still secretly hoping the new arrangement would turn out to be terrible. But from the worried look on Katie's face, I was pretty sure it was really good.

Oh, what the hell. It might actually end up being fun.

Either that or the most embarrassing experience of my life.

Ten minutes later, I sat in stunned silence as Annie played the new audition piece. It sounded nothing like the original version. Annie had somehow managed to change it from an operatic pile of drivel to a slow, sultry masterpiece. Having already sung a few songs with Katie the previous afternoon, I knew how well our voices blended. If we could pull this off, we'd bring the house down.

"Okay, Annie, you are indeed a genius." Joel bowed and winked at Annie. "I just hope Cole Porter doesn't roll over in his grave, or Professor Haines slap us with a year's detention for messing with a classic. Hey, what do you think about adding some congas? I reckon that sultry beat is calling out for them."

Annie smiled and opened her mouth to say something when the bell for our first class rang. She shrugged and looked at Katie. "Well, I guess we can talk about the details later. So... you think it sounds okay then?"

Annie was eyeing me nervously, and I suddenly realised I hadn't said a word since she'd started playing. "Are you kidding me? *Okay? That* is the understatement of the year. This new version is brilliant."

Annie beamed and shared a weird look with Katie. Okay, what weren't they telling me? I threw a suspicious look at Katie, and she started rifling through her bag.

"So... I guess we'd better get to class then," she said to Annie, grabbing her hand and dragging her out the door. "See you guys after English."

English and Math classes were the only ones sorted by gender. Apparently, separating boys and girls has been proven to increase concentration levels, especially in the male species. *Gee... I wonder why.*

Not that it helped when you couldn't get a particular girl out of your head. Which reminded me of that weird look the girls shared. It was still bugging me as we walked to class. "Hey Joel, did you happen to notice the weird looks those two were throwing at each other?" I finally asked.

Joel chuckled as we entered the classroom and found a couple of empty seats. "Yeah, they're definitely plotting something. And I hate to admit it, but I can't wait to find out what it is. I kinda like this new never-a-dull-moment when those two are around."

Yeah, he had that right.

I tried to pay attention to the lesson, but my thoughts kept drifting back to that look. As if it wasn't bad enough that I'd been sucked into doing this audition, I got the feeling there was something I was missing.

Knowing I couldn't concentrate on anything else until I knew what was going on, I pulled out my phone and hid it under the desk. This had to have something to do with the audition piece. I *Googled* "Songs from Kiss Me Kate" and found a *YouTube* clip of the audition song being performed, muting the sound so I wouldn't get busted.

You have got to be kidding me!! This Petruchio guy was prancing around in freakin' *tights* that showed his entire package. Katie couldn't seriously think I'd wear that? Could she? Suddenly, the nervous looks they'd exchanged started to make sense. No way in hell I'd be caught *dead* wearing *that*.

Shaking my head, I was just about to close the clip down when Petruchio pulled Kate into his arms and kissed her. Ookaay... maybe *this* was what they were worried about. Shivers ran up and down my spine as I sat glued to the image of the two characters sharing a passionate kiss.

Could I kiss Katie like that and make it look believable? Wait... did I *want* to kiss Katie like that... in front of an audience?

Umm... hell yeah, I did!

Yes, I wanted to pull her into my arms and watch those emerald eyes light up with anticipation. And then I wanted to kiss her like she'd never been kissed before, and I didn't give a toss who was watching.

Whoa... whoa... whoa. Hold the phone, Petruchio.

No matter how much *I* wanted it, there was no way that scenario was *ever* going to play out. Katie was already struggling with the whole concept of just being *friends*. She'd made it perfectly clear that she was *not, and never would be* into pretty-boys. The thought of kissing her and her not being into it turned my stomach. *No way* this would ever work. I wanted her to want *me* as much as I wanted *her.*

But wait... if the kiss was a necessary part of the audition, and it turned out to be mind-blowing, maybe she'd be tempted to cross the line from friendship and see where it led?

My stomach churned with equal parts excitement and terror. There was no way Katie would go along with this... *unless?*

Maybe I needed to take a leaf out of Annie-the-master-manipulator's book. What if I put up a token protest? Katie might just be stubborn enough to insist the kiss had to stay *because* I was against it. Then, I could begrudgingly give in because I knew the audition would be good for Katie.

It just might work. Katie was the queen of challenges. And damned if the whole idea didn't make me burn with anticipation. This must be what they called the *thrill-of-the-chase.* And I was in it for the long game.

"What are you looking at?" Joel whispered, leaning over to check out my phone.

"You have *gotta* see this, man." I passed the phone to Joel under the desk. "Play it from the start."

I watched Joel's face, chuckling when he screwed up his nose at what had to be the costume. "Keep watching. The surprises just keep coming."

I knew Joel had reached the kissing part when his jaw dropped, his eyes nearly popping out of his head.

I shivered and grinned. "So... do you think *this* might be what the girls were nervous about?"

Joel nodded and handed back the phone. "Nothing surer. So I assume you're gonna tell them where they can stick the whole audition idea?"

"Maybe... maybe not?"

"Seriously, Stone. You're not seriously considering wearing those—"

"No way. Not the costume part. But I might be up for the rest of the act..."

"*I knew it!*" Joel hissed, loud enough to make heads turn. I threw him a dirty look, and he chuckled quietly. "So you *are* into Katie. Look man, I know this sounds weird, with you being... well, *you,* and her being *her,* but I don't think you have a hope in hell of convincing Katie to be more than just friends. She's... ummm... well, she's just Katie."

Katie

"Okay, so I thought that went well. What about you?" Annie said, linking her arm with mine as we walked to class.

"Yeah, they liked the new arrangement. But there's no way Riley will go for the rest of it."

"Stop being such a wuss. We'll need the costumes *and* the kiss to pull it off."

Annie and I had *Googled* the song the previous night and watched the *YouTube* clip. After spending the first half of the song cracking up at the thought of Riley in tights, we'd both been gobsmacked at Petruchio and Kate's passionate kiss. Ookaay... I *so* wasn't expecting *that*. Just the thought of being kissed by Riley like that made my head spin and my heart race.

But Riley being forced to kiss me?

Because it was in the script?

No way.

Not gonna happen.

Riley had made it perfectly clear he wasn't attracted to me, and I would *not* be kissed by *anyone* under sufferance. No matter how much *I* wanted it.

But the thought of it still had me tossing and turning half the night, imagining how it would feel to be wrapped in Riley's arms and kissed – for all the right reasons. Which is why, when I'd woken up this morning, I'd made Annie swear she wouldn't mention the costumes or the kiss to the boys.

Just the idea of singing the new song with Riley was enough. No way I'd risk him cancelling the whole thing because of some stupid costume and a kiss.

Snapping back to the present, I stopped walking and planted my hands on my hips, giving Annie my very best death stare. "Remember: No costumes and no kiss. Got it? And don't even *think* about accidentally letting it slip. This audition will *only* be about singing... *okay?*"

"Fine... whatever. Come on, we're gonna be late." We entered the classroom and found a couple of empty seats. "But what if —"

The speakers above our heads crackled, the usual prelude to an incoming message.

All students intending to audition for the end-of-semester show on Friday should report to Professor Haines in the auditorium at the beginning of lunch. This will be the only opportunity to be added to the list, and special arrangements for rehearsal time will be advised upon registration. Thank you.

A buzz of excitement spread throughout the classroom following the announcement. I turned to look at Annie, my stomach suddenly in knots at the thought of performing on stage with Riley. "Oh shit... maybe this wasn't such a good idea. I hope Riley and Joel are outside at the end of class. We need to talk about this before—"

Annie reached out, grabbed my hand and squeezed. "Will you stop stressing and just breathe? Of course, they'll be there. Riley wouldn't make you do this on your own."

What the hell was I doing? This was insane. I wasn't ready to perform in public again yet. *No.* This whole thing had all the makings of an impending car crash. Time to put on the brakes and get out of the car.

Then the guilt crept in. Annie had worked so hard and done a fantastic job on the new arrangement. She'd be devastated if I pulled out now.

Wait... what if we just signed up, rehearsed, and then pulled the pin at the last minute? I could get sick or fake an anxiety attack or something. Yeah, that might work—

"Katie, stop it! I can hear your brain ticking over from

here. It's just a bit of fun. And it's not like you'll have to perform in the actual production. I seriously doubt our version is what they had in mind."

Okay... Annie was right. I let out the breath I hadn't realised I'd been holding. This whole thing was *supposed* to be just for laughs. Although that didn't stop me from stressing for the entire class. Maybe I *should* tell Riley about the costume and the kiss and let *him* pull the pin.

Yes... that was it.

Even Riley would have to back down from a challenge like that.

It was the perfect solution. I'd let Riley be the bad guy, and I wouldn't have to feel guilty about all Annie's wasted time. There'd be plenty of other opportunities to audition and perform later in the year. I just got here, for God's sake. I shouldn't be expected to handle this sort of pressure so soon.

But by the time the bell rang, I couldn't decide whether I'd be more upset if Riley pulled the pin or he *didn't*. Yep, I was a total mess. Chewing on my lip, I packed up my books and followed Annie out of the classroom.

Riley stood with Joel on the other side of the corridor wearing a confident grin. Although it faded pretty quickly when he saw the look on my face. "Oh-oh... that's not a good sign. Don't tell me you're getting cold feet again?"

I shrugged and sighed. "What makes you think—?"

"You're chewing on that poor, defenceless lip again. What's up?" Riley asked, moving to walk beside me as we headed for Maths.

"Did you hear the announcement?"

"Yep. So we need to go to the auditorium and sign up. Hey... I thought you liked Annie's new arrangement?"

"I do... it's just... why would you even want to do this? With me, of all people?"

Riley stopped walking and wrapped his hand around my elbow—*aaannd cue the tingles* —turning me to face him. "Which part of 'because-you're-my-friend' don't you get? I thought we sounded pretty good singing together yesterday. Wait... is that the problem? You don't want to sing with me? I know I'm not as good—"

"Don't be ridiculous. We *do* sound good singing together. It's just... I'm not sure I'm ready for this kind of pressure. When I sing my usual stuff, I'm confident I can do it. But this? Singing with someone else and totally changing the audition piece? It scares the crap out of me."

"Would it help if I admitted I feel exactly the same way? This is *way* beyond stepping out of my comfort zone. But you know what? Nothing ventured, nothing gained. We can totally rock this, Katie. You just need to trust me. Do you think you can do that?"

Please, no... not the "T" word.

I looked into Riley's beautiful blue eyes and desperately wanted to say yes. But the last time I'd trusted someone, it had almost destroyed me. Besides, if we were talking about trust, didn't I owe it to him to come clean about the 'costume-and-kiss' part of the song? Before someone else mentioned it, and he felt like he'd been blind-sided.

"Ummm... there's something I need to tell you. Annie and I watched the song on *YouTube* last night, and—"

"Is this about the costume, or the kiss?" he asked softly,

leaning in close to whisper in my ear. Which was *way* too close for me to continue breathing.

Say what? He knew?

I stepped back in shock. "What? How do you... I mean... when—?"

Riley shrugged, his mouth lifting into a sheepish smile. "I knew something was up when you and Annie looked so weird this morning after she finished playing the song. So I searched for and watched the *YouTube* clip in class."

What? How could he still want to do the song if he knew about...

My face was burning, and I *needed* the floor to open up and swallow me whole. "So we need to pull the pin... right?"

"Why? I'm sure we can work around those 'requirements' and still do the song."

"Yeah, right. Bloody Petruchio yells, 'Kiss Me Kate'. What would you suggest? That Kate says...*no?*"

The bell rang for class, and I wanted to scream. We needed to make a decision by the end of this class. Maybe I could just do what I was thinking earlier. Register and then pull out before the audition.

Riley blew out a long breath. "Look, how about we think it over during class? But whatever you decide, I'll be outside the auditorium at the beginning of lunch. If you're not there, I'll assume you changed your mind." My heart almost jumped out of my chest when he smiled and reached for my hand, squeezing it before shrugging and walking away.

What the hell? Why was he acting as if he'd be disap-

pointed if I chickened out? Damnit. I never wanted to do this stupid audition in the first place. And what? Suddenly, he was okay dressing up in tights and kissing the 'fat-chick' onstage? Why? So he could play the hero?

No, wait... maybe he wanted to be seen as the martyr who *suffered through* the experience of kissing the ugly girl for the sake of his art?

No thanks. He could find someone else to be his patsy.

Because I knew, without a doubt, there'd be no going back after kissing Riley Stone.

Chapter Fourteen

Riley

I leaned up against the wall outside the auditorium and stared at my feet. I didn't really expect Katie to show up, but I'd said I'd be here, and I'd wait until the last minute. This having a girl look horrified at the thought of kissing me was a whole new experience. And when I'd asked her to trust me, she'd looked at me like I was some kind of alien monster.

Seriously? This whole situation was all kinds of messed up.

Joel sighed and patted me on the shoulder. "Well, looks like you're off the hook, man. I told you Katie was different. She's probably— Well, I'll be damned."

I looked up to find Katie stomping toward me, her beautiful emerald eyes shooting sparks. I grinned as she stepped up in front of him.

"Fine. Let's do this," she said and turned to walk into the auditorium.

What the hell? I grabbed her elbow and moved in front of her to block her path. "Hang on a sec. We're either doing this as a team or not at all. You don't get to be all huffy and make out like you're doing me a favour."

Katie looked up, and all the fire was gone. She looked lost, and scared, and vulnerable. My heart twisted, and I slipped my hand down to take hold of hers, leading her over to a quiet corner of the foyer and pulling her down next to me on the lounge. "Okay... now tell me what's wrong? I thought we were friends. Just talk to me."

She gave a massive sigh and became fascinated by her fingernails. But then, I knew that was so she didn't have to look at me. "Fine. It's about the... ummm... kiss. I'm sure we won't be the only ones auditioning for Petruchio and Kate, and everyone will know there's *supposed* to be a kiss. So... if you *don't* kiss me, they'll all think it's because you couldn't stand having to kiss the 'fat chick', and if you *do* kiss me, then they'll think... well, they'll feel sorry for you having to—"

"Just stop, okay? How could you even think like that? You're doing it again... judging people by how *you'd* react. C'mon Katie, some small-minded people *might* think things like that, but most of them will be too gobsmacked by your amazing voice and incredible stage presence to care about who's kissing, or *not* kissing, who."

"You honestly believe that?"

I so wanted to pull her into my arms and kiss away all her worries. But it was too soon. If I wanted her to trust me,

I needed her to believe in herself first. Which meant I had to be content with friendship—for now, anyway.

"Yes, I do. And before you stormed up and declared war, I was going to tell you I came up with a solution to the kissing thing. How about you put your hands on my face, *look* like you're about to kiss me, then turn my head and kiss me on the cheek? Totally unexpected, and still in character."

Katie's eyes lit up, and she threw her arms around my neck. "Riley Stone... *You. Are. Brilliant!* I'm sorry I was such an idiot. I guess I *do* need to learn to trust you."

Alright! Katie was hugging me... again. Should I return the hug? Friends hugged, didn't they?

Aww, what the hell. I wrapped my arms around her waist and just enjoyed the moment. She smelled of strawberries and vanilla... and it was my new favourite scent.

I stifled a groan as she stiffened and pushed against my chest, her flaming face almost the colour of her hair. "Oh no, I did it again. Riley, I'm so sorry."

"Did you hear me complaining? That's what friends are for, remember? So... are we ready to do this?"

Katie jumped up and grabbed my hand, dragging me into the auditorium and up to the registration table. "Hello, Professor Haines. My name's Katie Sims, and Riley and I would like to audition for the *Kiss Me Kate* excerpt."

Professor Haines handed Katie the registration form, raising an eyebrow at me as Katie completed the form. "So you're auditioning together? I wasn't aware this was your kind of thing, Riley?"

I couldn't help grinning. "Just helping out my buddy Professor."

The woman actually smiled. "Well, I'm looking forward to your audition."

SITTING in the cafeteria twenty minutes later, I got this warm, tingly feeling watching the excitement on Katie's face as she told Annie about my idea. How had she managed to worm her way into my heart so quickly? I mean, I'd known her for what... forty-eight hours? And what did I really know about her? Absolutely nothing outside the walls of *Crescendo*. Where did she live? What was her family like? I wanted to know everything about what had made Katie into the person she was today.

She was so different from the girls I used to be attracted to, not only on the outside but on the inside as well. Now I realised how shallow and fake those girls were compared to Katie. Hell, even if Katie never returned my feelings, I wanted her to stay a part of my life. She challenged me and made me think outside the box. And she evoked a protectiveness I'd never experienced before without suffocating me with expectations.

"Riley?... Hey... earth to Riley!" Joel's elbow dug into my rib, pulling me out of la-la land.

Oh, man... I'm pathetic. Please tell me I haven't been staring at Katie like some love-sick loser. "Yeah, sorry. What'd I miss?"

Katie wore a dazzling smile, and something in my stomach wriggled.

Whoa, maybe I had worms?

"You mean, besides World War Three and the Zombie Apocalypse?" she giggled.

I groaned as heat rose up my neck and flooded my face. I seriously needed to get a grip on these stupid run-away emotions. "That bad, huh?"

Katie tilted her head, studying me as if trying to work out what was going on inside my head. "Everything okay?"

Sure... except that it's killing me not to lean across the table and kiss you. "Yeah. Just got a lot on my mind."

"You sure you're not the one getting cold feet this time? 'Cos we can always—"

"Don't even think about it. There's no way *anyone's* backing out of this now. So... now that we've dealt with the kiss, how about we address the *other* elephant in the room? You know, the costumes...?"

Silence...

Finally, Annie cleared her throat and sighed. "Okay. Well... ummm... I've been thinking about this. I definitely think Katie needs to wear something like Kate wore in the video clip. That red medieval dress with the whole popping cleavage thing—"

Katie gasped, blushed, and punched Annie in the arm. "Wow, Annie... overkill on the visual or what?"

Well, I certainly wasn't complaining about the visual...

Annie giggled and held up her hand. "Let me finish. And even though every female on the planet would give an arm and a leg to see Riley in those tights—"

"Which is *not* going to happen," I growled. *Yeah, okay, so maybe I needed to get a handle on the whole growling thing. But seriously...*

Annie did the hand thing again. "Which we *all* know is *never* going to happen. So, we need to come up with something else. Oh, and seeing Joel and I are part of the act, I think we should dress up too."

Joel's mouth opened and closed a couple of times, but nothing came out. I cracked up, returning the jab to his ribs from earlier. "This just keeps getting better and better. I know some students from last year got permission to use costumes from the school's wardrobe department. Apparently, it's huge. There'd have to be stuff we could use there."

Joel groaned, leaned back in his chair, folding his hands behind his neck and looking up at the ceiling. "Why do I get the feeling I'm being railroaded? I'm still trying to work out exactly when my life took the turn towards crazy-town?"

Katie was literally glowing with excitement, which convinced me even more that it was worth the embarrassment of auditioning to see her so happy.

Even if it was *killing me not being able to touch her.*

Without thinking, I reached out and covered her hand with mine. Hey, we were friends, right? Surely touching hands was okay? She gasped, and her eyes flew to mine.

"So whadya think partner? No more doubts? Sink or swim, right?" I squeezed her hand, and her eyes filled with tears. *Wait... that wasn't exactly the response I'd been looking for.*

"Thank you for doing this, Riley. You really are turning out to be an awesome friend."

Chapter Fifteen

Katie

"*Hell to the no!* I *cannot* be seen in public wearing this!" I stared into the mirror, my face burning. The girl in the red velvet and lace medieval gown reflected back at me was a total stranger. Apart from the dress being perfect and fitting like a glove, I was mortified at the thought of anyone seeing me wearing it.

No way. I looked like a total slut.

Annie stood beside me in the dressing room with her eyes popping. "Hot damn, Katie. It's perfect. You look... sensational."

"So... ummm... does your partner in crime get to have a say in this?" Riley's voice floated in from the other side of the curtain, sounding a bit husky. Of course. After Annie's embarrassing comment about the *popping cleavage*, any red-blooded male would want to see if the reality matched the visual. I *almost* giggled, and then memories of Mark's gross friend describing my boobs as 'ginormous puppies' flashed in my mind and made me want to throw up.

Nope. The dress had to go.

"Come on, Katie, it can't be as bad as those pantaloon things Joel and I have to wear. At least give us a look before you make up your mind." The image of Riley in his costume instantly banished all thoughts of Mark and his sleazy band of morons. Riley would never make me feel dirty and degraded like they had. Maybe I *could* do this.

Okay, so I had to admit the dress really *did* fit the part. I sucked in a deep breath—*oops, maybe not such a good idea with the threat of an escaping-boob-fest*—and closed my eyes. "Fine, but if either of you laugh, I *will* punch you in the face!"

Riley chuckled. "What, like you two didn't practically roll on the floor when we—

He stopped talking as I stepped out from behind the curtain. Holding up the bottom of the dress and keeping my eyes glued to my hands, I held my breath. The stunned silence was the *last* reaction I'd expected, and I lifted my eyes to see what was going on.

Wait. Riley's face was so red he looked ready to burst a blood vessel.

What was that all about?

Maybe he was upset about me looking so slutty?

"That bad, huh? Well, I did try to warn you..." I turned to head back into the dressing room, feeling like a complete idiot.

I stopped when Riley's hand—*wait... was it seriously*

shaking?—reached out and grabbed mine, letting the dress fall to the floor. "Are you serious? How is *anything* about this..." he swept his hand in front of me, "even close to being bad? You look... Jesus, Katie... you look incredible."

My eyes flew to Riley's in shock, and I was instantly lost at sea. Did this gorgeous guy really just say I looked incredible? This couldn't be happening. I needed to pinch myself, 'cos this had to be some fantasy playing out in a dream I was having. I tried to swallow, but my throat was so dry it was pointless. There was something in his eyes I didn't recognise. And whatever it was, *no one* had ever looked at me like that.

Annie cleared her throat and stepped out from behind me, wearing a similar dress to mine, but in blue, and I didn't miss the flare of appreciation in Joel's eyes.

Hmmm... interesting.

Thank the stars for Annie and her ability to defuse an awkward situation. Because if Riley had kept looking at me like that, I was either going to burst into flames or throw myself at him... again. And the *friends-hug* excuse was starting to wear a bit thin.

Annie did the clapping hands thing *and* giggled—*both of which I had given up caring about. Acting mature was so overrated.* "That's what I tried to tell her. Can someone else *please* tell her she *has* to wear it? It's perfect."

Joel dragged his eyes away from Annie and threw me a huge grin. "Yeah. Annie's right, Katie. You are seriously rockin' the part in that dress." He turned to Riley and raised an eyebrow. "What say you, Petruchio?"

Riley laced his fingers together on top of his head, stepping back and running his eyes over my entire body before returning his heart-stopping gaze to mine. "Ummm... they're right, Katie. In fact, I'm feeling much better about wearing the whole pantaloon thing already. 'Cos with you wearing *that*, no one will even *notice* what I have on."

Damnit. Why did he have to say nice stuff like that? He almost made me believe I looked... beautiful. "Yeah, right. Come on, Riley, you don't have to—"

"Don't, okay? Would it kill you to just take the compliment for once?" I was about to snap out a "fine" when he held up his hand, his eyes holding a distinct warning. "Graciously."

Annie snorted and threw her arm around my shoulder. "Girl... you have just been told!"

I shivered as Riley's eyes continued to hold mine.

Hot damn, he was mind-numbingly sexy when he was mad.

Pulling myself together, I adopted a cheeky grin, pursing my lips and throwing him what I hoped was a sultry look. Dropping into a curtsy, my heart hammering in my chest, I held his gaze throughout. "Many thanks, Petruchio. It pleases me to know you approve."

Holy cow! Was I seriously flirting?

Riley's eyes glittered, a slow smile lifting the corners of his lips. "Pity we're not doing the scene where Petruchio puts Kate over his knee and spanks her for being such a shrew."

A deathly silence hung in the air as if no one dared to breathe. I knew they were all waiting for me to explode, but I burst out laughing instead.

How did he even know about that scene?

Unless he'd watched the entire movie?

I mean, Annie and I watching it the previous night was one thing, but Riley sitting through the whole thing?

Joel was frowning and scratching his head. "Wait... what spanking scene? What'd I miss?"

Okay, so he hadn't watched it with Joel.

Annie grabbed my arm and dragged me back into the dressing room. "Come on, let's get changed. I'm not sure that dress will hold up under all your hysterical laughter."

Reining in my laughter, I allowed Annie to help me out of my dress. But I really had to know. "By the way, Riley... how do you know about that scene? Please tell me you did not watch the whole movie?" I called out over my shoulder.

Riley's chuckle floated through the curtains. "Fine. So, I *may* have wanted to know a little more about the characters. Now, can you two please hurry up before our allotted rehearsal time runs out? I'd like to at least have the song ready if I'm going to be seen in this ridiculous costume."

I giggled and nudged Annie. "I'm beginning to wonder how many times he watched the movie. He's starting to sound more like Petruchio every minute. Bossy and conceited."

"I heard that," Riley growled, and my heart skipped a beat. I loved it when we bantered and pushed each other's buttons. And as for that warning look he'd thrown out earlier? Dear God, I'd almost melted into a pile of goo at his feet. The thought of what he might do if I pushed him too far made me tingle from head to toe.

Nah... he wouldn't,... would he?

$$Chapter\ Sixteen$$

Riley

I was seriously struggling to breathe, not to mention feeling like I was having a heartache. Watching Katie flounce around in that beyond-sexy, should-be-declared-illegal, red dress, while belting out the lyrics of the new, improved—*and mind-blowingly raunchy*—version of *I Hate Men,* was playing havoc with my mental state.

How on earth was I supposed to sing?

Didn't using your vocal chords require a functioning brain?

Well, if it did, I was on the brink of an epic fail. 'Cos watching Katie had turned that, and every other organ in my body, to mush, except maybe my heart, which was functioning at triple time.

It was Thursday afternoon, and we'd agreed to do the final rehearsal in costume. *And lucky for me, we did.* At least there wasn't an audience to witness my mortification.

What was I thinking, letting myself get roped into this? Oh yeah, *Mission: Convince the Girl to Fall for Me.* And I'd already stuffed that up completely by suggesting we change what should have been a toe-curling kiss into a peck on the cheek.

Dufus to the max.

The worst part was that Katie had actually started to warm to me, letting me in a little more every time we spent time together. Maybe it was wishful thinking on my part, but there were times when I could have sworn she was flirting with me.

But we never got five minutes alone. Would she freak out if I asked her to go for coffee or something—just the two of us? I mean, I'd have killed to take her out to dinner, but there was no way I could afford it.

Damnit... why did everything have to be so complicated? I gulped as she sashayed past me again, those fiery eyes glittering as she directed the words about how much she hated men at me.

No. That's what *Kate* was singing to *Petruchio.*

I *needed* to believe that it wasn't *Katie* telling *Riley* that's how she really felt.

Damnit. She was either a brilliant actress, or I didn't have a hope in hell.

She was winding up to the finish of the solo part of the performance. I needed to get my act together... now! As she spat the last words at me, I grabbed her around the waist and pulled her close. Or rather, *Petruchio* pulled *Kate* close.

Okay, this was rapidly becoming the most ridiculous thing I'd ever agreed to. The fine line between Kate and

Petruchio's tumultuous on-stage romance, and Katie and Riley's reality, was starting to blur.

Wait... this might be just what I needed. Maybe Petruchio could convince the real Katie to give Riley a chance. What had Katie said about Petruchio when we were getting our costumes? Oh yeah... *bossy and conceited.* I sucked in a calming breath.

Okay, Petruchio, over to you...

And I sang...

> *So, kiss me, Kate, thou lovely loon,*
> *'Ere we start on our honeymoon...*

Well, at least I *sounded* normal. Katie's eyes widened as I slipped entirely into the role of Petruchio. Praying I didn't end up with egg on my face, I'd thrown caution to the wind to show Katie how I really felt.

Would she even realise this was how *I* felt, or put it down to my amazing acting ability? Aww c'mon. I wasn't an actor's bootlace. But did Katie know that?

Okay, something was working. Because there was no way she was protesting as strongly to Petruchio's moves as she'd done the last time we'd rehearsed it.

Were her eyes really softening?

Whoa, she hadn't worn that cheeky grin before, either.

I held my breath when she slipped her hands up to cradle my face, her emerald eyes blazing into mine. Our lips were almost touching when she sighed, turned my head and placed a gentle kiss on my cheek.

Stuff it! Time to go for broke.

I pulled her against me and whispered against her lips. "Now... can you please kiss *me*, Katie?"

I sighed with relief when she tilted her head and closed her eyes. My heart thundering in my chest, I closed the gap, pressing my lips against hers. Fireworks exploded in my head, my entire body sizzling as if I'd been zapped by a thousand volts.

Just... wow!

I'd kissed a lot of girls, but *nothing* could have prepared me for the emotions rampaging through my system when Katie returned my kiss. The world ceased to exist, and time stood still. Holding and kissing Katie just felt so *right*, the feel of her lips moving against mine making my head spin and my heart soar.

I ran my tongue along the seam of her lips, moaning in response to her soft whimper as she opened to me. I was free-falling through space with no desire for it to end.

And to be honest... it absolutely, positively terrified me.

Katie

Snap. Crackle. And Pop!

This was insane. Riley freaking Stone was kissing *me*—Katie Simpson, or Sims, or whoever the hell I was.

Every single fibre of my being was on fire. My hands had developed a mind of their own, slipping around Riley's neck, my fingers sneaking up to play in his hair.

Oh, please let this be real.

Wait... why was Riley...?

I shut down the thought before it could take hold. Nope, no rational thought allowed. I refused to let anything intrude on this magical moment in time. Being wrapped in Riley's arms, his lips and tongue playing havoc with my sanity, was exactly where I wanted to be.

Kissing Mar—wait... *he-who-will-not-be-named-while-kissing-Riley*—had done nothing to prepare me for the onslaught of emotions I experienced when Riley kissed me. How could I ever have compared this incredible guy to my douchebag ex-boyfriend? And how on earth could a kiss make me feel so warm, and safe, and maybe even a little beautiful? I never wanted it to end...

Oh no!

What would happen when it did *end?*

No matter how hard I tried to kick and scream against it, reality raised its ugly head. I must have stiffened or given myself away somehow because I felt Riley start to pull away.

I buried my flaming face against his chest as soon as his lips left mine.

Here it comes...

Now, we'd have to *talk* about what just happened. There was no way I'd be able to pretend I didn't have feelings for Riley any more. Not after the way I'd responded to his kiss. But I wasn't sure if I was ready to hear how Riley justified his actions.

"Okaaay then..." Annie's high-pitched voice pulled me back to earth with a resounding *thud*. How could I have forgotten she and Joel were in the room? "So...ar...

Joel. I'm thinking coffee in the cafeteria. How about you?"

Joel cleared his throat. "Ummm... yeah... good thinking. Let's go..." I groaned at the suppressed laughter in his voice. By the time the door shut behind Annie and Joel's uncomfortable exit, the silence in the room had become almost deafening.

"Katie... you need to breathe." Riley's soft, husky voice against my ear made her stomach do back flips. I shivered and released the breath I'd been holding. *Now what?* I had no idea what to say to him. But one thing was for sure... the feel of Riley's warm hand rubbing circles on my back had me wanting to stay where I was forever. *Talking was over-rated anyway...*

Riley sighed. "Thank you for trusting me. You have no idea how long I've wanted to do that."

No way! He did not *just say that.* So the kiss had been more than just a spur-of-the-moment thing? He hadn't just been immersed in his role?

Riley slipped an arm from behind my back, his fingers coaxing my chin up until I was gazing into his dreamy baby-blue eyes.

Okay, so maybe I wanted to stay like this *forever... the view was definitely better.*

My eyes slid down to the luscious lips I felt intimately acquainted with, and they broke into a cocky grin. "What? Nothing to say? 'Cos I have plenty."

"What?" My brain had obviously stopped functioning because I couldn't seem to remember how to string words together to form a sentence. This must be how it felt to be a startled deer caught in a car's headlights. *Man, was I in serious trouble.*

I shivered as Riley ran the back of his hand down my cheek, tucking a stray curl behind my ear. The gesture was so tender, tears welled up in my eyes. And there was that look again. The one I'd never seen in anyone's eyes before Riley.

How was this even possible?

"Please don't cry, beautiful girl. I'm not going to apologise for kissing you, but I won't do it again if you tell me not to. Even though *I* may start crying if you do..."

I giggled and blinked away the tears, the tension melting from my body at his words. This was Riley, my friend, and he *wanted* to kiss me... again.

"Why?" That one word represented a multitude of questions.

Riley chuckled, his chest vibrating against mine, making me aware of his arm still tightly wrapped around me. "I thought I'd made how I feel pretty obvious. But I need to know you feel the same way. I want to be more than friends, Katie, but if you regret kissing me, if it was just a heat of the moment thing, I won't—"

I pressed a finger against his lips, standing on tip-toes and pulling his head down until our lips were almost touching. "Haven't you ever heard that talking's over-rated? Actions speak *way* louder than words." Pressing my lips against his, I proceeded to show him *exactly* how I felt about him.

Chapter Seventeen

Riley

By the time we entered the cafeteria an hour later, I felt like I'd won the freakin' lottery. It was like Katie's hand *belonged* in mine, like she was the missing piece in the puzzle that had been my life. Spotting Joel and Annie sitting together at a table laughing, I squeezed Katie's hand as we crossed the room to join them.

Our friends stopped laughing as we approached the table, wearing matching looks that were a mixture of good-to-see-you're-both-still-alive and explain-now. I bit back a laugh at the relief on Annie's face when she saw us holding hands with no obvious bruises or limbs missing.

"Nice of you to join us," Joel said with a smirk, his eyes flitting between Katie and me, as if assessing the situation. "Interesting twist to the audition piece there. So, is it a permanent addition to the script, or what?"

Katie blushed, but her goofy grin never slipped as she

slid into a seat opposite our inquisitors. Wearing that same grin, I sat beside her, moving my chair closer so I could drape my arm across the back of hers, needing to keep touching her. "We wouldn't make an important decision like that without running it by the rest of the cast. Sooo..."

Annie took one look at Katie's fire-engine red face and reached across the table to grab her hand. "Hey, you look like you could do with a coffee, and I need a refill. Let's go." She dragged Katie out of her chair and then turned back to look at Joel and me. "Anyone else?"

I coughed to cover my grin at the sight of Katie standing behind Annie, mouthing the word 'help'. "Yeah, white with one, please, ladies."

Joel just shook his head and pointed to his still half-full cup. But the minute the girls turned to walk away, Joel's face broke into a huge grin. "Holy shit, Stone. I gotta tell ya, that was *one hot kiss*. At one stage, I thought Annie and I might be at risk of bursting into flames just from being in the same room."

I rubbed the back of my neck, cursing the heat flooding my face. Why did I feel like a thirteen-year-old caught kissing a girl behind a tree by the principal? I hadn't even thought about there being other people in the room when I'd decided to seize the day. And poor Katie had looked mortified at the thought of Annie's interrogation.

But then... who the hell cared anyway? No way I had any regrets. It would be worth whatever they dished out to know Katie felt the same way I did.

After the initial discomfort following our first kiss—well,

Katie's, anyway—we'd talked, laughed and kissed for the entire hour. We'd both avoided talking about anything serious, content to just enjoy the newness of... whatever this was. Or, at least, that's what I'd done. I could only assume Katie had been feeling the same way. But we *had* both agreed we needed to spend some time together, *just the two of us*, on the weekend.

Now I just needed to find a way to speed up time between now and then

"Hello... anybody home?" The irritation in Joel's voice finally broke into my thoughts. "Hey, don't worry about me. I'll just sit here and talk to *myself* until the girls come back."

Damn, how long had Joel been trying to talk to me while I was off in la-la-land... again? I needed to pull myself together and stop acting like a love-sick dork. "Sorry, man. I'm a bit scattered."

"Scattered? *That's* what they're calling it these days?" Joel threw his head back and laughed, slapping the table with his hand.

"Yeah, laugh it up, Kenny." *Maybe it was time he got a taste of his own medicine.* "Sooo... you and Annie seemed pretty cosy when we came in."

Joel's mood changed instantly. As if flicking a switch, he stopped laughing and frowned down at his coffee cup. "Nah, nothing to talk about there. Annie is great, but I'm pretty sure I've been *friend-zoned*. Besides, you know me. I'm not in the market for a relationship. Now a hook-up... that's a whole different ballgame. Wait... not that I'm saying I'd want to hook-up with Annie. Girls like her and Katie are different. They deserve... Aww, shit, I'm gonna stop talking now before my head implodes."

Wow. It sounded like Joel had it bad, even if *he* didn't know it yet. Maybe I should ask Katie if she knew how Annie felt.

I looked up to find the girls heading back to the table, my insides squirming as Katie's eyes lit up when they met mine. She was practically glowing, looking nothing like the defensive, world-weary girl I'd met four days ago. And I loved knowing I'd helped to bring about that change.

But I couldn't help wondering if she'd ever feel comfortable enough to tell me what happened in her past.

I could only hope.

Katie

As soon as we were out of the boys' line of vision, Annie squealed and threw her arms around my neck. "I gotta tell ya, that was the *hottest* kiss I have ever seen. And I gather from the goofy grins and the holding hands that it wasn't just a one-time thing? Come on, girl... spill. If I have to live my love life vicariously through you, I need details."

I chuckled, returning my friend's hug and then holding up a hand before Annie could continue to babble. "Maybe if you stopped gushing from the mouth long enough for me to get a word in, I'd tell you."

"Oops... my bad. Okay, mouth is sealed and I'm all ears."

By the time I'd finished giving Annie a blow-by-blow account of what had happened, she was fanning her face and practically swooning. "Okay. It *has* to be my turn to talk now, 'cos otherwise I'm gonna explode."

I laughed and took over making the coffees Annie had started while she listened. "Okay... aaand go."

Annie clapped her hands and did a little jig on the spot —*okay, so maybe it was more cute than immature. Huh, who knew eh?*

"So... you and Riley are, like, together, and the kiss is staying in for the audition, right?"

Blushing furiously, I shrugged and nodded. "Yep. Riley talked me into it. Unless you or Joel have a problem with it? I don't want to—"

"Puh-lease. As if Joel or I would have a problem with it. Although you might want to tone it down just a tad. Wouldn't want you blowing all the electrical circuits in the auditorium." Annie nudged me with her hip and reached to pick up her coffee. "You right with those?" She nodded toward the other two cups.

I rolled my eyes and gave her a filthy look. "Yeah, I think I can manage to carry two whole cups of coffee."

Annie winked. "Just checking. You know, with all this excitement and all..."

Wondering how long I'd have to suffer through Annie giving me a hard time, I shook my head and waved her forward. Not that I cared anyway... the reward *far* outweighed the price.

Riley's eyes met mine when we were halfway across the cafeteria, the intensity in his gaze waking the butterflies, which seemed to have taken up permanent residence in my stomach, from their short-lived hibernation.

"Here you go. White with one, right?" I placed the coffee in front of Riley, embarrassed to see my hand was shaking.

What was that all about?

How could I be nervous when Riley had gone out of his way to make me feel comfortable about us being together?

"Perfect... thanks. You okay?" *Of course, he'd noticed.* He reached for my hand and pulled me down beside him.

"Yeah, I'm fine. It might just take me a while to get used to all this..." I bit my lip and waved a hand between us. "You know... *us.*"

Still holding my hand, he turned and draped his other arm on the back of my chair, running a few strands of my hair through his fingers. "By the way, I hope you're not embarrassed by PDAs?" he asked softly, rubbing the thumb of his other hand over the back of mine. "Sorry, I guess I should've asked you that before. I don't mean this to sound weird, but I just kinda like touching you. And I couldn't give a toss who's watching." Riley blushed, a sheepish smile on his handsome face, his eyes searching mine for answers. Suddenly, he was frowning. "Wait... did someone say something to you when you went to get the coffee?"

I giggled at his cute burst of protectiveness and squeezed his hand. "Calm down, Captain Caveman. No one said anything. There were a few sour looks, but I can handle it. As for the PDAs, I kinda like touching you too.

I guess I'm just not used to it. My ex wasn't—" I slammed my mouth shut, horrified by what I'd almost said. Damnit, I was *not* ready to discuss anything about Mark with Riley, and now I'd gone and opened the door to his questions.

His arm tightened around my shoulder as he leaned over to place a gentle kiss on my forehead. "Good. Glad we feel the same way."

Wait... what?

He wasn't going to ask me about Mark?

No. Riley wouldn't do that. He'd seen my look of horror and regret at mentioning my ex. He would never push me to talk about something he knew I wasn't comfortable about sharing. He'd wait until I was ready to tell him.

Because he was amazing

... and caring

... and sexy

Oh hell... this guy was everything.

"So... are we all ready for tomorrow? I'm assuming the audition will play out exactly as it did today?" Joel waggled his eyebrows at his last words, and we all laughed.

Annie leaned into Joel, flashing him a mischievous grin, as if they were sharing a secret. "Well, I *did* suggest to Katie they should maybe tone it down just a little. I mean, we don't want the building going up in flames."

Joel blushed to the roots. Which was weird, right? Annie hadn't been talking about them. Until I realised it was more of a reaction to what Annie had *done* than what she had *said*. Just for a second, when Annie had leaned in close, Joel had looked like a stunned mullet. I made a mental note to ask Riley if he knew what *that* was all about.

How cool would it be if Annie and Joel got together? We could, like, double-date. I'd always wanted to do that, but Mark had never liked us being seen together in public.

Gee... I wonder why?

"Yeah, well, I'm not making any promises about the toning it down part," Riley said, grinning down at me and stealing all the air from around me. "Maybe someone should keep the fire extinguishers handy, just in case."

Chapter Eighteen

Katie

The auditions had been going on for almost two hours, and I was gobsmacked by the incredible talent of the students so far. With only two more auditions before we were up, the four of us had snuck out of the auditorium to change into our costumes. Now we stood anxiously waiting for Joel's friend, Mikey, to call us in.

"I am *so* nervous. That last couple were amazing." I chewed on my thumbnail, pacing back and forth, my heart threatening to jump out of my chest.

Riley reached out and pulled me against him, brushing a few strands of my wild hair back from my face and rubbing my arms. "Hey... deep breaths. We're going to bring the house down... trust me."

"Okay, maybe not *too* deep breaths in that dress, girl,"

Annie said in a loud whisper, and we all laughed. As always, she'd defused the situation like a pro.

Mikey's head appeared in the doorway. "Okay Joel... you're up." Before he pulled his head back inside, his face split into a huge grin when he saw our costumes. "Oh yeah... this is gonna be good."

Riley's arms tightened around me. "Knock 'em dead, babe," he whispered against my ear, his lips swooping in for a good luck kiss that ended way too soon.

I slipped out of Riley's arms and gave him a seductive smile. "I'll give it my best shot. Just don't forget who's the *real* boss here, Petruchio."

Throwing my hair back over my shoulder, I turned and was almost at the door when Riley's arm snaked around my waist, pulling me back against his chest.

"You can't say I didn't warn you," he chuckled against my ear. I could feel his heart pounding in his chest against my back. And then it happened. My jaw dropped as he slapped me hard on the butt and nudged me forward.

Excuse me?

He did not just...

Right! Now it was on!

Gritting my teeth, I moved ahead of him, my mind racing as I followed Annie and Joel into the auditorium. I could still hear Riley chuckling behind me.

Oh, he was gonna pay... big time.

Hands-on hips and boobs stuck out, I slipped into the role of Kate, the shrew, flicking my hair and swaying my hips. Turning to play-up to the audience, I threw death stares at Riley every time, as we moved down the centre aisle and up onto the stage.

Oooh... this was fun.

I growled out loud at the sight of the grin Riley was still wearing when he took his seat on a stool to watch me perform *I Hate Men*. But the warning in his eyes told an entirely different story. Flashing him a *you-ain't-seen-nothing-yet* smirk, I turned my back on him and the audience, scanning the stage for my first weapon.

Time for a little payback!

I had to bite back a laugh at the nervous looks on Annie and Joel's faces. I usually started the song standing centre-stage facing the audience—or at least I had in our rehearsals.

Surprise!

All my nerves had evaporated, and I was more than ready to play the shrew. I waited for Annie to play the intro., then spun to face the audience, almost growling the first words of the song in Riley's direction.

I hate men!
I can't abide them, even now and then!

The murmurs and surprised faces of the students at the unexpectedly raunchy rendition of the well-known song egged me on. *This just kept getting better.* Sneaking a peek at Riley, I thrilled at the sight of his Adam's apple bobbing up and down.

Hah!

Now *he was nervous!*

Good!

Okay, time to take it up a notch. Winking at Annie sitting stiffly at the piano, I worked my way across the stage toward the small table where a metal tankard sat. I was supposed to pick it up, pretend to drink, and slam it back down on the table. Or at least, that's what I'd done in the rehearsals...

I hate men!
They should be kept like piggys in a pen!

I lifted the cup to my lips, then turned and threw it at the wall above and behind Riley's head. The audience cracked up laughing as Riley rocked on his stool, shock written all over his handsome face. Then his eyes narrowed, a sly grin sneaking across his face.

O-oh.

Had I gone too far?

I bit my lip to hold back a giggle and ploughed on.

Right, I'd reached the final lines of my solo. Should I go ahead with the rest of the plan or behave? What would Kate do if Petruchio was sitting there with that challenging smirk?

Oh yeah... do it, Katie.

But ladies, you must answer to,
"What would we do without them?"

Sashaying across the stage towards Riley, I sang the words in a silky sweet voice... And then I did it. Before he could work out what was going on, I planted my foot against his chest and pushed him off the stool, scampering out of reach to the other side of the stage.

The sight of Riley sprawled on the floor almost brought me undone, but I would sing the last damn line if it killed me!

Still I hate men!

Finally able to release the laughter, I curtsied and played up to the audience as they cheered, whistled and catcalled. Vaguely aware of Annie starting to play the intro to the duet, *Kiss Me Kate*, with Joel accompanying on the congas, I squealed when Riley's arm clamped around my waist and pulled me back against him.

Wait... where did he come from?

He was supposed to start singing from the other side of the stage.

Oh no.

"My turn, wildcat," he whispered and broke into raucous laughter, making Annie repeat the intro before he started singing.

So, kiss me, Kate, thou lovely loon,
'Ere we start on our honeymoon.
So kiss me, Kate, darling devil devine,
For now thou shall ever be mine.

I tried to prise his arm from around my waist, wriggling and squirming in the hope he'd let me go.

Nope.

His arm was suddenly made of rock.

Fine!

I'll never be thine!

I stomped my foot down on one of his as I sang the words, smiling as Riley yelped and let me go.

But the look!

OMG... those eyes!

My legs were threatening to give way beneath me. We continued to goad each other throughout the song, playing a game of cat and mouse. I ducked and dodged as Riley tried to trap me in his arms again, until the air felt so charged with electricity I thought I might spontaneously combust. Annie and Joel sang the lines written for the chorus, urging Kate to kiss Petruchio with rising excitement.

And then Annie and Joel sang the final line:

Ah... kiss him, Kate

Riley pulled me into his arms, his eyes burning with an intensity that set my blood on fire, my entire body quivering with need. Reaching up to cup his face with shaking hands, I tried to turn his head to kiss him on the cheek. But Riley just shook his head, grabbing both my hands and pinning them behind my back before swooping in for the most explosive, toe-curling kiss ever. All further thought processes were instantly shut down.

It wasn't until Annie and Joel stepped up beside us,

allowing reality to burst the perfect bubble we'd been caught in, that we reluctantly separated. Crashing back to earth, I became aware of the tumultuous applause and cheering from the audience. I looked up at Riley and grinned, rewarded by a wink and another softer slap on the butt. My eyes widened, but then I giggled and slapped Riley's chest... *softly.*

'Cos I sure hoped we were even.

Riley

As KATIE SLIPPED her hand into mine, it felt like electricity zinged along every nerve ending in my body. Holding tight as we left the stage and headed out of the auditorium, I grinned at the students laughing and clapping us on the back as we passed.

Wow. Who knew performing onstage with Katie would turn out to be the most exhilarating experience of my life?

Annie ripped Katie away from me as soon as we burst out the exit door. I wanted to protest, but seeing them throwing their arms around each other, then jumping up and down, squealing, was so cute I couldn't stop grinning.

"Damned if that wasn't a total head-rush, eh?" Joel nudged me, wearing the same goofy grin I knew would be on my face. "Never thought *anything* could come close to the buzz from playing in a band, but *wow...* that was a blast!"

"Yeah, who knew, right?" I couldn't focus on anything but Katie's glowing face. Although, if she kept jumping around like that in her dress, things could get embarrassing real quick.

Katie caught me watching her over Annie's shoulder, the connection sending my pulse rate jumping to an all-new high. Giving Annie one final squeeze, she moved back to throw her arms around my neck.

Katie's sweet lips were almost on mine when Annie pushed an arm between us. "Oh no, you don't. Before you start with the kissy-kissy thing, you two have some major explaining to do. I was nearly having a heart attack up there, with no idea what was coming next. I mean, it was awesome to watch, but man... a bit of a heads-up would have been nice."

Katie's eyes glittered as she looked up at me. "He started it. With that—"

I chuckled and kissed her forehead. "Wait. Before you rip me a new one, I was only trying to help."

Katie leaned back and tilted her head. "Sorry? You're seriously going with that one?"

"You were nervous. I thought I'd try to distract you. How was I to know a slap on the butt would turn you into a screaming banshee?"

Annie's eyes were like saucers. "Oh, *you did not*. You're lucky that cup she threw didn't break your nose."

Katie shrugged and grinned. "Yeah... well... I knew he needed to be able to sing."

Annie cracked up laughing, shaking her head and laughing more every time she looked at us.

Joel just stood and scratched his head, his eyes flicking from Katie's face to mine and back. "So... ummm... I don't know about you guys, but I'd *really* like to get out of these pantaloons and tights. Certain *important* parts of my body are threatening to revolt unless they're released soon."

Annie's eyes widened—*yeah, it was pretty hard to ignore the visual*—before she was doubled-over in hysterical laughter again. Which, of course, started Katie and then me. Tears rolled down Annie's face as she held her stomach, in between spluttering 'no more... please' and 'Katie... stop laughing... dress' when she could draw breath.

Joel just huffed and threw his hands in the air. "Fine. I'm not waiting for you bunch of laughing hyenas any longer. My... *needs*... can't wait any longer. See you in the common room."

Chapter Nineteen

Riley

"So... you sure you're up to the task of dating Katie?" Joel asked me once we were settled in the common room to wait for the girls. "I mean... you don't think you might have bitten off just a *little* more than you can chew, so to speak?"

I chuckled and ran my hands through my hair. "She is pretty feisty, eh? But no way I'd call dating her a task. I... like... feel more alive when I'm around her, ya know? I know it sounds corny, but... yeah... I'm really into her. I think she might be the *one*."

Great, I sounded like some corny, blushing idiot.

But I was past caring.

I was way too happy to even be embarrassed.

"Yeah, well, I guess I'm just kinda jealous," Joel mumbled, his face turning even redder than mine.

Poor Joel. The guy was in so much deeper than I'd

thought. "You... ah... got anything you wanna get off your chest? Maybe something to do with a cute blonde named Annie?"

"Aww shit. Is it that obvious?"

"Nah. I just know you better than you think. All this stuff you keep sprouting about being just friends and her being too good for you? That's absolute bullshit, man. Time to drag your sorry arse out of the denial stage and find out whether she feels the same way."

Joel groaned and covered his face with his hands. "Are you shittin' me? You mean, like... ask her out or something? What if she says no? I don't want to risk stuffing up the friendship the four of us have going. Ya know... awkward?"

I sighed and rubbed my chin. "Look, I know where you're coming from. I was the same about making a move on Katie. But sometimes you've gotta just throw caution to the wind and take the leap. 'Cos eventually, the not knowing will do your head in, and you'll start making excuses to avoid her anyway. Sorry man, but it's a lose, lose either way until you deal with it."

"Aww, man. I can't believe I let this happen. Falling for a girl was *not* part of the plan for this year."

"Yeah, sucks bigtime, eh? It wasn't exactly on my 'to-do' list either. But hot-damn, I feel good right now."

Joel looked up and grinned. "Gee, never would've noticed. Maybe I'll—or not."

Turning to see what Joel was looking at, I grinned as my eyes met Katie's across the room. Damnit... she was so beautiful. I just wanted to pull her into my lap and kiss her senseless. Although I *did* feel a pang of guilt for being so happy, with poor Joel sitting opposite me, pining for the girl walking beside my girlfriend.

My girlfriend.

Wow, who'd have thought that word could make me feel this good?

Huh! Wonders would never cease.

Some of the students sitting around in the common room smiled, giving Katie a 'thumbs up' as she walked past. By the time she slid onto the couch beside me, she looked totally bewildered.

"Okay. That was weird. Who knew being your girlfriend would turn me into an instant celebrity," she said, snuggling in beside me.

Unbelievable! She was doing it again. Anger burned through my chest at Katie's usual self-deprecation. "Don't you dare! *That* had nothing to do with you being my girlfriend. You *earned* those looks *and* the praise. You have no idea how amazing you were up on that stage today. So, can you please just learn to smile and say thanks when someone compliments you?"

Damn, I hadn't meant to snap at her, but it was too late to take it back. So I just held my breath and waited for the inevitable explosion.

My jaw dropped when Katie just giggled, her lips curling into a smile, her dazzling eyes looking up at me in wide-eyed innocence. "Thanks," she said meekly, batting her eyelids. "Like that, you mean?"

She looked so cute my insides turned to mush. Releasing the breath I'd been holding, I groaned and kissed the tip of her nose. "Damn you, woman. I have no idea how you'll react from one minute to the next."

"Good... so my evil plan is working then."

"Which is?"

I tilted her head so my lips hovered just above hers, smiling as she sucked in a breath, her eyes wide and inviting. "Ummm... what was I saying again?" Her tongue slipped out to lick her bottom lip, and I almost gave in to the overwhelming desire to kiss her. But she hadn't answered my question.

"Evil plan...?" I whispered.

"Oh yeah... that," she breathed against my lips. "To... ummm... keep you on your toes, of course."

"Hmmm... two can play that game." Holding her gaze, I lifted my head slightly, increasing the space between our lips, fighting the urge to cave at the disappointment in her eyes.

I knew I'd won when the disappointment turned to the blazing fire I loved.

"Fine, you win."

When she slid her arms around my neck and pulled my lips back down to hers, I knew I really had won.

Katie

MY HEART FELT ready to explode when Riley's lips finally pressed against mine. This guy threw me off balance; my usual control shot to pieces when he looked at me with those soul-stealing blue eyes. Being wrapped in Riley's arms made me feel safer—*and more terrified*—-than I'd felt in my entire life. I tried to push down the doubts and fears rising to the surface, wishing I could just hit the delete button on my past and start with a fresh page.

And the ultra-scariest part? What did I know about this guy who already held a piece of my heart? We knew nothing about each other's lives outside the walls of *Crescendo*. Okay, so I knew he was kind, and talented, and supportive, not to mention gorgeous (*duh!*).

Unbelievable. I was doing it again. What was wrong with me? What kind of idiot thinks about this kinda stuff while being kissed by the hottest guy ever to draw breath?

And the worst part, was that Riley seemed to know something was wrong. I felt him pulling away, and when I opened my eyes, his were full of questions.

You. Are. A. Complete. Moron. Katie. Simpson.

Riley sighed as his eyes searched mine, before leaning his forehead against mine. "So... I was thinking. Now that the audition is over, and with tomorrow being Saturday, how about we have some just you-and-me time somewhere away from here? Maybe go for a walk and have a picnic in Hyde Park or something?"

Ookaay... so there it was again. That thing where he considered my feelings before his own. He knew something was wrong, but he was prepared to wait until we were on our own to talk about it. *Wow.* The list of amazing-things-about-Riley-Stone just kept growing. Now I needed to add considerate, patient and wise.

This guy was seriously too good to be true.

And *BAM*, just like that, my insecurities were questioning his motives again. *Why* did he have to be too good to be true, just because he liked me?

Oh God, maybe my Mum was right, and I did *need to see a shrink!*

Annie leaned over and cleared her throat. "Ummm... sorry. Didn't mean to eavesdrop, but aren't your parents expecting you home this weekend?"

Oh shit. I'd totally forgotten about asking Dad to pick me up Saturday morning. I'd arranged it before he dropped us off at the beginning of the week, worried I'd end up spending my first weekend bored and lonely. But I knew my parents would be ecstatic to hear I'd made some friends, so cancelling shouldn't be a problem.

Riley's smile was still in place, but he couldn't hide the disappointment in his eyes. "Hey, it's okay. If you've already organised—"

I pressed my finger against his lips. "Hang on. Let me think about this for a minute... weekend with Mum and Dad... picnic with Riley." I pretended to weigh the options in my hands like a set of scales. "*Huh!* It's a no-brainer. I'll call Dad tonight and cancel."

Riley grinned, his face lighting up like a Christmas tree. I just about melted when he kissed my finger before removing it from his lips and wrapping my hand in his. "Sure you don't need to think about it for a bit longer?" he asked in a low, soft voice.

I shook my head, giggling when he squeezed my hand,

and I was back floating in a sea of contentment. *Could my life possibly get any more perfect than this?*

Which was when the guilt hit me. Spending all day alone with Riley meant I'd be deserting Annie. She hadn't said whether she wanted to come home with me for the weekend, but now I'd taken the option away completely. "Wait. Now I feel awful. What are you gonna do all day?"

"Excuse me? Like I can't entertain myself for one day. I managed for almost six months when..." Annie blushed and looked ready to bite off her tongue. "... when you... ar... were away."

I froze, hoping no one would address the elephant Annie had just dropped into the room. I needn't have worried. As always, the pregnant silence didn't last long. I looked up into Riley's eyes, knowing it must have been killing him not to ask, but he just smiled and kissed my forehead. *Seriously... how did I get this lucky?*

"Hey... I'm not doing anything tomorrow either, Annie." Joel, who hadn't said a word since Annie and I arrived, sat forward on the couch. "Maybe we could do the popcorn-and-a-movie thing here in the common room. I mean... if you want."

"Yeah? That sounds great, Joel. What kind of movies do you like?"

I sighed with relief as Annie and Joel started chatting about movie choices. I desperately wanted to spend some time alone with Riley, but I'd hated the thought of Annie being bored and lonely all day.

"So I guess that means we're free to do our own thing? Unless there are any other obstacles you can think of?"

Riley wore a mischievous grin, the challenge in his eyes making my heart flutter, as usual.

"Well... I do still have to break the news to my parents..."

"Having *seen* your acting ability, I'm sure that won't be a problem. Or do you require a little more persuasion to change your plans?"

I shivered in anticipation as his lips moved closer. "I'm *always* up for a little *persuasion*..." I whispered, sighing as he closed the distance between us.

Chapter Twenty

Katie

Riley rolled his eyes and groaned as I practically dragged him into the music store. *What? Did he really expect me to walk past such a treasure trove without going inside? Seriously? It was a music shop.*

"Fine," he said as we entered the store. "But this is the last one. I need coffee and food."

We'd left *Crescendo* after breakfast and had been walking—*okay, so maybe you could call it shopping*—for almost two hours, during which time I'd pulled him into a bookstore, an electronic games store and now the music store. And, for a guy, he'd been incredibly tolerant.

But I had to admit I was ready for our picnic as well. We'd chatted about our favourite movies, books and music, but neither of us had volunteered any information about our past or families. Maybe that was why I'd been subconsciously put off sitting down to lunch. I knew what was coming.

Flicking through a pile of sheet music for something I thought Annie might like, my eyes drifted over to Riley. I smiled at the look of awe on his face as he lifted down a guitar, running his hands over its sleek body. He strummed a few chords, closing his eyes as the sweet sound resonated in the air.

Abandoning the sheet music, I moved over to stand beside him. "Wow... what an amazing sound. Let me guess. It's one of those 'every-guitarist's-dream-instruments', right?"

"Yeah, something like that. It's a *Gibson Les Paul*. Beautiful, isn't she?"

I caught sight of the price tag and sucked in a breath. "Seriously? Is it really $5000?"

Riley shrugged and hung it back up on the wall. "'Fraid so. Way outta my price range. Nice to dream, though..."

"What about if you... like... put a deposit on it and paid it off or something?"

A sad look flickered in Riley's eyes, but then he just sighed and tucked my arm around his. "Ready to get outta here and have some lunch?"

"Yep, let's go." I bit my lip, wishing I'd never mentioned the price.

Why did money—whether it was having too much or not enough—always have to be such an issue in life? Pushing the thought aside, I smiled up at my gorgeous man. "So whadya feel like for lunch?"

"There's a great little food van near the entrance at this end of the park. They make great coffee and sell pies and sandwiches and stuff."

"Sounds perfect," I said, smiling up into Riley's face as we left the shop.

Just like you.

Riley

I COULDN'T BELIEVE Katie had suggested putting a *deposit* on a $5000 guitar. Yeah, right, like owning a *Les Paul* was ever gonna be within the realms of possibility. Katie may not act or dress like her family had money, but even *suggesting* something like that told me they weren't exactly lacking it either.

Whatever. I needed to push the image of the oh-so-perfect-but-unattainable guitar out of my head and not let it affect our day. Slipping my backpack off one shoulder, I held my coffee out for Katie to hold and pulled out the blanket I'd stuffed in there at the last minute.

Katie's face lit up, and all thoughts of guitars vanished. "Wow. You're brilliant. I never even thought of bringing a blanket."

"You obviously haven't been on many picnics then. Sitting on the grass is for squirrels."

Katie laughed and handed my coffee back, flopping

down onto the blanket with a sigh. "I'm not arguing. Aargghh, whose stupid idea was it to 'walk' for two hours?"

"The 'walk' should have only taken half an hour. It was the 'shopping' along the way that took up all that time."

Katie blushed, not a fire-engine red blush, but a cute pinkening of the cheeks. "Yeah, sorry about that. It's a girl thing. Can't walk past a shop you've never been into. Hey, at least we only went into the ones I thought you'd like, too. We passed a shoe shop that made me salivate... but I refrained."

I sipped on my coffee, content to watch the expressions flit across her face. She really was beautiful, and I was rapidly discovering how much I preferred 'big girls' to 'stick-thin Barbies'. "So tell me about your family. Where did you grow up? Any brothers or sisters? You seem to get on well with your Dad. What about your Mum?"

Katie smiled and patted my leg. "Whoa. Slow down. One question at a time."

"Well, it sorta *was* one question. I just threw in a few cues."

"A-huh... 'cos you haven't noticed yet that cues, a bit like scripts, are wasted on me?" But her smile had slipped, and she looked down at her hands.

Okay... so she didn't like talking about herself. Maybe I should have let her warm up to it. "Sorry, I shouldn't have been so nosy. What would *you* like to talk about?"

Katie looked up, the smile restored and turning mischievous. "Ummm... let me think... how about... *you*? Same questions apply."

I chuckled and shook my head. *Shoulda known that was coming.* "Ah, I see how it is. Fobbing me off when I ask questions about *you*, but *I'm* supposed to just blurt out my life story?"

I wanted to kick myself when her eyebrows drew into a frown. "Apparently, we both have issues talking about ourselves. To be honest, I guess I don't want the realities of the outside world to burst the happiness bubble I've been floating in since... well, pretty much all week." She sighed, tilted her head and gazed into my eyes. "But it shouldn't matter if we come from completely different backgrounds... should it? Our past doesn't define who we're striving to become... right? I feel like we have similar passions and goals in life, as well as likes and interests. That should be enough... right?"

The passion in her words blew me away. I leaned over and kissed her softly on the lips. She was absolutely right... about all of it. Besides, if we were going to judge each other on where we'd come from, I got the feeling we wouldn't have much hope of moving forward together.

Okay, Riley, you're up. "You're right. So, I'll go first. I grew up in Campbelltown, in the western suburbs of Sydney. I have an older brother... Sean, who's five years older than me. My Mum raised us on her own. Dad fell victim to the old 'grass is always greener' scenario when I was five and never looked back." I sucked in a deep breath, focused on the coffee cup in my hands, and pushed on. "I got into *Crescendo* on a full scholarship and worked my butt off before and after school before that so I'd have enough money saved to survive. Otherwise, I wouldn't have had a hope in hell of being here." I wasn't ready to tell her about my crazy Mother or my brother's irresponsible years yet. I could only take so much pity in one day.

Still focused on my coffee, I lifted it and took a sip. I could feel Katie's eyes burning a hole into the top of my head. Damnit, I didn't want to look up and see the pity or condescension in her eyes.

"Well... that just proves how incredibly talented you are," she said so softly I had to lean in to hear her. "Only the very best musicians get scholarships for *Crescendo*."

Say what? I lifted my head and looked at Katie's smiling face in shock, her eyes shining and filled with admiration.

Wow. She didn't care that I was some poor nobody from nowhere. *And* she liked me *despite* my pretty boy looks.

How did I ever get this lucky?

I held her gaze and squeezed her hand. "Okay... your turn."

Katie chewed on her lip. Was she trying to decide how much she wanted to tell me? Okay, I could relate to that. "Right... well... mine's pretty boring. I grew up in the Northern Beaches, Palm Beach. I'm an only child unless you count Annie, who's always been like a sister and a best friend rolled into one. My parents are both workaholics, who didn't want to take the time away from their busy lives to have any more kids."

Okay, so her family had money. Just being able to afford to live in Palm Beach told me that much. But she didn't seem to be affected by it, not like the other rich kids who flaunted Mummy and Daddy's wealth and looked down on people like me.

Hah... maybe our different backgrounds wouldn't affect our chances of having a relationship after all. My face felt like it might split from the grin I couldn't seem to lose. "See, that wasn't so hard... was it?"

Katie leaned against me, dropping her head onto my shoulder. "Nah. Much easier than having a tooth pulled... *just.*"

Slipping an arm around her waist, I kissed the top of her head. "Hey, I've been meaning to ask you. How did your Dad take being dissed for a hot date?"

"Ummm..."

"You didn't tell him you were going on a date, huh?"

Katie groaned. "Only child remember? Teenage girl. I'm not sure my parents got the memo that I'm sixteen yet. They tend to be a little over-protective when it comes to me 'dating'."

"So, have you dated much?" As soon as the words were out of my mouth, I wanted to rip out my tongue. Katie stiffened, and I braced for impact.

"Have you?" she asked softly.

My mouth was suddenly as dry as a desert. "Depends on what you classify as dating. I don't usually do the whole 'girlfriend/boyfriend' thing?"

Katie didn't move. *Wait, was she even breathing?* "So you're usually just the king-of-the-hook-ups, huh?"

I slipped a hand under Katie's chin and lifted her face to look at me. "I thought we weren't going to let our present be affected by our past? I can't change where I came from, or who I used to be, any more than you can. All I'm asking is that you give me a chance to prove I'm more than just a product of my past."

I caught the tears in her eyes before she threw her arms around my neck, burying her face against my chest. I leaned back until we were lying on the ground, loving the way Katie snuggled in beside me. "Hey, this is supposed to be a picnic... you know, lots of laughing and fun. Maybe talking about this kind of stuff was a bad idea."

Katie sniffled and sighed. "You may have noticed I'm not real good with the big 'T' word either... you know... trust."

"Do you wanna talk about it?" I whispered against her ear.

Katie was still for a good minute, and I'd just about given up hope of hearing her secret when she started to talk.

"The answer to the dating question is: Only once... before this. Mark was a pretty-boy who played guitar and sang in a band." *Aww, shit, she could have been describing me.* "We went out together for three months until I caught him and his friends laughing over a video of me topless, with my ex fondling my... ummm... boobs, or the 'ginormous puppies', as one of them called them. I pulled out of school and finished the second half of Year-Ten online."

It took everything I had to bury the rage burning inside me. How could *anyone* do something so cruel? No wonder Katie's self-esteem was in shreds. I felt her tears soaking into my shirt, and my gut churned. I wanted to hunt this guy down and beat him to a pulp. But right now, I needed to find the words to help this amazing girl in my arms deal with the heartache of her past.

Propping myself up on my elbow, I wiped a tear away with my thumb, wanting nothing more than to erase the sadness in her beautiful eyes. "Well, I guess that just proves how amazing *you* are. You didn't let some puffed-up arsehole stop you from coming to *Crescendo* and proving to the world how talented you are."

Chapter Twenty-One

Katie

I gazed into Riley's eyes in awe at his unexpected words. He'd used the same ploy I'd used on *him* to make *me* feel better about my past, and damned if it hadn't worked. I'd never even considered it from that point of view. I may have allowed Mark to ruin last year, refusing to attend the Year Ten formal, or any of the parties to celebrate the end of the school year. But I hadn't let what he did stop me from following my dreams and coming to *Crescendo*. I smiled as some of the pain dissolved. Maybe I *could* crawl out of the hole I'd been living in and move on after all.

Riley's eyes warmed when he saw my smile, and I sighed as he leaned over to brush his lips against mine. The kiss was sweet and gentle, nothing like the other toe-curling kisses we'd shared, but it was perfect. I shivered when he lifted his head and gazed into my eyes, the baby-blue a little darker than usual. "So... any more secrets we need to share?"

Damnit. This was where I should be telling him about Dad. I wanted to trust him, to believe it wouldn't make a difference, but Mark's cruel words echoed in my head... *if it wasn't for the fame and fortune her Daddy's gonna bring us, I could have a* real *girlfriend.* Nope, I wasn't ready to share *that* yet.

Instead... I deflected. "Hmmm... let's see. I wanted to be a prima-ballerina when I was eight until I realised I was too chubby for the cute costumes."

Riley chuckled. "I wanted to be an astronaut until I was ten, but then I went on a plane for the first time and had to use the sick bag."

I giggled—*totally unashamedly... maturity, blah*—my heart skipping a beat at Riley's playful banter. His ability to disprove everything I'd ever believed about myself made me feel beautiful... and wanted.

Please don't let him be acting.

Riley brushed my hair back off my forehead, his touch gentle and feather soft. I shivered as he ran his hand down its length, wrapping the ends of a few strands around his finger. "So... I was thinking."

I grinned. "Sounds dangerous."

Riley chuckled and tugged on the strands of hair. "Be wery wery careful... "

"Why... we huntin' wabbits?"

I sucked in a breath as Riley threw his head back and laughed. He looked so happy and carefree. I loved knowing I had that effect on him. A rare surge of contentment flooded through me. Until I noticed we'd drawn the attention of a group of girls sitting nearby, as well as another two walking past. They were all staring wide-eyed at the laughing god-like man in their midst.

That laughing man who'd chosen me!

And then the bubble burst with a sickening pop.

"Did you see the fat chick he's with? Man... what a waste..." The voice of one of the passing gorgeous, size eight girls was like an arrow straight to my heart.

My world imploded. I couldn't breathe. *Who was I kidding?* I couldn't date someone like Riley. It didn't matter that he was everything I'd ever wanted in a guy. He would always be one of the-beautiful-people, and I could never survive in that world.

Jumping up from the blanket, I started gathering our rubbish, not wanting Riley to see the tears in my eyes and praying he hadn't heard the girl's nasty words. I just needed to get back to my room. *Now!*

"Hey." Riley had moved to stand behind me, his warm breath against my ear. His arms slipped around my waist, pulling me back against his chest. I closed my eyes and leaned into him, trying to resurrect that happy, carefree feeling we'd shared. But seriously, what was the point? This... *us*... was never going to work.

Riley sighed, gently turning me around and lifting my chin. The sadness in his eyes sucked the air from my lungs. It was as if he felt my pain, and it hurt him too. "Who cares what she thinks?"

"*I do!* And you should, too. I'm sorry Riley, but this—"

Riley growled deep in his throat—*damnit, I'd miss that*

sound—and the sadness was replaced by a look of fierce determination, re-awakening the butterflies in my stomach and morphing them into hornets. "Why? So I can let them dictate who I should go out with? Listen to me, Katie. *You. Are. Beautiful.* I've hooked up with plenty of girls like that bit—" Riley blew out a breath, running his hands up my arms, and I desperately wanted to believe him, but... "Katie. I don't want *them*. I want the girl who pushes my buttons and makes me feel alive. Who makes me laugh and doesn't judge me. Whose voice renders me speechless when she sings." He pulled me against him and whispered in my ear. "Sound like anyone you know?"

The tight knot in my stomach began to unravel. He sounded so sincere. No one had *ever* described me like that. I wanted to be with him; I really did. But the hateful looks and words *hurt*. Maybe if we could be together without—? "Hey, what if we kept *us* a secret? You know, not be together in public—"

Okay, there was that growl again. *Sooo sexy.* "*Not. Going. To. Happen.* Damnit Katie. Will you please listen to me for once? I don't give a rat's arse what people think. Stop running and hiding. It's time to *own* who you are and call these judgemental arseholes on their shit. Hey, I'm living proof you can do it... you've sat me on my arse enough times."

Riley was *almost* right. I could be that person— when I was performing... shutting the world out and not allowing their judgement to affect me. But that was the *pretend* world, where I was confident in my singing ability and who

I was on stage. But the *real* world was a whole different ballgame.

Would I ever be able to look in the mirror and be happy with who I was? *Believe* that I was desirable and deserved a boyfriend like Riley? Maybe knowing Riley wanted me just the way I was could be the first step towards that—

"Wow. I would *kill* to know what's going through your head right now. It's like watching a wrestling match. Who's winning?"

"Ummm... you *may* be starting to get the upper hand. But the logical part of my brain is still putting up a good fight."

"That's my girl," Riley said softly, leaning down to capture my lips with his. The kiss was so tender it brought tears to my eyes... again. Like I hadn't done enough crying today already. His hands cupped my face, his lips a caress, his tongue seeking entry. I sighed and gave in to what my heart wanted, shutting down my brain and all its negative thoughts. With my heart beating so fast I thought I might pass out, I welcomed his tongue with my own.

Being in Riley's arms... kissing him... felt *so* right. How could I doubt his feelings when they felt so much like my own? Riley *wanted* to be with *me*, and *he* wasn't afraid to show the world how he felt. Maybe it *was* time I allowed myself to stand tall and fight for what I wanted. I deserved happiness just as much as those jealous *Barbies*.

Feeling empowered, I wrapped my arms around Riley's neck and pressed myself against him, deepening the kiss and running my hands through his hair. I wanted him to know how much I trusted him and what his words meant to me. I felt free for the first time in my life... free to just be...*me*.

And okay, *maybe* I also wanted to send a message to anyone watching. I would *not* give anyone the satisfaction of being embarrassed about kissing my hot boyfriend in public.

Mine!

Suck rocks, Barbies.

I couldn't stop the whimper of protest that slipped out when Riley lifted his head, his breathing ragged, his eyes as dark as midnight. I rested my burning face against his chest, inhaling his musky scent as I leaned against him, my legs seriously threatening to quit their job.

"*Wow.* So *that's* what it feels like," Riley whispered against my ear.

"What *what* feels like?"

"Kissing you... being kissed *by* you... and not having to worry you're gonna bolt any minute. It was incredible."

I lifted my head, my eyes locking with his. "How did you—?"

"Oh, Katie, I was intrigued the first time I saw that fiery-eyed, challenging glare you use as armour against the world. I wanted... no, I *needed*... to know the girl inside the armour. You lowered it a few times, and I got a glimpse. But just then, when you kissed me, it was like you'd finally peeled it off and let me in."

Snap. Crackle. And... Pop.

How was it possible that this gorgeous guy I'd only known a week understood me so well? It was like he could see inside me, past the barriers and walls I'd built to protect my damaged heart.

And maybe... just maybe... he'd even begun to repair a tiny bit of that damage.

Riley

I MUST HAVE DIED and gone to Heaven!

Katie's mind-blowing kiss had tipped my entire world off its axis. Knowing what she'd been through and that she was willing to trust me made my heart swell with pride. Now, all I needed to do was keep proving to her that I was worth it.

I've no idea how long we stood there, grinning at each other like a pair of goofy ten-year-olds, before my brain finally kicked back in. "Now, can we please sit back down so I can finish telling you what I was thinking about? *Without* the wisecracks."

"Sure." Katie's raised eyebrows and cheeky grin made my stomach churn—in a good way—as we settled back onto the blanket. I loved that I never knew what to expect from my beautiful, feisty girl.

"Okay, you have my complete and undivided attention." She batted her eyelids, folding her hands in her lap and trying to look serious.

Sooo cute.

"Well... what do you think about you, me, Joel and

Annie forming a band? I know you write music, and I have a few songs I've written—"

Katie's face lit up. "Absolutely... I'm in. And I'm sure Annie would love it too."

"Okaaay... you don't want to think about it then?"

"Are you serious? This is... like... something I've always dreamed of doing. I loved performing with you guys in the audition. So can we do covers as well? Maybe some of those duets we worked on?"

"Whoa... slow down. Don't you think it might be a good idea to see what Joel and Annie say first?"

"Fine."

I bit back a laugh. *Was she seriously pouting?* "Okay, what's wrong?"

"Well... now I really wanna know if they're interested, but I don't want our picnic to end. Wait. What if we ring them and ask? Then we could stay here and start—"

"We'll have plenty of chances to have other picnics. Come on, let's go talk to Joel and Annie and get the ball rolling."

I jumped up and held out my hand, helping Katie to her feet and pulling her against me. "But before we go, I just need another one of those amazing, armour-free kisses."

Katie's eyes glittered as she threw her arms around my neck, stood on tiptoes and kissed me.

Yep, that was the one.

My world tilted all over again as my beautiful girl once again succeeded in blowing my mind.

Chapter Twenty-Two

Riley

"So... how was the movie?" I asked, flopping down on the lounge and wrapping an arm around Katie's shoulder as she snuggled in beside me. Annie and Joel both blushed, but I figured it was probably best to pretend I hadn't noticed.

Damnit, I'd forgotten to ask Katie if she knew what was going on with them. I'd been *way* too busy working on my own love-life to worry about anyone else's.

Whoa... love-life?

Seriously, Riley, settle down.

You've known the girl for a week!

But I had to admit, it would be easy to fall in love with Katie. She was so real, somehow managing to make *everything* more exciting. I was so over people pretending to be something they weren't. Katie never failed to call me on my crap, and it was exhilarating.

Annie giggled. "Yeah, it was great. Joel agreed to watch *Pitch Perfect*, and although he'll never admit it, he enjoyed it as much as I did."

Joel rolled his eyes and shrugged, but a sheepish smile snuck across his face. "Just call me another musician suffering for his art."

"So, Joel and I were talking about—"

"So, Riley and I were talking about—"

Annie and Katie had both spoken at once, stopped and looked at each other, then burst out laughing.

I raised my eyebrows and grinned at Joel. "You mentioned the band thing too, huh?"

"Wait—"

"What—?"

The girls had stopped laughing the minute I said the 'band' word, and, as if on cue, Joel and I cracked up. I knew we were drawing the attention of the other students in the room, and I couldn't care less. I was enjoying the camaraderie of our new group and felt lucky to be a part of it. Truth be told, most of the students watching us probably wished they were a part of it, too.

Katie sat up and scooted to the other end of the lounge, putting her hands on her hips and giving me the evil eye. I instantly missed the feel of her body snuggled against mine.

"Riley Stone! I thought you said we needed to run the idea past Annie *and* Joel before we made any decisions. So how does Joel even know what we're talking about?"

Okay. I was in trouble. But instead of the old feeling of trepidation, excitement ran through me. I loved it when she got all feisty and challenged me. "Well... ummm... Joel and I *may* have sorta talked about the possibility of asking you and Annie."

Adopting a sheepish grin, I reached out and tried to pull her back beside me, chuckling when she slapped my hand away. *She was sooo hot when she was fired up.* Folding my arms in front of my chest, I shrugged and threw Joel a 'bit-of-help-here-would-be-good' look, trying not to show how much I was enjoying myself.

Joel sighed and looked down at his shoes. "Look. We didn't actually *discuss* it. We just sort of agreed that it would be great if—"

"Wait. When was this?" Annie asked, jumping on the bandwagon. Joel just looked at me and shrugged.

God help us... I'd forgotten how irrational girls could be. "C'mon, does any of this really matter? Joel didn't know I was gonna mention it today, and I didn't know he would. Like Joel said, we never really talked about it; we just agreed that we'd both be interested. So how about we stop trying to dissect the who, what, when, where, and why and move forward?"

Katie looked at Annie and blew out a long breath. Annie held her gaze, some secret message passing between them, before giving a slight nod. Then they both broke into big cheesy grins and shared a high-five. *Damned if they hadn't been playing us.*

"Hell yeah... I am definitely in!" Annie did that weird little hand-clapping thing and threw her arms around Joel's neck. "This is *so* awesome."

As if realising what she'd just done, she blushed beetroot red, scooting to the other end of the lounge and muttering her apologies. Joel just sat there, looking like he'd been hit by a stun gun, until a smug smile emerged. That conversation I planned to have with my roommate was becoming more interesting every minute.

My pulse rate sped up as I pretended not to notice Katie sliding back across the lounge, her warm body snuggling against mine. "Fine, I'll let you off the hook *this* time. But you owe me another picnic…"

Wrapping my arm back around her, I chuckled and kissed her forehead. "As you wish, Buttercup."

Katie giggled. "No way. You have *not* watched *The Princess Bride*?"

"Inconceivable! How could you doubt my appreciation of such a classic?"

Joel was scratching his head. "Ummm… I hate to show my ignorance, but what the hell is *The Princess Bride*?"

Annie sighed and shook her head. "Looks like we need to have another movie-watching session. You've lived a sad life up to now, Joel Kenny."

Joel groaned and slumped down on the lounge. "Oh yay… and Stone? No more chick-flick movie references, okay? I'd like to watch at least *one* action or horror movie this semester."

Annie just grinned, shrugged and stuck out her tongue. "Welcome to the hardships of having girls for friends. Suck it up, princess."

Katie

BY SUNDAY NIGHT, I was so tired I couldn't stop yawning as I struggled to finish my homework for Music Theory. Not that I was complaining. I'd had the best weekend of my life, and the goofy grin on my face had become a permanent fixture. Which probably explained why it was taking so long to finish my stupid homework. Every blissful moment spent with Riley was on permanent replay in my besotted brain.

After our picnic, I'd spent Saturday night snuggled on the lounge in the common room with Riley, kissing and 'watching movies'. Well, more kissing than watching... I couldn't even remember what had been on.

I'd woken up Sunday morning and prayed before I'd even opened my eyes that it hadn't all just been a dream. But after spending the day in Studio Five bantering, laughing and singing with Riley, Joel and Annie, I was finally convinced my life had really changed. I couldn't remember a time when I'd been happier.

"You almost done?" Annie asked, closing her laptop and packing away her books.

"Yeah, just on the last question."

"So... ummm... can I ask you something?"

"Sure. What's up?"

"WhadyathinkofJoel?" Annie's words came out in such a rush I wasn't sure I'd heard them right. But I knew I had when I looked up to find her blushing furiously.

"Joel? I think he's great. But more importantly, what do *you* think of Joel?"

I studied Annie's face as she took off her glasses and cleaned them, as if she were trying to sort out exactly how she felt before answering. Honestly, I'd never understood why more guys weren't attracted to my petite friend. At five-foot-three inches, Annie's spiral-curled blonde hair and blue eyes made her look a bit like a doll—well, a doll who wore glasses. Okay, so maybe she came across as shy and reserved when you first met her, but once you broke through that thin layer, she was feisty, vivacious and heaps of fun.

Annie heaved a huge sigh and slipped her glasses back on. "I really like him when he's not acting like a self-conscious idiot. I mean, we can be in the middle of laughing and talking like friends, and suddenly, he gets all weird and shuts down. And it's annoying the hell outta me."

"So when you say you *like* him, are we talking just friends, or would you be interested in more if *he* was?"

"Hell if I even know. I watch you with Riley, and I kinda wish I had that too. But I don't know whether I just want that with *someone* or I want it with *Joel*. Does that even make sense?"

I slipped off my bed and sat beside Annie, throwing my arm around her shoulder. "Of course it makes sense. It's not like either of us has any experience with this sort of thing. But you don't want to start something with Joel just because he's the only guy available. Maybe you need to check out what or *who* else is around. What about that friend of his, Mikey? He's cute and was definitely checking you out in that blue medieval dress you wore for the audition."

"Really? He was checking me out? Huh, I was too nervous about the audition to even notice. But now that I think about it... yeah, he *is* pretty cute. All that messy blonde hair and big blue eyes. Hmmm..." Her eyes lit up. "Hey, I think Joel said he plays bass guitar. Maybe we could sound the boys out about him joining the band? Invite him to sit with us at lunch to talk about it or something?"

"Okaaay... although it might change the band's dynamics a bit if it turns out Joel *is* interested in being more than just friends. But hey... it's time that guy either stepped up or stepped back. All's fair in love and war. How about I ask Riley about Mikey tomorrow? I mean, we don't know anything about him except that he's cute. He might turn out to be a complete jerk yet."

Annie leaned her head on my shoulder and sighed. "Thanks for listening to my drivel. I love having my best friend as a roommate. Imagine how hard it would be sharing a room with a stranger?"

My stomach twisted as I thought about how close I'd come to blowing off the Academy and sending Annie on her own. I'd never told Annie what I was thinking of doing or how Mum was pressuring me to study online for another year. But somehow Annie had known about my internal battle, and never pressured me either way. She knew I had to make my own decision, for all the *right* reasons, and I knew she would have stuck by me no matter what. *That's* what best-friends do for each other.

"Lucky for us we'll never have to find out then, eh?"

I WAS SITTING and playing with my breakfast on Monday morning, waiting for the right opportunity to ask Riley about Mikey, when the guy in question turned up at our table, wearing a huge grin on his cute face.

"Hey, you guys. Congrats on getting the spot in the end-of-semester show. Not that I'm surprised. You totally nailed the audition. So... is the meeting over already?"

"Sorry—?"

"Say what—?"

"Huh—?"

I was the only one not to say anything, rendered utterly speechless by Mikey's words. Instead, I stared at Mikey as if he'd lost his mind.

Did he just say we had to perform Kiss Me Kate in the actual show?

No way!

The audition was a joke.

Mikey looked at our faces and chuckled. "I'm guessing from your reactions you didn't know, right? Now that I think about it, you guys left straight after your audition, so you wouldn't have heard the announcement. The results were posted last night, and there's a cast meeting and breakfast in the auditorium... ummm... now."

I didn't know whether to laugh or cry. Not only would I have to repeat the performance, but it would be in front of all the students, faculty, and par—

Oh my God, my parents would be there.

There was no way I could do that toe-curling kiss in front of them. Anyone watching could see *that* wasn't an act. *How the hell did I get myself into this mess?*

Riley! This was all his fault. *"We'll just ham it up and give them a good laugh,"* he said.

Yeah right. How the hell was I supposed to repeat that performance?

Damnit, I couldn't breathe.

And what about the band?

How would we squeeze rehearsals—?

"Breathe, babe." Riley's breath was warm against my ear, his arm sliding around my waist. "Come on, deep breaths—in and out."

I looked up to find Mikey, Joel and Annie watching me nervously. How long had they been standing there? *Oh no. I'd almost gone into a full-blown panic attack right there in the cafeteria.*

Okay, I needed to pull myself together.

I'd performed onstage hundreds of times...

Yeah. Not kissing a hot guy in front of my parents, though...

Riley looked up at Joel. "How about you and Annie go on ahead and tell them we're coming? Maybe explain to Professor Haines why we're late?"

"Yeah sure. We'll... ar... see you there..." Annie threw me a 'will-you-be-okay-if-I-go' look, and I nodded, trying to paste on a smile.

As soon as they left, Riley sighed, wrapping his other arm around me and pulling me closer. "Katie? What's going on? I know this isn't what we planned, but —"

"Damnit Riley. You don't understand. I can't do that performance in front of my par—"

Riley stiffened, his arms loosening their hold. "So this is about kissing me in front of your parents? Worried they won't *approve* of your dirt-poor boyfriend?" The hurt in his voice was like a vice squeezing my heart. How did he always seem to know what was going on inside my head?

Was that what I was worried about? After the whole Mark debacle, would my parents try to convince me Riley was just another pretty-boy trying to use me to further his career?

No wait... Riley didn't even know who my Dad was... did he?

But what if someone had found out who I was and told him?

Aargghh!

I just wanted to run back to my room and bury my head in my pillow. Why hadn't I told him everything at the picnic? Because there was still a part of me that didn't believe he could want me for myself. I'd figured if I didn't tell him, there was no risk of looking into his eyes and seeing he'd been lying all along.

Riley groaned. "So I guess that's my answer then, huh?" I couldn't even look at him, but the hurt in his voice made my heart ache. "Damnit, Katie, can't you at least have the guts to tell me the truth?"

"I don't *know*... okay? My head is all over the place right now. Can we please talk about this later? Right now, we need to get to this stupid meeting."

Riley turned my face to him, looking into my eyes, his

hand brushing a stray curl behind my ear. I desperately wanted to throw my arms around his neck and kiss away the hurt in his eyes. But I needed to sort my own head out first. And *that* needed to wait until after the meeting.

He sighed again and stood up, hesitating before holding his hand out as if he wasn't sure what to do. I slipped my hand into his, the spark I got every time I touched him kick-starting my scrambled brain.

This was only the beginning of week two of the semester. The show would run for the whole of week ten. There'd be plenty of time to introduce Riley to my parents as my boyfriend before then and convince them to give him a chance.

I squeezed Riley's hand and smiled up at him as we walked to the auditorium, but the pain in his eyes told me the damage had already been done. Somehow, I needed to fix things or risk losing the best thing that had ever happened to me.

It was time to tell Riley everything.

Chapter Twenty-Three

Riley

I sat in the auditorium, not listening to a word Professor Haines said. Not that it mattered; I'd get the rundown from Joel later. I was too busy wrestling with the fact that Katie thought her parents wouldn't approve of me. After everything she'd said about not judging a person on their past, or where they came from, she'd still freaked out about her parents seeing her kiss me on stage.

Typical. I'd had the best weekend of my life and could feel the happiness crumbling away already. You'd think I'd be used to this kind of thing by now. *Why did I keep expecting the good stuff to last?*

I'd already been stressed after receiving Sean's text last night, saying he suspected Mum was lying about taking her medication. And my *older* brother couldn't handle the stress of being responsible for her all the time. What did he expect *me* to do? Wave a freakin' magic wand and make it all better? *Unbelievable!* Like *I'd* enjoyed being Mum's carer for the previous five years while Sean trotted off to uni. and didn't look back.

And now this? Damnit. Having Katie in my life made me feel like I could breathe for the first time in years. I know it sounded ridiculous after such a short time, but I didn't even want to contemplate going back to the empty life I was leading before we met. *Seriously... what did I ever do to make the universe hate me? Was it so hard to just let me be happy for once?*

Katie's reaction to the thought of her parents seeing us kiss had floored me. Were her parents the type to tell her to stop seeing someone? Would she listen to them? Hey, it wasn't like I was some bum living on the streets. I was here, at a renowned school, trying to make something of myself.

Wait... didn't Katie say this scumbag Mark was a guitarist? Maybe her parents had something against 'pretty-boy musicians'. Well, if I wanted to keep Katie in my life, I'd have to prove to them I wasn't just another one of *those*.

The sound of chairs scraping across the auditorium floor snapped me back to earth. Before I could even move, Katie squeezed my hand and leaned over. "I'm gonna skip my first class and stay in my room. I'd really like to talk... if you want."

Slipping her hand out of mine, she smiled and walked out with Annie.

If I want?

Of course I wanted to talk.

I grabbed Joel, told him I was ditching class, and then headed back to my room. Okay, I'd give Katie ten minutes to get her head sorted out, and then I was going in. I'd suspected when she was telling me about Mark that there was more to the story. Maybe whatever it was had something to do with her parents' reaction to her dating. *What else did the slime-bag ex do?*

I paced the room, running my hands through my hair and trying not to picture any of the possible scenarios playing in my head. No, Katie would be a *lot* more messed up if *that* had happened. I checked my watch—seven minutes since she'd left the auditorium.

Stuff it! Time to exorcise some demons... whatever the hell they are.

Katie opened the door at my first knock as if she'd been standing in front of it waiting for me. The worry in her eyes made my heart ache. I stepped in the door, closed it behind me, and pulled her into my arms.

Damnit... she was shaking.

What was going on?

Tilting her chin up so our eyes met, I moved to kiss her, stopping with my lips almost touching hers, scanning her eyes to make sure she wanted me to. My knees went weak with relief when she sighed and slid her arms around my neck, closing the gap and answering the question I'd been afraid to ask. I shivered as her fingers played with the hair at the base of my neck, her kiss setting me on fire. I wanted this girl more than I'd ever imagined possible.

Whoa there, Casanova.

You're here to talk!

Wrestling my raging hormones back under control, I broke the kiss, my eyes drinking in the beautiful girl in my arms. Katie's eyes held a glow I was pretty sure matched mine. They told me everything I needed to know. She wanted me just as much as I wanted her. No way I was letting *anyone* take her away from me.

Aaand my goofy grin was back. Guiding her to sit on the bed, I pulled up her desk chair so there was some distance between us. I wasn't sure who I was more worried about giving in to temptation... me or Katie.

"So... ar... you wanted to *talk?*" I winced at the husky tone of my voice.

"Ummm..." Throat clearing. "Yeah, right."

Apparently, I wasn't the only one struggling with the concept of *talking* when we were alone... in her bedroom.

Get your mind out of the gutter Stone and pull yourself together.

Blowing out a long breath, I leaned forward and rested my elbows on my knees, studying my hands. "How about we start with your reaction to the thought of kissing me in front of your parents? What are you worried about? Is it because I'm a musician, or too much like Mark, or —"

"Riley, I need to tell you something, but I'm worried you'll be mad at me..."

I looked up and saw... *was it fear?...* in her eyes. I resisted the urge to pull her back into my arms... *barely.* "Jesus, Katie. Just tell me already."

Katie sucked in a huge breath and squared her shoulders. "Okay. So, have you heard of the recording label *Simpson Records?*"

"Yeah, of course... who hasn't?"

Wait. Surely not...

The puzzle pieces all started to fall into place. Katie Sims... Simpson... shit.

This couldn't be happening! That would mean... Katie was the daughter of a millionaire?

My stomach churned at the implications. Of course she'd hidden who she was, because she didn't want some ambitious and unscrupulous musician at *Crescendo* trying to use her to get to Daddy.

"The look on your face tells me you worked it out, huh? Well... at least you look surprised."

Wait...why wouldn't I be—

"Please don't look at me like that. Like I'm someone different. None of this changes who *I* am. Please, Riley, you're the first person, besides Annie and my family, who ever liked me for me, and not what they could get from me."

"What do you mean I look surprised? Why wouldn't I be?"

The last piece of the puzzle hit me like a punch to the chest.

She'd thought I might have already known and was using her just like all the others.

A tear slid down Katie's beautiful face, her teeth chewing on her lip. "I'm so sorry, Riley. I wanted to tell you on Saturday, but I was so happy. I didn't want to know if you were just—"

"Using you?" I sucked in a deep breath, trying to push the hurt and anger down. I couldn't decide what was making me angrier. The fact that she thought I'd do something like that or that this meant she was *way* out of my reach.

Life totally sucked! I needed to get out of there. "Yeah... look... sorry Katie. I have to go. I... ar...need some air."

Before she could say another word, I jumped out of the chair and bolted out the door. Taking the stairs two at a time, I raced out of the building, my mind reeling from Katie's revelations.

I don't know how long I walked without thinking about where I was going, but eventually, I found myself in Hyde Park, where we'd had our picnic.

Yeah, I was hurt that Katie had questioned my motives for wanting to be with her. But I kinda understood that her lack of trust had more to do with her insecurity and her awful past, coupled with her fear of believing in a guy she hadn't known long.

But that wasn't the biggest problem. Katie would probably laugh if she knew how much I wished she *wasn't* who she was, that she was just a normal girl from a middle-class family.

Because, in the end, I knew it would come between us, no matter how hard we fought against it.

'Cos there was no way a man like Reece Simpson would *ever* believe I didn't want anything more than his daughter's love.

Katie

I was still sobbing into my pillow when Annie popped in between classes. Okay, so I'd expected Riley to be mad at me for not telling him who I was at our picnic. But what I *hadn't* expected, was for him to look at me like I was a stranger. I was so confused. Shouldn't he have been happy or excited to find out he was dating the daughter of someone like Reece Simpson?

Annie dived onto the bed and wrapped her arms around me. "Oh, Katie. What happened? Did you tell him?"

I groaned and punched my pillow. "Yep, and he hates me."

"What?" Annie's hand rubbed my back, and I could almost *hear* the thoughts jumping around in her head. "No. There's no way he hates you. Where is he?"

Annie moved back as I sat up and hugged the pillow to my chest, trying to settle my breathing. "No idea. He... he just s-said he needed some air and... bolted out the door like I was diseased or something." *Where* was *he?* "Have you... ummm... spoken to Joel? Does... does he know what's going on?"

"Yeah, I saw him, and no, he doesn't know about you or anything else. He was waiting outside when I walked out of class, looking totally freaked out. He said Riley had *never* skipped a class, and he wanted to know what was going on.

I sorta told him it had something to do with the panic attack you almost had at breakfast and that Riley was helping you deal with it."

"Thanks. Do you think I can trust him with my secret? Joel, I mean. He doesn't seem like a douchebag-Mark type of person."

"Yeah, I think he'll be cool about it." Annie had that look on her face that told me she wanted to ask me something but wasn't sure if she should.

I sighed and grabbed her hand. "Go on... just ask, whatever it is."

"I just need to know what brought on the panic attack this morning. It's not like you've never performed on stage before. What the hell happened?"

"In a nutshell? The thought of my parents being in the audience when Riley and I practically devoured each other onstage. You know what they've been like since Mark. I don't want them to scare Riley off."

"Okay, so maybe Riley's a pretty-boy-up-and-coming-guitarist. But that's the *only* thing he has in common with Mark. Surely your parents will... ah shit. No, you're right. They'll never believe it. You're screwed."

I almost choked on a laugh at her forthright summation of the situation. Annie never was one to beat around the bush. "Yeah, goodonya. Way to make me feel better... *not!*"

Annie grinned. "Yeah, but at least I got you to laugh. Come on, Katie, it's not like you to throw in the towel before the fight's even started. We need a plan."

I groaned again. I hadn't had a chance to tell Annie that

Riley was dirt poor and at *Crescendo* on a scholarship. "Hang on... there's more."

I watched Annie's face as I told her about Riley's background and knew what she was going to say before I'd even finished talking.

"Sorry, Katie, but there's no way your Dad won't do a background check on Riley as soon as he hears you're dating him."

Yep, I was definitely screwed. "Exactly. I was kinda not planning to tell them for a while... like, until the memories of the Mark fiasco had faded a bit more... like, maybe graduation?"

Annie rolled her eyes. "Katie... there's no way you can hide a boyfriend from your parents for two years! You have the worst poker face *ever*."

I jumped at a loud knocking on the door.

"It's me, Joel."

Annie climbed off the bed and opened the door. "What's up?

"I just got a text from Riley saying he's in Hyde Park and asking me to cover for him the rest of the day. What the hell is going on?"

Feeling the tears threatening to break through again, I grabbed Annie's hand. "Sorry, Annie, but I need to sleep for a while. Can you please go... both of you. Oh, and maybe you should tell Joel everything. I don't care who knows any more... In fact... I don't fucking care about anything."

I rolled over and faced the wall, curling up in a ball and wishing it could all be over. As soon as I heard the door close behind Annie and Joel, I buried my face in the pillow and let the sobs take over again.

It so wasn't fair! It felt like I'd had Riley for, like, five minutes, only to lose him because we lived in a world where people were judged by what they had, or didn't have, instead of *who* they were. And here I'd thought it was all about being a 'fat-chick'.

I hate my life!

Chapter Twenty-Four

Katie

I tried to eat the dinner Annie had brought to our room, but everything tasted like cardboard. According to Joel, Riley still hadn't returned to the Academy, and my stomach was in knots worrying about him. Fine, I got that he didn't want to talk to—*or see*—me, but why hadn't he at least come back to the school?

I was still lost in the irony of being *rejected* because of *who* I was. That was definitely one for the books. Giving up on trying to eat, I moved the plate to the bedside table, sliding back down under the blankets and staring at the ceiling.

Okay, maybe it was time to put things back into perspective. I'd missed an entire day of classes—for what? So I could wallow in misery all day over some guy I'd only known a week?

Idiot.

Moron.

Sook.

Get over yourself and move on.

I picked up my iPad and tried to get back into the book I'd started reading before I left home. Reading had *so* not been a priority since I'd met...

I gave up pretending to read when I realised I'd read the same sentence ten times and still had no idea what it said. Sighing, I put the iPad carefully back in the drawer, somehow resisting the urge to hurl it against the wall like I wanted to.

I just couldn't get the look on Riley's face before he left out of my head. Damnit... who was I trying to kid? No way was he just 'some-guy-I'd-met-a-week-ago'. I thought we'd found something special. And I'd stupidly thought he felt the same way.

Damnit... there needed to be a tap you could just turn off to stop loving someone.

Because, let's face it, I was totally in love with Riley Stone.

Just the thought of not being able to talk and laugh with him every day, with no right to touch or kiss him, made me want to curl up in a ball and never get up.

I jumped at the soft knock on the door, my blood turning to ice.

What if it was Riley?

Did I even want to see him?

Or for him to see me like this?

I must look like something-the-cat-dragged-in after spending the entire day in bed crying. But then, why would it matter how I looked? For once, it wasn't my *looks* that had turned a guy off. Besides, it was probably just Joel running *another* errand for Annie. At least, that was his *excuse*. They'd taken turns checking on me all day.

"Yeah, come in... it's open." I rolled over and faced the wall again. "And before you ask, I'm fine. Just grab whatever it is and go."

"Katie?"

It was Riley.

I froze, torn between wanting him to stay and telling him to leave. I heard him sit down on the office chair, his breathing erratic, as if he'd been running. I stayed perfectly still, not that I would have been able to move if I wanted to. Every muscle in my body felt like it had shut down.

What was he even doing here?

And what was I supposed to say to him?

Riley gave a huge sigh. "Okay, I get that you don't want to look at me. But can you please just listen?" The pain in his voice made my heart ache even more. He sounded like he'd been through the wringer just as much as I had. But I still didn't move, waiting for him to explain why he'd walked away and left me here alone all day.

"I'm so sorry, Katie, I was an idiot. No, a complete jerk. But then, you know that already... In fact, I'm sure you came up with way more colourful language to describe me. I just need you to know *why* I freaked out and ran away with my tail between my legs. And can you please breathe?"

I released the breath I hadn't realised I was holding. Even from way over there he could see how tense I was. Okay, I was ready to hear it—whatever lame, piss-poor excuse he had for brushing me off.

"The thing is... I *really* like you, Katie. So much, that finding out you're the daughter of a millionaire, which makes you completely out of reach for someone like me, sent me into a blind panic. A bit like one of those 'panic-attack' things you have. I was just so blown away that we couldn't be a *normal* couple, dealing with the usual shitty stuff life throws at us as it happens. But *this*... man, I don't have a clue how to be the boyfriend your parents want for you. And from your reaction this morning, you know exactly what I'm talking about."

Wait... what? Was he seriously saying he ran away because he thought he wasn't good enough for me? That he didn't deserve to be in my life?

A tiny ray of hope blossomed in my chest. He'd raced out the door before I had a chance to tell him I was prepared to *fight* my parents to keep him in my life.

Well I'll be damned.

But... and this was a huge *but...* he hadn't said he was willing to fight for *me* either. So maybe this was still just him saying goodbye.

"So I figured it would be easier for both of us if I walked away." I sucked in a breath and felt the tears threatening again.

Here it comes...

I flinched when the bed dipped beside me, unable to breathe as a shaky hand gently stroked my hair. "But I can't do it... shit, I don't *want* to walk away. So, if you still want me in your life... if you can find a way to forgive my 'jerk-of-the-century' reaction... I'd really like to learn how to be that guy your parents would approve of."

I lay in stunned silence. Was he saying he was willing to take on my parents for me?

Okaaay... this was like a freakin' miracle.

I rolled over and looked into his beautiful blue eyes, seeing the same hope blossoming in their depths.

Hell yeah, I could forgive him!

I sat up and threw my arms around his neck, our lips crashing together. My heart soared —I was back in Riley's arms, being kissed like I was the most precious thing in the world. No way I was letting my parents' bias, or snobbery, or over-protectiveness, or whatever the hell they thought, drive Riley away.

We both froze as the door burst open, our lips still locked, a familiar giggle floating over from the doorway. "Ummm... don't mind me... I was just leaving. Wait... make that *cheering* and leaving..." The door closed with a click, the kiss ending as we both burst out laughing.

Riley leaned his forehead against mine, his hands resting on my hips. "I am so, so sorry, Katie. By the time I got my head straightened out, I was sure you were going to tell me to take a hike. I missed you..."

"Well, Mr Stone, if you'd hung around a little longer this morning, I'd have told you I'd decided I don't give a damn what my parents think. Actually, my life would probably be a lot easier if they disowned me. And just so you know... I *really* like you too. You don't need to change, or be anything more than the Riley Stone sitting right here..."

Oh yeah... right here... on my bed... with just me!

I buried my burning face against his chest, trying to ignore the mental images of what we *could* be doing right now. And just like he always did, Riley seemed to read my mind, his husky chuckle rumbling under my cheek.

"Yeah, well, under the circumstances, me *sitting right here* may not be such a good idea. I'm only human, you know." I giggled as he kissed the tip of my nose and moved back to the office chair. Although he *did* make sure it was close enough to the bed to keep holding my hands. Wearing a sheepish smile, his beautiful blue eyes captured mine. "So... *we're* okay then?"

Riley

Oh God. Please, please, please say yes.

I held my breath as I waited for her answer, that feeling of an impending heart attack freaking me out as I gazed into Katie's beautiful emerald-green eyes.

"We're better than okay... we're awesome."

I sighed as I watched the old coat of armour she'd resurrected slide from her shoulders and fall to the ground. *My Katie was back, and she still wanted me.* This beautiful, feisty girl was willing to fight to keep me in her life. For the first time since I'd walked out her door this morning, I could breathe again, like I could sprout wings and fly...

Yeah, it's probably not a good idea to try it, though... dork. "So... do you have any brilliant plans about how we can *intercept* your parents' evil plans?"

"Not a clue," Katie said, a cheeky grin on her face. "But

let's leave that problem for another day. I was thinking maybe we could go snuggle on the couch in the common room and *pretend* to watch a movie again?"

"I love the way your mind works. But... ummm... you might want to change first."

Not that she didn't look cute in her Minnie Mouse pyjamas, her glorious hair tousled, her face glowing from our kiss. I sooo wanted to...

Brakes... now!

She raised her hand and tried to run her fingers through that riotous hair tumbling around her shoulders. "Oh my God. I must look like a banshee. Maybe you go ahead. I'll be there in ten minutes." She giggled—*man, I loved that sound*—blushing a pretty pink. "Maybe fifteen tops."

"You look beautiful... I kinda like the bed hair and cute pyjamas look on you."

Oh shit, I need to get out of here before my hormones override my common sense.

I helped her off the bed, unable to stop myself from wrapping my arms around her and pulling her close. She felt so good pressed against me. Katie sighed, resting her hand against my chest before giving me a gentle push.

She stepped back out of my arms, and our eyes met. Yep, from the look in her eyes, it was definitely time to leave. We were both hovering way too close to the precipice.

"I'll see you soon," Katie whispered, her hand shaking against my chest as she brushed her lips over mine.

I summoned every last ounce of willpower I possessed and fumbled for the doorknob behind me. Finally tearing my eyes away, I turned, opened the door and stepped out into the hallway. As soon as the door closed behind me, I leaned against the wall beside it and blew out a long, slow breath.

Okay, that was a first. The old 'Riley-the-chick-magnet' would never have walked out of a room knowing the girl wanted him as much as he wanted her.

Wow... who knew, eh?

I walked to the common room feeling like I was floating on air. I probably should have been terrified by the emotions rampaging through my body, but all I could think about was how awesome it had felt when Katie said I was worth fighting for.

Knowing—*and way beyond caring*—that I was probably wearing a ridiculous goofy-grin, I spotted Annie and Joel in their usual spot and crossed the common room. They both looked up with raised eyebrows, and I almost laughed. They were alike in so many ways... maybe it was time someone gave them *both* a nudge in the right direction. But right now, I flopped onto the lounge and braced myself for the *Spanish Inquisition* I knew was coming.

Fair enough... I deserved it.

Annie went first, railing at me about how badly I'd hurt her best friend. I sat quietly through her tirade, knowing she needed to vent after what I'd put them all through that day. Besides, it wasn't like she called me anything I hadn't already called myself. I just hoped I hadn't ruined any chance of repairing the damage I'd done to our friendship.

"Okay, I'm done," Annie said, her shoulders sagging as she leaned back into the couch. "So... you wanna explain what happened?"

I told them everything, starting with Katie's reaction to having to perform in the end-of-semester show. When I'd finished, Annie and Joel's expressions were way less hostile. "So basically, I'm everything you just called me, and I know I screwed up. What can I say? Katie is worth fighting for."

Annie jumped up and threw her arms around my neck. "*That's* what I was waiting to hear. But know that I *will* kick your arse from here to eternity if you hurt her again."

"Ditto, man. Katie's good people. Glad to hear you got your shit together... keep it that way." Joel had sat quietly throughout the entire conversation; his fists clenched as if prepared to hit me if I said the wrong thing.

"Excuse me? Am I interrupting something here?" Annie's arms were still around my neck, and she jumped away, blushing scarlet red and looking at Katie with horror in her eyes.

"Aww, c'mon Katie... I was just—"

"Jesus, Annie... chill. I was playing." Katie grinned as she dropped down on the lounge beside me, the feel of her thigh pressed against mine doing crazy things to my equilibrium. "So I gather Riley told you everything, and you decided to forgive him? Or was that a choke hold, and you were about to strangle him to death?"

I smiled as the heavy cloud of tension hanging in the air evaporated. Seeing Katie so happy had obviously convinced Annie and Joel to let go of the last of their animosity. These people here were real friends, not the 'fair-weather' friends I was used to. And I'd do everything in my power not to screw up again and risk losing them.

Annie picked up the remote to press play on the movie,

which was currently frozen on the screen. Katie and I cracked up when we recognised the scene from *The Princess Bride.*

Damn Annie was good.

Joel rolled his eyes, trying to disguise his grin with a long-suffering sigh. "What can I say? She was in a filth... I had to think quick." Annie nudged him in the ribs, and he allowed the grin to shine through. "Okay, so maybe it's not a bad movie. The 'I've-been-mostly-dead-all-day' scene was a crack-up."

Annie folded her arms and threw him a smug smile. I chuckled, leaning over to whisper in Katie's ear. "Whadya reckon? Annie -Two: Joel - Nil? It might be time I had a word in that guy's ear."

Katie shivered, and I couldn't help breaking into a smug grin. She always reacted like that when I whispered against her ear. Katie saw the grin and cupped my face, turning my head so her lips were against my ear.

Holy shit, no wonder she shivered.

"Nothing like a taste of your own medicine, eh Petruchio?" I swear I almost burst into flames when she pressed her lips against the spot right below my ear.

Lucky she hadn't done that *when we were alone in her bedroom.*

Chapter Twenty-Five

Katie

The first few days of our second and final week as buddies flew by. By Thursday night, after four days of classes, rehearsals for the show, and trying to squeeze in band meetings, I was exhausted. I climbed into bed with a blissful sigh, snuggling down under the blankets and wishing I was spooned against Riley, drifting off to sleep imagining myself wrapped in his arms.

Until the sound of my phone buzzing on the bedside table interrupted my thoughts.

Who the hell... ooh wait, it might be Riley.

I scrambled to pick up the phone, my heart sinking at the displayed caller ID... *Dad.*

"Hey, Dad."

"Hey, honey. How are things? Judging by the distinct lack of phone calls, I gather you're enjoying yourself." He chuckled, but I didn't miss the hurt in his tone. Guilt flooded in when I realised I hadn't rung home all week. In fact, the only time I'd rung was to cancel going home for the weekend.

"Yeah, sorry about that; I've been crazy busy. *Crescendo* is awesome. I'm so glad I came."

"That's wonderful, Katie. You deserve some happiness after... well... Anyway, your Mum and I were wondering if you plan to come home this weekend? We miss you."

"I miss you guys too. But there's a welcome ball this weekend, and I need to be here. Would next weekend be okay? I thought I might bring Annie and a couple of other friends home with me..."

"Sounds great, honey. We'd love to meet your new friends. I'll make sure the poolhouse is cleaned, and you can all bunk out there. How does that sound?"

Oh great... here we go... "Ummm, the other two friends are boys, Dad, so maybe they could bunk out there, and Annie and I can stay in the downstairs guest room."

Please don't overreact.

Long pause. "So these *boys* are just *friends* then? And they know who you are?"

"Actually, they're our buddies. The professors at *Crescendo* allocated all the new students a buddy on our first day. The boys have been awesome, helping us settle in and find our way around. That's the other reason for the ball. It's an *End of Buddyship* celebration. Oh, and yes, they know my secret and understand why I don't want anyone else to know."

"Oh... well, it' sounds like you have everything under control then. Your Mum and I are very proud of you, Katie."

"Thanks, Dad. Listen, I was already in bed and almost asleep when you rang. Can I call you next week when I'm a bit more awake? Maybe we can sort out the arrangements then?"

"Of course, sweetheart. I'm pleased to hear you're being sensible and having early nights, and not out partying."

Yeah, right, 'cos heaven forbid I'd be doing what normal sixteen-year-old kids do. "Nah. Not with my crazy schedule. I'm totally exhausted by the end of the day."

"Okay, well, goodnight, sweetheart. Mum sends her love, and we'll talk to you soon."

"Night, Dad, and give Mum a hug for me."

"Will do. Love you."

"Love you too."

I hit the end button, dropped the phone back on the bedside table, and slumped back under the covers.

"We're *all* going to your house for the weekend?" Annie's sleepy voice floated across the room. "Are you sure that's a good idea?"

"Honestly? I have no idea. But I was thinking that if Mum and Dad met Riley as my school-mandated buddy, and we're just friends, maybe they'll see him for the great person he is... *Before* they cast judgement about his suitability as a boyfriend for their daughter."

"I hope you're right. 'Cos this plan has more holes than a block of Swiss cheese, and we all know how you feel about that—something about it being too flimsy, wasn't it?"

"Yeah, yeah, smartarse," I replied with a grin.

"Seriously though, you and Riley are gonna have to be on your best behaviour twenty-four-seven. And coming from someone who spends a lot of time around you two, I seriously doubt you can pull it off."

"Do you have a better suggestion for preventing the shockwaves if they see that kiss in the show with no warning?"

"Nope. Not a one. But I promise to visit when you're under house arrest... if they let me in the front door."

"Oh, come on, Annie. They're not *that* bad." *Are they?*

"You just keep telling yourself that, honey. Whatever helps you sleep at night."

Great. Suddenly the sleep I'd felt tugging at me before the phone call seemed a long way off.

"So... my Dad rang last night. Wanted to know if I was coming home for the weekend." If I hadn't been studying Riley's face when I told him about the call, I might have missed his first reaction, a worried frown. It was gone in an instant, but I'd seen it.

"Did you tell him about the ball?" Riley tried to act nonchalant, but the tension in his shoulders was obvious.

"Yeah, and he understood. But I think I'll have to go home the following one." Annie threw me a you-going-to-tell-them look, and I quickly shook my head.

"Did you... ar... mention you'd made any *friends*?"

Riley said, his eyes asking an entirely different question. *Do they know about me?*

"Yeah, as a matter of fact, I told Dad about the professors assigning us buddies for the first two weeks and how the ball was to celebrate the end of it. Dad said he'd love to meet you guys."

The silence at the table was deafening. I almost jumped out of my skin when the bell for English rang, not sure whether I was relieved or disappointed by the interruption.

Riley threw his arm around my shoulders and kissed my forehead. "Maybe we can talk about it at lunchtime. Come on, I'll walk you to class."

He stood up and reached for my hand, his smile not quite reaching his eyes. Okay, I needed to give him time to process what I *hadn't* said. That it would be good if he *offered* to come home and meet my parents. Smiling, I slipped my hand into his and we headed for class.

Well, I'd planted the seed. Now, I just had to wait and see what Riley had to say at lunchtime. I'd decided against telling him it was all arranged when I'd seen his first reaction. I needed to let *him* decide whether he was ready or not. If he didn't offer to go home with me, then I'd go alone.

Damnit. I'd totally messed up. I should never have said anything to Dad without talking to my friends first. Why *should* they have to put up with the judgemental crap my parents were sure to dish out? Fine. I'd just have to put on the old big-girl-panties and deal with this on my own. Maybe it would be better for everyone if I told my parents I had a boyfriend *before* they met Riley.

Yep, I needed to let my friends off the hook.
It was the right thing to do.

Riley

I SPENT the next three hours stressing over what to say to Katie about meeting her parents as her buddy. I should at least offer... right? What could be so hard about that? All I had to do was not touch her, or kiss her, or look like I *wanted* to do either of those things.

Yeah right... piece of cake...

Okay, so all I had to do was prove to Katie's parents that I wasn't after her money or what her daddy could do for me. *Yeah, right... even though everything about the situation screamed that I was.* Maybe if I dressed up as a nerdy, boy-next-door type, I might have a better chance. 'Cos from the sounds of things, turning up as a pretty-boy-wanna-be-guitarist would have me instantly labelled a Mark-clone, and I'd be sent packing.

Unbelievable! Who'd have thought I'd ever wish I *wasn't* good-looking? Hell, I was way out of my comfort zone here, with no clue how to play this game. I'd always avoided people with money for this very reason. People *with* money *always* assumed those *without* wanted theirs.

"So dya reckon Katie was dropping a hint or what?" Joel leaned in and whispered when we sat down for our second class of the day. He hadn't said a word about the conversation at breakfast until then.

"You thought that too, huh?"

"Well... you did say she wanted them to meet you before the end-of-semester show. Maybe showing up the first time as her buddy isn't such a bad idea. Although you might wanna put a hold on the whole kissy-kissy-touchy-feely thing for the weekend."

I groaned, rubbing the back of my neck. "So that's the way you'd play it if you were in my shoes?"

"Hell if I know, man. Wanting to date the daughter of a millionaire record producer is way outta my realm of possible fantasies."

"Mine too, damnit. I seriously hate that Katie is one of those. But she is, and I have to deal with it somehow. *Shit.* What a freakin' nightmare."

"Look, man, as your friend, I just gotta say this, okay? Maybe it's better if you *don't* meet the parents. I mean, there's no guarantee you and Katie will still be together by the end of the semester. Don't get me wrong... I really like Katie. She's great. But why put yourself through all this when you've only known each other for, like, five minutes?"

I *so* wanted to just take Joel's advice and forget all about meeting Katie's parents. But Joel didn't get it. Whatever decision I made here could end up being the *reason* we were either still together at the end of the semester or not. I'd promised Katie I'd fight for the right to stay in her life. And I was gonna run and hide at the first opportunity to prove my worth?

"Thanks, man. I appreciate the advice. But there's more

to it than that. And right now, I need to stop thinking about it and work out what this class is about. It's not like *either* of us will have the notes at this rate."

Joel shrugged and nodded, then turned his attention back to the lesson. I just wished I could do the same.

Chapter Twenty-Six

Katie

It had quickly come to my attention that trying to put on mascara without poking out an eye when your hand wouldn't stop shaking was a physical impossibility. *And why was I so nervous?* Because tonight's inaugural *End of Buddyship Ball* would be the first time I'd gone out 'officially' as Riley's girlfriend. Sure, we'd hung out together in our common-room and the cafeteria, but the entire staff and student population would be there tonight.

Annie stopped pacing behind me, shook her head, and reached for the mascara in my hand. "Oh, for God's sake Katie. Just let me do it. At this rate, the ball will be over before we even get there."

Annie looked stunning in her body-hugging sleek silver dress, her hair and make-up perfect. Although I couldn't help thinking that with the measly amount of fabric it took to cover her body compared to mine, her dress should have cost half the price. Maybe I should just be grateful the manufacturing industry didn't charge by the metre.

Enough with the pity party, Katie. I giggled when I realised the voice in my head wasn't mine but Riley's. Damn him... now even *inside* my own head, it was two against one.

Annie jumped back and glared at me. "Did you seriously just giggle while I was trying to apply mascara? Do you have a death wish? And more importantly, do I want to know why?"

I giggled again at Annie's ferocious frown. It felt *so* good to be happy. I'd forgotten how liberating it felt. "Sorry... won't happen again. Do your worst."

Annie's eyes filled with tears. "Oh, Katie, it's so good to hear you laughing and giggling again. I didn't realise how much I'd missed you being like this. Remind me to give Riley a big hug tonight."

"You just keep your hugs to yourself, missy. He's mine. Or better still... save them for Joel."

"Whoa... possessive much? Claws in sweetie. And as for the rest... *pfft.*"

"More information required. Not sure I know the definition of *'pfft'.*

I breathed a sigh of relief when Annie stepped back, shrugged and put the mascara away. "Definition: Joel freakin' Kenny's mixed messages. To be honest, I'm over it. From now on... just friends. And you can stop looking at me like that. I'm fine. Now get your butt out of that chair so I can take a selfie of us before we go."

Great. Just what I needed. A photo of my voluminous body next to Annie's petite curves.

Annie rolled her eyes and grinned. "And don't give me that long-suffering look either. If we're gonna start making comparisons, I'd rather not have my poor little non-boobs next to your cleavage poppers, but I *still* want a photo."

What the... could everybody read my mind these days?

"Fine." I stood up and smoothed down my emerald-green silk dress. Knowing how much Riley had *appreciated* the red dress I'd worn for the *Kiss Me Kate* audition, I'd found a dress with a similar style, although it was *slightly* less cleavage-popping.

I stood beside Annie in front of the mirror, both of us grinning like a couple of Cheshire cats. And for the first time, I tried to see myself through Riley's eyes. And *maybe* I didn't hate my reflection as much as I used to.

Riley

I'd come to the conclusion that the Tuxedo was invented by a woman, *solely* as a form of torture. I hated wearing the bloody things. Sitting in the foyer outside the auditorium waiting for the girls, Joel and I must have looked like a couple of squirming penguins.

But the sight of Katie walking down the stairs, looking like a goddess, made it all worth it. Suddenly the stiff collar and bow-tie weren't the only things making it difficult to breathe.

Aaand... hello, goofy grin.

She had no idea how beautiful she was. I wanted to pull

her against me, wrap her in my arms, and kiss away the shy smile on her lips and the uncertainty in her eyes.

Ah, hell, I couldn't wait another second.

I needed to do it right now.

Her eyes widened as I took three strides and had her right where she belonged, in my arms. Her lips were soft and yielding, tasting of strawberries and... Katie. She slid her hands up my chest until they were clasped around my neck. Her heart pounded against mine as her fingers sent shivers up and down my spine as they raked my hair. A growl rumbled in my chest, my hands slipping down to her hips to pull her closer.

The sounds of a giggle and someone clearing their throat penetrated my befuddled brain, and I remembered where we were. Katie's lips smiled against mine, and when I opened my eyes, the uncertainty in hers had been replaced by a confident glow.

I grinned. *Mission: Accomplished.*

Damn she looked hot.

"Did I mention how stunningly beautiful you look?" I whispered against her lips.

She giggled. "Well, maybe not with words... but I think I got the message."

"Can we *please* go in now? Or would you two prefer to just get a room?" I finally turned to look at Annie, grinning at the sight of all five-foot-three of her silver-wrapped body shaking with indignation.

With a huge sigh, I unwrapped myself from Katie's gorgeous body and gave Annie a hug. "Wow...you look absolutely beautiful too, Annie."

Annie blushed and giggled as I moved back to take Katie's hand in mine. Wait... where was Joel? I hadn't seen or heard from him since the girls came down the stairs. I turned to find him still sitting on the chairs behind us.

Wait... was he seriously studying his phone?

Wow. No wonder Annie had looked so indignant. What the hell was wrong with this guy? "Hey Joel. You plan on joining us tonight or what?"

He looked up with a weird expression, his face so red it was painful to watch. His eyes slid over Annie before moving to Katie.

"Yeah, sorry." He slipped his phone into his jacket pocket. "I... ar... just had some stuff to deal with. You girls look... great."

Oh God. He and Annie needed to sit down and have a serious conversation before one of them imploded.

Annie seemed to deflate at his words. She shrugged and moved toward the auditorium. "Whatever. I'll see you guys in there." And then she was through the doors and out of sight.

"So... any idea what's going on there?" I whispered to Katie.

"I probably know about as much as you do. Annie keeps telling me she's sick of Joel sending her mixed messages, so she's decided they should just stay friends. But the way they're both acting, I'm worried their friendship may not even survive."

"Right. But do you think she's into him?"

Katie shrugged. "I think that would depend on what

day of the week it was and Joel's mood when you asked her."

I looked back over at Joel to find him frowning at the door Annie had disappeared through. *Man, this was getting ridiculous.*

Katie squeezed my hand and nodded towards him. "You should go talk to him. I'll go find Annie and meet you inside."

"Damnit. I really wanted us to walk in together. You know, so I could show the world how proud I am that you're my girl."

Katie blushed, her eyes shining. "I don't think 'the world' is here tonight, but just knowing you *wanted* to is enough. Now let's go fix our friends." She stood up on tiptoes, her lips hovering over mine. "Just don't be long."

"I won't... trust me." I closed the distance between our lips, nipping at her lower lip as I pulled away.

"You've got five minutes, Petruchio, then you're mine." Katie's words, uttered in a deep, sexy growl, almost brought me to my knees. I stood transfixed as she turned and disappeared through the doorway.

Wow... just... wow.

I *almost* gave in to the temptation to go after her and leave Joel to sort out his own problems. But he looked so freakin' miserable I knew I couldn't do it.

I walked over and flopped down into the seat beside him. "Hey man... what's going on?"

Joel lifted his head and ran his hands through his hair, almost pulling it out by the roots. "Damn woman. Just when I'd convinced myself we're better off friends, she turns up looking like... well, *that*. C'mon man, did you see her? She looks freakin' gorgeous."

"Okay, this is the last time I'm gonna say this. If you really *like* her, you need to grow some balls and tell her. 'Cos if you don't—looking like she does tonight—someone else will. Now... there are two beautiful girls in there waiting for us. You ready to go in? Or would you rather sit out here and wallow all night?"

"Yeah, yeah. I'm comin'. And thanks, man." Joel shoulder nudged me, a sheepish smile on his face.

"Hey. That's what friends are for... right?"

Chapter Twenty-Seven

Katie

Getting out of bed Monday morning had taken a Herculean effort. I'd have killed to just turn off the alarm, roll over and go back to sleep, but missing another day of school wasn't an option. So I'd compromised—hitting the snooze button for about an hour, skipping breakfast and making it to Music Theory with seconds to spare.

The last two days had superseded the previous weekend's title of best-weekend-ever, and I was still floating on a cloud. Slow dancing with Riley at the ball had been like something out of a Cinderella story, exceeding my wildest expectations and fulfilling every fantasy I'd ever had. Well, *almost* every fantasy.

The only blemish in my perfect world was that Riley still hadn't mentioned the trip home next weekend. Not that I could blame him. Hell... *I* was dreading it, and they were *my* parents. I'd decided to bring it up again at lunchtime today and tell my friends I thought it best if I went alone. Oh, and that I would be breaking the news to my parents about Riley and me. Now *that* should be an interesting conversation.

"Whoa... you look wiped out. Do I look that bad?" Annie said, pulling her laptop out of her bag and opening it on her desk.

"Gee, thanks. Way to make a girl feel good about herself."

Annie patted my shoulder and giggled. "Sorry, hun... you know me... honest to a fault."

Before I could think of a snappy reply, Professor Willis, our Music Theory teacher, entered and walked toward the front of the room.

"Good morning, all. You may not have heard, but one of our students, James Tebbet, had to leave the Academy due to his family relocating overseas. As a result, the next person on the wait list was offered a place at *Crescendo* starting today. Mark, could you please stand up and say hello? Everyone, please welcome Mark Barnes to *Crescendo*. Since the buddy system ended..."

And, just like that, my perfect world imploded, crumbling into tiny pieces at my feet. A burning sensation flooded through me, like all the blood was being drained from my body.

No way!

He couldn't be here.

He didn't get accepted!

Wait... he was on the waiting list? Nooo... this couldn't be happening. I shuddered at the sound of his voice coming from somewhere behind me. It was like listening to fingernails on a chalkboard.

Unbelievable! Why did the universe keep doing this to me? Just when I'd finally got back on my feet and started to live again. What was I supposed to do now? What if he still had the video and showed... no, I needed to *not* go down that road.

Slowly, the shock faded, and the blood I'd previously thought gone started to boil. No freakin' way I would give him the power to hurt me again. I wasn't the same naïve girl he'd tried to destroy last year. I had friends here, people who didn't judge me for my looks and who thought I had talent.

Screw Mark Barnes.

Mr Scumbag had a few lessons coming his way!

"You okay?" Annie whispered, her worried eyes flashing with sparks of anger as she rubbed my shoulder.

I sucked in a shuddering breath. "Yeah... I'm fine."

I almost smiled at the sight of Annie's fiercely protective streak kicking in. She looked ready to rip Mark Barnes a new one. "Holy shit Katie, Riley is gonna spit chips. And I want a front-row seat when he finds out the arsehole is right here, in this class."

Oh my God... Annie was right. I hadn't told Riley the name of my ex-boyfriend. Riley and Joel still sat at the back of the classroom. Shit, for all I knew Mark could be sitting right next to them. Not that I wouldn't love to see Riley kick Mark's butt, but I didn't want Riley getting into trouble. The last thing he needed was to be kicked out of *Crescendo* for starting something. I needed to talk to him *before* he found out who Mark was. I pulled out my phone and sent him a text.

Katie: Hey, I'm leaving right on the bell. Can you meet me outside Studio Five between classes?

Riley: Sure, babe... what's up? 😗 **"**

You have no idea. **Katie: I need to talk to you alone.**

Riley: Hey, is everything ok?

No Mark freakin' Barnes is here. **Katie: Yeah, all good.** *Not even slightly.*

Riley: Okay... talk soon <3

"I texted Riley. He's meeting me outside our studio between classes. I'm gonna be ready to bolt at the bell," I whispered to Annie.

Annie nodded and mouthed *good idea*. Right. So now all I had to do was be ready to run out of class as soon as the bell rang. *Oh God*, maybe I should leave early. If I looked half as sickly as I felt, I'd definitely be excused from class.

Stop it, Katie.

He has no power over you unless you give *it to him.*

You're fine. You can do this.

I had no idea what Professor Willis said for the rest of the lesson. My mind wouldn't stop replaying that nightmare scene from last year. I tried to push it away, to focus on images of Riley's handsome face as he pulled me in for a kiss, but it was as if Mark's presence in the room brought all the horror back like it happened yesterday.

I blinked away the tears gathering behind my eyelids. There was no way I'd give Mark bloody Barnes the satisfaction of seeing I was upset. Five more minutes... that's all I had to hold on for.

Hold it together Katie.

Do. Not. Cry.

I started packing my things away with one minute to go. I'd carry my laptop and put it in my bag later. I jumped when the bell rang, even though I'd been counting down. Grabbing my bag, I slammed my laptop closed, scooped it off the table, and bolted for the door.

"Katie...?" I didn't stop at his voice; I just ploughed toward the door.

How dare he speak to me? What, did he think I'd want to stop and chat about old times?

I pushed the door open and almost ran to the studio, leaning against the wall and waiting for Riley. Where the hell was he? He shouldn't have been that far behind me.

Come on Riley. Where are you?

I bent down to put my laptop in my bag, sighing when Riley's shoes appeared in front of me. Looking up into his eyes, the tears finally burst through. I caught the shocked look on his face before he pulled me up against his chest and wrapped me in his arms. I slipped my arms around his neck and sobbed.

"Hey, baby. What's wrong? Did someone say—"

I shook my head, trying to pull myself together enough to get the words out. The bell would go any minute... I didn't have time for this stupid crying shit.

Sucking in a deep breath, I lifted my head and looked into Riley's piercing blue eyes. "The new guy... M-Mark... he's the one... m-my ex."

Riley's arms stiffened, his eyes turning to that dark, midnight blue as they stared off into the distance. I cradled his face with my hands, pulling his gaze back to mine. "I'm... I'm okay. It was just the shock. But... but I need you to promise me you won't do anything stupid. Please Riley—"

Riley growled, the sound rumbling in his chest. "Jesus, Katie... he was sitting two seats away. That prick almost destroyed you. Why would you defend him?"

"I don't give a damn what happens to *him*. I just don't want *you* getting into trouble because of me. Please, Riley... let me deal with this." My mouth lifted into a half-smile. "Or at least wait until we can get him in a dark alley away from the school."

Riley seemed to come back from wherever his thoughts had been, his eyes studying mine, before leaning down to kiss me. I felt warm and safe wrapped in his arms, the kiss gentle, soothing, his lips moving over mine, a hand sliding up to caress my hair. And I knew it would all be okay. I was back floating on that cloud of contentment, all thoughts of Mark and that horrible day shoved back in their box. I wanted to stay like this forever, shivering when his lips left mine and moved to that spot just below my ear.

"Okay... I promise," he whispered against my ear. "But if he—"

I leaned my head back and put a finger to his lips. "Yeah... I know. The dark alley scenario."

"YOU'VE GOT to be effing kidding me! The douchebag is

here? At *Crescendo?*" Annie slapped her hand over Joel's mouth, her face red as a beetroot.

"Goodonya Joel... subtle much? I don't think they heard you in Adelaide!"

"Whadidyouexpectmetdo?" Joel's mouth was still going under Annie's hand.

"Ewww... keep your saliva to yourself... and your voice down!" Annie removed her hand and wiped it on Joel's shirt. "Now... what did you say?"

"I said." Joel's voice had dropped about ten decibels. "What did you expect me to do? Public enemy number one has entered the building."

I had to laugh at Joel and Annie's *unusual* relationship. The pair had disappeared for a while at the ball, but neither would talk about what happened. Well, at least it appeared they were back to being friends.

Annie huffed. "Can I please finish what I was saying now? I haven't even had a chance to tell Katie this yet."

I snuggled closer against Riley's warmth, where I'd been since lunch started. To be honest, I was a bit shocked by how well I'd handled Mark's reappearance in my life. But then, I was a very different person from that girl I'd been a year ago. And it was all thanks to this amazing guy sitting beside me and holding me tight. "Okay, I'm intrigued. What?"

Annie wore a look very similar to that of a cat who'd swallowed a canary. "Well, while you were off talking to Riley, *I* had a word with a certain sleazebag."

My jaw dropped. "And you didn't tell me this, why?"

"Well, you did run into Maths late... and I could hardly

tell you the whole *I-said-he-said* with the Professor prowling around."

Riley growled—*yep, I was getting used to it now*—his hands clenching into fists. "What did the jerk have to say for himself?"

"Well... it was surprising, actually. I, of course, went in with guns blazing. Told him he'd better stay away from us and not to even *think* about pulling any of his low-life crap here. I was still firing from both barrels when I realised he was sitting there nodding and agreeing with everything I said. Which kinda made me stop and *look* at him for the first time, and I was gobsmacked. Seriously Katie, he looks terrible. Nothing like the cocky jerk we went to school with last year. Something awful must have happened in his life—"

Now it was my turn to clench my fists. "Like I give a shit *what* happened to him. He deserved whatever it was... and more. Do you honestly expect me to feel *sorry* for the jerk?"

Annie held her hands in front of her face. "Hey... you're not supposed to shoot the messenger, remember?" She reached across the table and put her hand on my clenched fist. "I'm just telling you what happened... okay?"

I blew out a long, calming breath, unclenching my fist and squeezing Annie's hand. "Sorry. I just—"

"You don't need to apologise, honey. I get it... I really do. But just let me finish... okay?"

Riley must have realised his own anger wasn't helping the situation and placed his hand on mine when Annie withdrew hers. Resting my head against his shoulder, I nodded to Annie to go on.

"Right. So, when I stopped ranting, Mark sucked in a deep breath and said: *What I did to Katie ended up being the biggest wake-up call of my life. I know what I did was unforgivable, and I did try to contact Katie to tell her how sorry I was. But she'd changed her mobile number and her email address. I even wrote a couple of letters, hoping she'd at least read them.*

Katie never did anything to deserve the way I treated her. I made sure no-one else ever saw the video. Hey, I even threatened to beat up the guys who saw it if they ever said a word to anyone. She's a good person, and I hate myself for what I did. I get that she's uncomfortable with me being here, so I'll see if I can get my classes changed so she doesn't have to be in the same room with me. Then he just picked up his bag and walked away."

I felt like I'd been hit by a stun gun. Would it have helped if I knew he felt remorse for what he'd done? The main reason I'd missed the end of Year-Ten was because I was sure he'd turned me into the laughingstock of the entire school.

Damnit! Why didn't I get the letters? Would I have even read them? I'd never know because I wasn't given the choice. Because someone had taken that choice away from me... intercepted them before—

Oh God, no...

My bloody, over-protective parents had decided for me. They probably thought they were doing what was best for me, but... *how dare they?* What if something in those letters could have helped me move past the whole nightmare? Annie had told me no one ever mentioned it at school. In fact, a few kids had even asked where I was. But I'd always assumed my dad had dealt with Mark and made sure the whole thing was hushed up.

Aargghh... I needed to get out of my own head. I was drowning. *Did my parents open the letters and read them? Had they even considered how much more pain their interference may have caused me? Did they even care?*

Oh shit. No... no, no, no. I tried to suppress the new horror story taking shape in my head, but the door I'd opened refused to close. Suddenly, I was seeing my parents' attitudes in a whole new light. Mum and Dad were both slim. Mum was an upstanding pillar of society, always perfectly dressed and perfectly made-up. I'd inherited my Mother's hair and eyes, and my Father's smooth, olive skin. But my overweight genes were apparently a throwback from some previous generation.

I was flooded with memories of my Mum *strongly encouraging* me to try every new diet going. It had always annoyed her that she couldn't control what I ate at school, as if I was only overweight because I stuffed myself with junk food at school. *Because my weight problem couldn't possibly be her fault.*

Now that I thought about it, she'd been eager to support my idea of pulling out of school and hiding from the world. Hell, maybe they'd thought if they kept me locked away for long enough, people would forget I existed, and she wouldn't have to make excuses for producing such an imperfect daughter.

Oh. My. God... Could my own parents really be ashamed of me? I was the gross, overweight daughter who didn't fit into their world of beautiful people. Who knows—Dad might have actually offered to help Mark in his career if he promised to continue to date his fat-and-so-un-datable daughter.

Unbelievable!

How had I not seen any of this before now?

Well, at least I knew Riley was for real.

Didn't I?

What if...?

No. I wasn't going to do this. Riley's reaction to finding out who I was had been too genuine to be an act. I groaned at the memory of almost pushing him away because I was worried about what my controlling, selfish, judgemental parents would think of him!

"Katie... baby?" Riley's whisper in my ear jarred me back to reality. "What about we go to the studio and play some music?"

Music! Yes, that's what I needed. It never failed to pull me out of my own head. Funny how Riley already knew that, even though we'd only known each other for two weeks.

I squeezed his hand. "Yeah... that'd be great."

He smiled and kissed the top of my head. I became aware of the worried looks on Annie and Joel's faces. Damnit, I'd done it again.

They must all think I'm a basket case.

Hell... I am a basket case!

My heart swelled with gratitude for Riley, Annie, and

Joel. Without them in my life, I'd probably be locked up in a padded room—or my parent's house, which was just as bad.

Riley kept a firm hold on my hand as we walked to the studio. No one had said a word since we'd left the cafeteria, and their wariness was giving me the creeps. Maybe, once we got to the studio, I needed to tell them what had been going through my head. These were my friends. They cared about *me*. They didn't care who I was, or what I looked like.

They just accepted me without question.

Chapter Twenty-Eight

Riley

My heart was breaking at the lost, desolate look in Katie's eyes. No way this was just about what the douchebag had said to Annie. *What the hell was going on inside my beautiful girl's head?* I needed to know so I could at least *try* to help her fix it. No one had said a word since we'd left the cafeteria. The walk to the studio was like we were in a damned funeral procession.

It hadn't taken long to realise that music soothed Katie's soul, just like it did mine. Luckily, I'd remembered we had studio time booked for rehearsals this afternoon.

I pushed open the studio door, expecting Katie to head for her locker to grab her microphone. Instead, she waited for Annie and Joel to enter the room and gave a huge sigh.

"Look, I'm really sorry I keep doing that spacing out/panic attack thing, but I think I've worked out some stuff in my head that I need to run by somebody..." She smiled sadly at the three of us, "or *somebodies*. Would you guys mind if I, like, download some of the stuff floating around in my head? *Before* we have to call the men in the white jackets?"

Annie threw her arms around Katie's neck and breathed a huge sigh of relief. "I would *love* to help you sort through that minefield you call a brain. I really think it will help if you talk about it... whatever it is."

Joel grinned and patted Katie's shoulder. "Yeah, I'm always up for some brain-draining. Not that I've ever had a girl want my input on anything. But hey... I'm a fast learner."

Annie and Joel headed over to the lounges in the corner, and I wrapped Katie in my arms, looking down into her pain-filled eyes. Whatever this was about had sure messed her up, and I was relieved she wanted to share it.

"Whatever it is... we can fix it. Okay?"

She stood on her tiptoes and brushed her lips softly against mine. "I don't know what I did to deserve you, but I'm glad I did it."

"Right back at ya, beautiful." We moved over to the lounges, but when I sat and tried to pull her down with me, she smiled and shook her head.

"Nah. I think I might need to move while I talk."

Katie sucked in a deep breath and shared everything she'd been thinking since hearing about the letters Mark had written, the ones she'd never received. She kept pausing as if waiting for one of us to tell her it was all a load of crap. But the sad truth was, it was all making sense. And by the looks on Annie and Joel's faces, they agreed. If anything, Annie was getting angrier and angrier the more Katie said.

"Wait... you have *got* to be kidding me! I should have known! Heaps of times I came over to take you out shopping or to a movie, and your Mum told me you weren't up to seeing anyone. She always asked that I not mention my attempted visits because she didn't want you to feel guilty for letting me down. You know... I've never been a huge fan of your parents. I always thought they were grossly overprotective. But this is sick!"

Katie had stopped pacing and was staring at Annie. "Seriously? Annie... I had no idea. I used to hang for your visits, but I figured you were really busy studying for finals and stuff."

Annie's eyes narrowed in her stormy face. "Oh, God... Katie. Did your parents ever *suggest* you not start at the Academy with me? Was that why you couldn't decide?"

Katie breathed out a huge sigh and nodded, her shoulders sagging as tears filled her eyes. I reached out and grabbed her hand, coaxing her into my lap. "They tried to sabotage your music career? Seriously?"

"They wanted me to study online for another year. Until I was... *fully recovered from the incident*. But from what Annie's saying, I'm starting to think it was more about wanting *her* out of my life, too. Annie was the only one who could ever drag me out of my slump and push me to move on."

Joel just sat shaking his head. "Man... sorry, Katie, but your parents are seriously screwed up. Hearing this is making me rethink the whole *get-rich-life-plan*."

Katie made a strangled sound that was half laugh, half sob. It was a miracle she'd retained her sense of humour after all she'd been through. She had no idea how strong and resilient she was. I didn't know whether to feel humbled or filled with pride by the amazing girl in my arms. So I went with both.

"Hey, don't apologise, Joel. I don't even have *words* to describe them. In fact, I don't even know who they are any more. I guess what people say about 'money being the root of all evil' is true. And to think, all this time I thought *I* was the head case."

That was my Katie. How could I have even *considered* walking away because of what her parents thought? She'd had enough rejection in her life from people who said they loved her.

Not that I loved her. I mean, how could I? We'd only known each other for two weeks. Love didn't happen that fast... did it?

But there was no denying that the pain in my chest when she was hurting, and the overwhelming desire to protect her, sounded a lot like what I'd heard it feels like to love someone. And having her here, wrapped in my arms, trusting me not to hurt her, made me feel something I'd never felt before.

"Well... now you all know about my miserable life. Guess I'm just another cliché—*poor little rich girl*. Well, except for the *little*—"

"Don't you dare," I growled. I hated the way she was always putting herself down. I tilted her face up so she was looking into my eyes... the ones I hoped told her how I felt.

"Unless you were going to change it to poor *beautiful* rich girl."

Damnit, she was beautiful. Why couldn't other people see that?

Why couldn't she see it?

Maybe because the judgemental, egotistical morons in her life had done a great job of convincing her she wasn't. Well, no more. Not if I had any say in it.

Running my hands through her silky soft hair, I was lost in a pair of emerald eyes set in the face of an angel. Her soft lips were practically begging me to kiss her, *needing* me to show her she was desirable.

She met me halfway, and the feel of her lips under mine took my breath away. Kissing Katie was like nothing I'd ever experienced before. Warmth spread through my entire body, making my head spin and my heart race. She whimpered as I ran my tongue along her bottom lip, her lips opening to allow her tongue to meet mine. Electricity raced along every nerve ending. She made me want... everything.

Who the hell was I kidding? It didn't matter how long we'd known each other; I was absolutely head-over-heels in love with Katie Sims.

"Ahem..." Katie's lips lifted into a smile against mine at Annie's less-than-subtle reminder we had company. Although it was probably a good thing we *weren't* alone... in her room... sitting on her bed. And I got the distinct impression Katie felt exactly the same way.

God help me, this girl was going to be the death of me.

Okay, so Annie looked like she had something to say. And we *were* being rude, making out in front of our friends. I lifted my head and smiled down into Katie's flushed face, her beautiful lips swollen from our kiss. Damn, I could just sit and look at her all day.

"*Finally!!* Look, I'm sorry, Katie, but this changes everything about... Well, I'm scared to let you go home alone next weekend. What if they lock you in your room and won't let you come back or something?"

Katie giggled. "Don't you think you might be slightly over-dramatising things, Annie? You're making my life sound like some weird version of *Rapunzel*."

Annie blushed. "Okay, so maybe your hair isn't *quite* long enough."

A weight lifted off my chest as I decided something I should have done days ago. "Actually, Annie's right about one thing. There's no way *I'm* letting you go home alone either." Her parents had perfected the art of manipulation, and I had no intention of losing her. "What if we all went with you? Didn't you say they would *love* to meet your new friends? *Hah!* Not half as much as I'd *kill* to meet them."

Joel's face broke into an evil grin. "Hell yeah, I'm in. No way I'm missing out on *this* party."

"Wait... so you guys are seriously offering to enter the lion's den with me?" Katie's eyes filled with tears. "I... I don't know what to say. Except maybe... that I think you're all out of you freakin' minds."

I wiped a tear from her cheek. "Wait... what happens if your parents play the money card when you confront them? Aren't they paying your fees for *Crescendo*? They could refuse to keep paying unless you toe the line and ditch the loser boyfriend." I nearly fell off the lounge when

Katie cracked up laughing. That was the *last* thing I'd expected her to do. "So, I'm obviously missing something here. What's so funny?"

"Yes, they're paying my fees at the moment. BUT... Dad set up a trust fund in my name when I was little. He said it was his way of guaranteeing I'd have the money for a car when I turned sixteen. That way, I'd be set up for life, even if his company went bust."

Unbelievable!

Another tiny piece of information she'd neglected to tell me—that she was *independently* wealthy. But at least it proved her parents hadn't always been complete arseholes. Maybe they did love her in their own warped and twisted way.

She turned to me with an apologetic smile. "And no, I didn't deliberately not tell you about the trust fund. To be honest, I haven't thought about it in ages. I don't even know how much it is. Dad always just called it *our secret little nest egg*."

I chuckled and shook my head. "Only *you* could have a possible fortune at your fingertips and not know or care about the details. Wait... does your Mum even know about it?"

Katie smiled. "Of course, Mum would know about it. As if Dad would... I mean, Dad always said it was our... Oh. Shit ... maybe Mum has no idea about the trust fund."

"I've kinda noticed that you talk more about your Dad than your Mum. I just put it down to the old *daddy's little girl* syndrome." I looked down into Katie's eyes, throwing her one of those *don't-even-think-about-it* looks. She grinned and shook her head, looking so cute I wanted to kiss her again.

"Bloody hell, Katie, now that I think about it, your Dad was never home when your Mum told me I couldn't see you. I think Riley might be right. This sounds way more like something your Mum would do. I always liked your Dad, but your Mum scares the bejeepers out of me."

I could feel Katie disappearing inside her head again, no doubt replaying scenes from her past. Time to stop talking about this stuff and play some music. I caught Annie's eye, flicking my eyes down to where Katie was snuggled up against me and then toward the keyboard. Annie smiled and nodded.

I rubbed my hands together and gave Katie a squeeze. "Right, time for some music. Katie, it's your turn to pick the first song to rehearse. What are you in the mood for? Babe?"

Katie gave me a startled look, a smile spreading slowly across her face as she scrambled out of my lap. "I'd... ummm... like to add a new song to the setlist if that's ok?"

Annie, Joel and I looked at each other and nodded.

This should be interesting... "Sure, babe. What is it?"

"I've never sung it before, but I'd love to try it. Could we maybe learn Kelly Clarkson's song...? *Because of You.*"

I smiled, jumping up and dragging her towards the locker holding her microphone. "Absolutely."

Damn! Hearing about what her parents had done to her put my own life back into perspective. My Mum may be mentally ill, but I'd never doubted she loved me and wanted the best for me.

Growing up poor suddenly didn't seem so bad.

Katie

"MAN... WHAT A DAY!" Annie moaned as she dropped down onto her bed. "I gotta tell you, Katie... you seriously owned that version of *Because of You*."

I flopped down on my bed and frowned up at the ceiling. "Thanks. It's amazing how easy it is when the lyrics relate so well to your own life."

Annie rolled onto her side facing me, propping her head up with her elbow. "God, Katie. My head's still spinning from today's crapola, so I can't even imagine how you must be feeling."

I rolled onto my side and mimicked Annie's position. "Ya know, it's funny. Well maybe not funny exactly... but I've been feeling heaps better since we worked out Dad wasn't a part of all this. Somehow, it's not that surprising to learn Mum is a manipulative bitch, but I was totally crushed at the thought of Dad being involved. I get the feeling there's a lot I don't know about my parents' relationship."

"Parents are weird. Mine used to fight constantly, and I'd be the one running from one end of the house to the other with messages. *Mum said dinner's ready. Dad said he's not hungry.* God, I felt like their friggin' answering service."

I threw her a sympathetic look. "By the way, thanks for suggesting I not go home alone this weekend. I'd decided not to ask the guys unless Riley offered.

"Yeah, well, you dropped enough hints at breakfast the other day. But so much changed today. It was like being on a freakin' roller-coaster ride."

I snorted—*yes, that's right, I snorted. But it was only in front of Annie so...* "Tell me about it. And who'd have ever thought that Mark the jerk would end up being responsible for me figuring out Mum's bullshit. Not to mention that the guy actually tried to apologise. Don't get me wrong, I'm a long way from forgiving him for what he did, but I had visions of him starting here and showing that video around." I shuddered at the thought of it still existing. But if what Mark had told Annie was true, it had been deleted a long time ago.

"Yeah, I *almost* felt sorry for the creep. But then, who the hell videos themselves making out with someone and then shows it to their friends? *Nah!* He deserves to be miserable."

I had to admit it was a relief to know I wouldn't be running into him any time soon. Who'd have thought he'd *ever* be considerate enough to offer to change classes so *I* was more comfortable? It also reduced the risk of him and Riley crossing paths.

Just thinking about Riley made me feel warm and fuzzy all over. The guy was every girl's dream of the perfect boyfriend, and he wanted to be with *me*.

Totally crazy, fairy-tale material right there!

I'd practically melted when he pulled me onto his lap in

the studio. Well, apart from being terrified I'd squash him. But he hadn't even hesitated. It was like there was some invisible connection between us that just made everything feel... *right*. And that kiss. *Phew!* Every part of my body had been on fire, as if the temperature in the room had soared.

A huge sigh from the other side of the room pulled me back to earth. Some friend I was, lying here drooling over my boyfriend instead of talking to Annie about her and Joel. "So... any new developments in the Annie and Joel story?"

Annie sighed again. "Are you kidding me? After watching what you and Riley have been going through, I may swear off men for life."

"Hey, it's not like you and Joel would have to deal with the *fat-millionaire's-daughter-with-a-psycho-Mum-dating-the-hot-poor-guy* scenario. At least both yours' and Joel's families are relatively normal."

"Jesus, Katie, I hate it when you call yourself the fat girl. So you're not some skinny-arsed model... who cares? Besides, did you ever think Riley might not be interested if you were? And seriously, you know I'd kill to have your boobs. Wait... I'd kill to have *any* boobs. Having *yours* would be like winning the lottery."

I snorted—*yeah, again.* "Trust me... having big boobs is over-rated. I'm terrified I'll get two black eyes if I break into a trot. And let's not even *mention* the thought of me going bra-less. Oh, and nice attempt at deflection, by the way. I seem to recall we were talking about Joel?"

Annie blushed and rolled onto her back, staring up at the ceiling. "Yeah, okay, I do really like him. He apologised for acting like such a dork before the ball and said he had some personal stuff he was dealing with. But I still have no idea whether he feels the same way I do. Besides, we've become really good friends, and I'm not sure I want to risk losing that."

"Yeah, I get it. But I still think you guys would be *so* good together."

Annie shrugged and sighed again. "Oh well… guess we'll never know. Unless, by some miracle, Joel feels the same way and gets up the guts to do something about it."

"Hey… personally, I've always been a big believer in miracles."

<h1 style="text-align:center">Chapter Twenty-Nine</h1>

Katie

I woke up Thursday morning to a text message blinking on my phone. Rolling over with a smile, my heart fluttered at the thought of reading another one of the cheesy good-morning messages Riley had started sending me.

My smile froze as I read the text, my heart sinking to my toes. The message was from Riley, but it wasn't what I'd expected. It had been sent at 2.30 am.

Hey babe... I'm so sorry, but something has come up at home and I need to deal with it. I don't know how long it will take to sort it out, but I'll do everything I can to be back by Saturday morning. Missing you already xxxxx

My stomach twisted, a feeling of dread washing over

me. Riley had gone home? *Something had come up? Seriously?* He'd used the oldest line in the book of excuses for how-to-get-out-of-something-I-don't-want-to-do. Was there really an emergency at home, or had he just decided I wasn't worth the crap he'd have to go through on the weekend? And if the emergency was real, why hadn't he talked to me about it?

I'd bared my soul to him, told him every ugly detail of my life, and I suddenly realised I knew absolutely nothing about his. All I knew was that he had a brother and a Mum. Now that I thought about it... he'd shared *nothing* about his past.

Damnit, here come the tears again...

"Message from lover-boy? Honestly, you guys are pathetic. You'll see each other in, like, an hour..." I hadn't even realised Annie had moved until I felt the side of the bed sink and a hand on my arm. "Oh no... Katie, what's happened?"

I handed Annie my phone, unable to meet my friend's eyes. Annie's breath came out in a loud whoosh.

"Damnit, Katie... you frightened the life out of me. I thought someone had died. Come on, I get that you'll miss him... but tears... seriously? It's only two days."

"What if he's changed his mind? What if he's running away? It's not like he hasn't done it before. And if there is an emergency, why didn't he tell me what happened?"

My eyes flew to Annie as she groaned, jumped off the bed, and started pacing the tiny amount of room between the bed and the door. Which meant she was practically walking in circles. I was getting dizzy just watching her.

She finally stopped, put her hands on her hips and glared at me. "Nope. I'm not buying it. Your idea of him running away, I mean. Damnit, Katie, I've watched you guys together for the last couple of weeks. Whether he realises it or not, Riley is head over heels in love with you. Seriously—he thinks the sun rises and sets around you. He would not leave you to face this weekend without him unless he had no other choice. What do you know about his home life? Anything you can think of that might have happened?"

"That's the thing. I don't know *anything* about Riley's home life. Except he was raised by his single Mum and has a brother."

Our eyes flew to the door at the sound of soft knocking. "Hey, it's me, Joel. Anyone awake?"

Annie opened the door before he'd even finished speaking. "Ssh, are you trying to wake the entire floor? Get in here before someone sees you."

"Sorry," Joel mumbled, shuffling in the door and looking around the small space for somewhere to stand. Annie sighed and pointed to her office chair.

"Have you spoken to Riley? Do you know what's going on?" Annie was like a drill sergeant. Poor Joel's shoulders slumped.

"No. I was hoping he might have spoken to you?" His eyes flicked to me, but he looked away before I could interpret the look in his eyes. Did he know something, or was he thinking what I'd thought... that Riley had chickened out and bailed?

Annie handed Joel the phone, and he read the text and

shrugged. "Pretty much what he told me, too. I'm a heavy sleeper, but he managed to wake me about 1 am and said he had to go home and deal with some family stuff."

"Did you believe him?" I whispered, focusing on picking at a loose thread on my blanket.

"C'mon Katie, I was half asleep. Not exactly a good time to try and analyse what was going on in his head. But he did seem pretty freaked out..."

Right... but was he freaked out about *his family emergency*, or the thought of sticking around to deal with my pathetic life? Even Joel wasn't rushing to his defence at my insinuation Riley had done a runner. Did he know more than he was telling us?

As if she'd read my mind, Annie moved to stand in front of Joel, feet apart and hands on hips. "Okay... spit it out, Kenny. What *aren't* you saying?"

Joel sighed and returned Annie's heated gaze. "Look, I honestly don't know any more than you do. *But*... I did overhear him arguing with someone on the phone the other night. I think it might have been his brother, and Riley was yelling at him, something about *taking some responsibility for once in his life*. That it was *his turn*. Riley never talks about his home life... it's always been one of those *off-limits* topics."

Annie sighed. "Okay. So it sounds like some serious stuff has been going down with his family. But I need to ask you something—as Riley's best friend. C'mon, you share a room with the guy. Do *you* think there's any chance he bailed because he's too gutless to tell Katie he can't go through with the visit to her parents?"

I held my breath as I watched Joel deliberate over Annie's question. The pause told me way more than his words ever could. He honestly had no idea. He was just as clueless about what was going on inside Riley's head as I was.

Joel rubbed the back of his neck and looked miserable. "Look. Just because I share a room with the guy doesn't mean we have heart-to-hearts about the meaning-of-life kinda stuff. That's a girl thing. But I do know he's a lot happier since he met Katie, way more than in the year I've known him. I just can't see him throwing that away... ya know? So yeah, I believe something happened, and he had no choice but to go home and deal with it."

Okay... so the jury was out. Except maybe in this case, Riley was guilty until proven innocent. Guess I'd know the truth soon enough.

Riley

I WAS LYING in bed awake, thinking about Katie—hey, when was I ever *not* thinking about Katie—when the text from Sean came in just before 1 am.

Mum tried to OD on pills. Mount Druitt Hospital. Come now!

It felt like all the air had been sucked out of the room.

How the hell had she gotten her hands on enough pills to overdose?

Wait... she *tried*... that meant she was still alive.

Shame washed over me as it registered that I wasn't as relieved she'd survived as I should have been. How many more times would I have to go through this?

Shit, what kind of son was I to have those thoughts when my mum had tried to kill herself? Horrified at my own selfishness, I pushed that particular self-analysis away for another time. I'd have plenty of time after I got to the hospital to indulge in the self-loathing session I deserved.

Diving out of bed, I threw some clothes into an overnight bag, wondering if trains even ran at that time of the night. Then, I wasted almost five minutes trying to wake Joel to tell him I was leaving. I planned to text Katie from the train station.

I had to wait almost two hours for the first train out of Central Station. Then, I spent the entire two-hour journey beating myself up for being such a lousy son. I stepped off the train at Mount Druitt station just on daylight.

No matter how I looked at everything that had happened, I kept coming back to the same conclusion... this was all my fault. I should have known Sean was incapable of overcoming his own selfish nature long enough to keep Mum on her meds. But then... was I really any better? I'd been so desperate to go to *Crescendo* that I'd ignored my gut instincts and run.

Swallowing down the unrelenting nausea, I pushed the doors to the ICU open and forced my feet toward the nurses' station. Hell, the only reason I was still functioning was thanks to the combination of adrenaline and caffeine pumping through my system.

I tried to get the attention of the young nurse on duty. She looked practically dead on her feet—about how I felt right then. "I'm looking for my mother... Irene Stone?"

"Oh...ummm, yeah... bed ten, around the corner on the left." She blushed and batted her eyelids, running her eyes over my body. *Seriously?* My mum was in the ICU, and the nurse was *flirting with me.* Where were the old, grey-haired, motherly-type matrons when I needed one?

I walked past the curtained beds until I came to bed ten. Sucking in a huge breath, I stepped through the curtains, groaning as my eyes fell on my mother, surrounded by beeping machines attached to fluid-filled tubes.

"Hey." I turned toward the soft, broken voice of my brother coming from a chair in the corner. Sean looked wrecked.

"Hey," I said, dropping into the empty chair beside him.

"I'm so sorry, man. I swear I was only out for a couple of hours. She must have lifted the key to the medicine cabinet from my jacket after dinner. I only left the damn jacket on the back of my chair for, like, twenty minutes max. It'd been so long since I'd seen her happy and chatty that I guess I let my guard down.

I went in to check on her before I went to bed, and... oh man... I'm so, so sorry... she's... she's in a coma. The doctors don't even know if she'll wake up. They pumped her stomach, but we don't know how long the drugs were in her system or what kind of damage they'd already done..." Sean dropped his face into his hands, his shoulders heaving as he let go of the emotions he must have been holding in check until I got there.

I knew I should be trying to comfort my brother, alleviating some of the guilt and telling him it wasn't his fault. But I just felt numb. All I could do was stare at Mum and wish I could somehow fix this.

Sean lifted his head, wiping away the tears with his sleeve. "It's okay… I get that you can never forgive me. I screwed up… like I always do. I'm supposed to be the big brother, the responsible one. She deserved so much better than me for a son."

"Sean… don't. This is just as much my fault as yours. I knew you weren't handling it, but I was too selfish to give up what I had and come back. I convinced myself it was my *turn* to enjoy life for a while. Going to *Crescendo* was like scoring a *get-out-of-jail-free* card. I guess I always knew it had a short expiry date. But I'm here now. I'll just need to go back and get the rest of my stuff, and I'll apply to defer until next year."

The thought of not seeing Katie's smiling face again— the one tattooed on my heart and brain—made my entire body ache. Maybe it was all for the best. I'd deliberately never told Katie anything about my mum's mental illness, or my home-life, for a reason. I couldn't stand to see the pity in her eyes. And then there was that deep, dark secret I tried never to think about. I'd done enough research on mental illness to know that it was often hereditary.

But the worst part was that I also knew Katie would think I'd bailed because of the situation with her family.

Maybe it would be easier to just let her believe that's what I'd done. But if I just disappeared *and* dropped out of the Academy, she'd know it was more than that. *Damnit...* I couldn't think about it anymore. I needed to focus on Mum, and by the looks of Sean, I'd need to help my brother survive the trauma, too.

Chapter Thirty

Riley

It was weird waking up on Friday morning back in my bed, in my old bedroom. I reached for my phone, surprised Katie or Joel hadn't tried to call or text me. My stomach dropped as I stared at the dead phone in my hands. *Yep, that'd explain it.* I jumped up and rifled through the bag I'd packed in the middle of the night, swearing when I realised I must have left my charger in my room back at the Academy.

I'd been so shattered the previous night, already suffering from sleep deprivation *before* spending the entire day at the hospital, and I'd passed out the minute I got home. But I *had* decided to tell Katie everything. I couldn't live with myself knowing she'd think I'd rejected her.

A quick look at the clock on my bedside table squashed any hope of having time to buy a new charger this morning. Sean and I were meeting the doctor treating Mum in less than an hour. I grabbed a change of clothes and dived into the shower. There'd be a public phone at the hospital. I'd ring Katie from—

Aww shit! Her number was saved on my phone. I'd never studied it long enough to commit the numbers to memory. Damnit... it was like whatever entities ruled the universe were conspiring against me. Either that, or they were nudging me toward my original idea... let Katie think I was just another jerk who didn't care about her enough to get past the obstacles.

But what would she do if she knew the truth? She had money... and she'd want to use it to fix my problems, put Mum in an expensive home, or hire a full-time nurse. But that would make me look just like Mark. *Not. Gonna. Happen.* I'd worked too hard to convince her I didn't care about her money. No way I would accept her help. I loved her too much to allow her doubts to creep back in.

I heard Sean moving around in the kitchen as I stepped out of the shower, dried myself and got dressed. Good, hopefully, he'd made coffee. At least Sean had a car, so we wouldn't have to use public transport to get to the hospital. And I could throw down my coffee on the way.

"Hey man... ready to go?" Sean nodded to the coffee sitting on the bench-top, chuckling as I groaned over my first sip. My brother looked a lot better than he had when I'd first arrived at the hospital.

We'd spent hours sitting beside Mum's bed, talking about random memories of growing up. Even though it had been years since we'd spent that much time together, I was surprised by the depth of the bond that still existed between us. It was almost cathartic talking about the pressure of dealing with Mum's illness.

By the time we'd driven home from the hospital in comfortable silence, we'd done more than forgive each other for letting our mother down. We'd accepted that we'd both done the best we could, in a situation that should never have been the responsibility of a couple of kids. There was nothing we could have done differently to change the outcome.

We arrived at the hospital with ten minutes to spare, so Sean stopped to get us coffee from the vending machine while I headed to the ICU. I stood beside Mum's bed, watching her chest continue to rise and fall only because the machine beside her told it to. She looked exactly the same as when we'd left the previous night.

"Here you go, bro." Sean handed me a coffee and sat beside the bed in one of the butt-numbing chairs.

"Good morning... I'm Dr Martin." I turned to find a grey-haired man in a white coat standing behind me.

"Hey, Doc. I'm Riley, and this is my brother Sean."

"Yes, Irene's sons, right?"

We nodded, both keeping our eyes glued to the doctor's face.

"I'm afraid I don't have good news, boys. Your mother is currently on life-support due to her brain being deprived of oxygen for too long. The tests we've run show minimal neural function..."

I stopped listening when the doctor started to ramble about medical terms and survival rates. Why did doctors always feel they needed to do that? Was it to show the patient's family they knew all the correct terminology, or designed to ease the family into understanding the bottom line?

Sean's voice pulled my attention back to the room. "Sorry, Doc, but that all sounded a bit like Swahili. Could you give us the English version?"

Yeah... what he said.

"Basically, your mum's body is shutting down. I'm sorry, but she won't be coming back from this."

"H-how long?" Sean's voice shook.

"Every case is different. But I'd say sometime in the next week."

My legs had gone to jelly, my brain telling me it was time to brave the butt-numbing chair beside Sean. So, Mum had finally got what she wanted. It was over. I swallowed down the bile rising into my throat as the self-loathing kicked back in.

How dare I be feeling relief?

This was my mother!

What kind of a monster was I?

I sat beside Sean for the next hour, neither of us talking, each lost in fighting our own inner demons. I wondered if Sean was feeling the same relief warring with the gut-wrenching guilt wracking my body.

Sean stood and dropped his hand on my shoulder. "Come on. I think it's time we had a break. I don't know about you, but I could do with a very large bottle of Jack about now."

I'd never been much of a drinker; I could take it or leave it at the best of times. But maybe talking to my older brother over a couple of drinks might help me deal with the relentless freak show playing out in my brain.

Katie

WHEN I STILL HADN'T HEARD FROM Riley by Friday afternoon, I was convinced he'd decided I wasn't worth the effort. Yep, he'd opted for *exit-stage-left, head-for-the-hills, get-the-heck-outta-Dodge*, or one of those equally corny clichés. I'd skipped my last class and taken some time out to sort through the maelstrom of emotions whirling around in my brain.

I was mortified by the fact that I'd texted and tried to call him enough times over the last two days to qualify as a stalker. Then there was the crying, ranting, begging, and praying to whatever godly entity might be listening. But none of it had changed a thing. It was time to let Riley go and move on.

The worst part was that I couldn't really blame him. I should never have accepted his offer to go home with me in the first place. I didn't need anyone's help confronting my mother.

Okay, so now I'd accepted the whole goodbye-Riley-thing—*yeah, right, like that was ever gonna happen*—I needed to focus on my game plan for the weekend.

In the rare moments I hadn't been obsessed with thoughts of Riley, I'd spent some time replaying past events with Mum, viewing them from an entirely different perspective. How could I have not noticed how cruel and manipulative my mother was? I suddenly realised I'd been walking around wearing rose-coloured glasses my whole life. Mum had been sabotaging my self-esteem long before Mark came into the picture. There were so many memories I could now see in a whole different light.

Like the destruction of my dreams of becoming a prima ballerina when I was eight. Mum had insisted the costumes for my end-of-year ballet concert be changed because they 'made her little girl look fat'. The other girls had all loved the costumes—*hey,* I'd *loved them*—and blamed me for having to wear the baggy new ones. Mum had pulled me out of ballet classes the following year, sprouting something about protecting me from the other girls' nasty, snobby comments. That was the same year Dad had set up the 'secret nest egg'. *Coincidence much?*

Then there were the never-ending veiled insults—too many to count.

No darling, you don't want that *dress. I know it's lovely. But frills just make big girls look bigger. Plain colours look best on you.*

Oh, Katie. Those jeans are looking tight. Do we really *need to go shopping for a bigger size?*

Oh, and the comments I'd overheard Mum make to Dad when she didn't know I was listening.

You know we can't have fattening food like that in the house; it's not fair to tempt Katie, and I don't want her sneaking food.

Maybe we should holiday somewhere away from the beach this year. Katie in a swimsuit is not her best look.

She'd always managed to word it as if she *cared* about me and how I looked. *What a load of frog-shit.* The only thing Mum had ever cared about was how her daughter's ugliness affected her social image. *What kind of Mother did that?*

... and then there was Daddy. He'd set up the trust fund just after the ballet fiasco. Why would he do that? What kind of hold did she have on him that he couldn't just call Mum out on her superficial lies? None of it made any sense. I'd never had any doubt my Father loved me. So why hadn't he stopped her?

Wait... a memory of an argument I'd overheard just before I left for Crescendo popped into my head.

Dad: Please, Olivia, she's miserable. You've had four months, and it's made no difference. Let her start at Crescendo with Annie.

Mum: So, as usual, you're putting her wants and needs before mine. Why am I not surprised?

Dad: You know that's not true... I've tried everything to make up for—

Mum: Do not even speak those words. Katie needs to be fixed before I can allow her to go back out into the world. As if it wasn't bad enough already, but this incident with the boy...? How am I supposed to deal with the fallout of that?

My face flamed with a mixture of anger and embarrassment. I'd been too busy wallowing in my own personal pity party to notice the pained tone in my Dad's voice. He knew what she was doing... and had let it continue.

"Hey, roomie... how ya doin'? I'm glad to see your head hasn't exploded... yet. Is it safe to enter the war zone?" Annie stood in the doorway, one eyebrow raised, her eyes searching mine for an indication of my mood.

I managed a half smile. "War zone? I'm the only one here."

"Yeah, but the internal battle could still have some serious fallout. I'm not a big fan of brain matter splattered on the walls..."

I laughed, feeling some of the suffocating tension leave my body. At least I still had Annie's slightly wacky view of the world to keep me grounded.

"So... still nothing?" Annie nodded to the phone sitting in my lap. I shook my head, biting my lip to stop the tears from starting again.

"I still think we're missing something. Maybe he lost his phone on his way home?" Annie shrugged at my eye roll. "Well... it does happen..."

I sighed and put my phone on the bedside table. No point waiting for a call that was never coming. "Anyway, I've been thinking—"

"Always dangerous—"

"Haha... I'm letting you and Joel off the hook this weekend. I'm a big girl, and I don't need—"

"Stop right now. I understand that you're going through a lot of heavy stuff at the moment, but un-inviting your friends to a weekend away is just plain rude. C'mon, Katie, Joel's been packed and ready to go for two days. It's not every day he gets to spend the weekend staying in a pool house at some mansion. Plus, *I* have a few words to say to your Mum, and I'm not missing out on saying them because you decided never to speak to her again after this! So, what time does the ferry leave tomorrow morning?"

I laughed and climbed off the bed, throwing my arms around my best friend. "Fine. The ferry leaves at 9 am. But if—"

"Nope. Not listening. Joel may have been packed for two days, but I haven't even *thought* about what I'm taking. Come on, neither have you. Something tells me this will be a weekend we'll never forget.

Chapter Thirty-One

Riley

I sat across the kitchen table from my older brother, swishing the amber liquid in its glass tumbler, the same drink I'd been nursing for the last hour. Even the thought of getting rip-snorting drunk didn't dull the pain in my chest. My emotions had been in such raging turmoil over the previous forty-eight hours I couldn't think. Just breathing had become a chore.

And I missed Katie more than I'd ever have thought possible.

Sean leaned forward, resting his arms on the table. "So, what else is going on in that head of yours, bro? And don't even *try* telling me you don't know what I'm talking about. You literally *reek* of a guy suffering from girl troubles."

I grunted and looked up at Sean, wondering if I should tell him about everything that had happened. It had been a long time since I'd asked my big brother for advice. We'd been close once… before the pressure of our mother's illness had driven us apart. Maybe it wasn't too late to repair our friendship.

"Yeah, there's a girl. But I'm pretty sure I've totally screwed it up."

"Ya know. My mates tell me I'm a pretty good listener. I know I've been a total failure as far as big brothers go, but sometimes it helps to get an outsider's point of view. I mean, if you feel like talking about it."

I shrugged and ran my hands through my hair. Sean was offering an olive branch, and he seemed to genuinely want to mend the fences between us. *Aww, heck, why not? Maybe Sean could come up with something I hadn't thought of.*

I started to talk, surprised by the way the whole story poured out of me. I told Sean everything that had happened since I met Katie, right up to where I'd left without telling her anything about my family, and not contacted her since.

"Are you serious right now? She's the daughter of a freakin' millionaire? And you're totally in love with this girl? Aww man… no wonder you look like death warmed up."

I nodded miserably, taking a large swig of the drink I'd been avoiding.

Sean scratched his head. "Okay, so I get that you were going to give up your girl and your dreams when you thought you'd have to move home and look after Mum again. But that's all changed. Mum's not…" his voice broke, and he looked like he was fighting tears.

"Seriously, Rye, you deserve to be happy. This girl… Katie… sounds like she's *the one*. And you're gonna walk away and let her think you didn't want to fight for her? Over some stupid shit with her parents? Come on, man… you're better than that! Hey, I've spent the last five years feeling like a lousy failure, wishing I could be strong and responsible like you. You're not the type to promise to be there for someone you love and then let them down. You need to get your sorry arse back to that school and tell her everything."

"How am I supposed to do that, huh? Mum is lying there in a hospital bed dying, remember? And what? I should just walk away? I'm not you, Sean. I can't just turn my back and hope it'll all go away."

Sean flinched as if I'd hit him. But it was the truth, and I'd bitten back those words for years. "Yeah, fair enough. I deserved that. And I know it's probably too little too late. But both of us sitting at the hospital all day, every day, for the next however many days, is not going to change the outcome. It's not like Mum's gonna wake up and ask where you are.

Ya know, I was a lot older than you when Mum got sick, and I spent a lot of years being angry about how much she changed. Maybe that had a lot to do with why I had to get out of here. But the Mum I remember from when we were little would have wanted you to be happy. Go do what you need to do. Your girl needs you. I'll stay with Mum… I got nowhere else I need to be. And it's time I stepped up and acted like the big brother for a change."

I stared at my brother as if he'd handed me the key to the Gates of Heaven. Sean was right. I'd spent years doing everything I could for Mum. Now, there was nothing more

I could do for her. But if I followed through with my promise to Katie to be there for her, it would change everything.

Maybe there was *still hope...*

Katie

I DROPPED my head onto my arms where they rested on the outside rail of the ferry, my heart shattering into a million pieces as we pulled away from Circular Quay. Until that moment, I'd clung to a last tiny shred of hope that Riley would turn up at the last minute, pull me into his arms, and tell me why he'd left. Big fat tears rolled down my face as I finally accepted what I'd suspected all along. Riley had walked away. It was over. And when he came back to *Crescendo*, we'd be nothing more than *acquaintances.*

Dear God. How was I supposed to act normal around him? Yes, he was a selfish jerk for running away, instead of admitting he couldn't deal with facing my parents. But that didn't mean I could just stop loving the bastard. Riley's rejection had hurt a thousand times more than what Mark had done to me. Because I understood now that Mark had never held a piece of my heart. Being with Riley had made me feel beautiful and special. But it was over... and I needed to deal with it and move on.

"Hey... you okay?" Annie's arm slid around my shoulder, pulling me against her in a side hug. "Aww shit, sorry.

Of course you're not okay. Why do people always ask such a dumb question when the answer is staring them in the face?"

I lifted my head and tried to smile at Annie's rambling attempt to cheer me up. Wiping away the tears, I rested my head on my friend's shoulder. "You're right... I'm not okay. I'm sad, and angry, and frustrated, and confused... and completely devastated. But I will be okay... won't I? I mean, I have to be *eventually*... right?"

"Yeah. You've survived worse."

"That's just it. I thought I had... but this is... damnit, this hurts more than I ever thought possible. It's like I've lost a part of me I didn't even know existed before..."

"I'm so sorry honey. I can't believe he did this either. I mean, I saw how he looked at you, and I'd have sworn he was totally in love with you too."

"Yeah, well, he sure proved us wrong, eh?"

"So... is this a private party? Or can anyone join in?" Joel stepped out of the doorway and moved to my other side, a hesitant smile on his face. "I know I'm a guy, which probably makes me on your hitlist right about now, but I come bearing gifts. Does that help?" He reached back inside the door and handed Annie and me each a coffee, before grabbing his own and returning to the railing.

I took a sip of coffee and sighed. "Okay... you're safe from extermination for now. But only because you supplied the caffeine."

"Look, I still think—"

Annie growled—a sound so like Riley's that it caused a stabbing pain in my chest. "If you so much as *try* to come up with an excuse for that dirtbag's behaviour, I will seriously pour this coffee over your head. Which means you'll *also* be guilty of depriving me of this much-needed caffeine fix."

I stared down at the white foam pushing against the side of the ferry as the boat ploughed through the sparkling blue water. Which was, of course, the exact colour of Riley's eyes when they gazed into mine.

I would be okay... eventually...wouldn't I?

Riley

Damnit. I was too late.

I dropped my head and planted my hands on my thighs, sucking in huge gulps of air as I watched the ferry gather speed, taking Katie away from me. I'd been so close... ten minutes earlier, and I'd have been holding her in my arms, telling her how much I loved her and why I'd had to go home.

Okay... what now? I didn't even know her address. I'd had it all planned when I set my alarm and climbed into bed the previous night. But thanks to bloody track-work on the line, the train had been late pulling into the station.

I knew if I went back to the Academy to grab my phone charger, I'd miss the next ferry as well. Besides, I didn't want to try and explain it all over the phone. I needed to do this in person and be there for her when she confronted her mum. Who could I ring that would know Katie's address?

Maybe if I rang the Academy and explained what had happened, they'd give me her address? Professor Haines seemed to know a lot about Katie. Wait... there *was* someone at the Academy who knew where Katie lived.

No way, I couldn't ask the mongrel who'd almost ruined Katie's life for help... could I?

Before I could talk myself out of it, I found a public phone, looked up the number for Crescendo, and entered it. A cheery voice answered the phone and asked how she could help me. I swallowed back the nausea rising in my throat and asked to speak to Mark Barnes.

"Hello, Mark Barnes speaking."

Act calm, and stop gritting your teeth. You need his help. "Hey Mark, this is Riley Stone. You probably don't even know who I am, but—"

"I know who you are. You're Katie's boyfriend. Why are you calling me?"

"Look, I don't have time to explain, but I need Katie's address."

A pause. "Why? Surely if she wanted you to have it, you would."

"I was supposed to be going home with her this weekend, but I had some family stuff to deal with and missed the ferry."

"So, do you really care about her, or are you just screwing with her? Because she—"

Okay, it was time to spit it out and hope Annie was right about this guy. "I love her, okay? And she needs me to be there for her this weekend. Shit... *I* need to be there for her..."

Another pause. "Fine. Have you got a pen?"

I breathed a sigh of relief and smiled for the first time that day. "Nope. But I have a good memory. Oh, and I'll need directions for how to get there after I get off the ferry."

Chapter Thirty-Two

Katie

My stomach was in knots as we walked up the long driveway to my house, the sound of Joel and Annie bantering fading into the background. I'd decided to hold off confronting my mother until Sunday, so at least my friends would get to enjoy their weekend before all hell broke loose. Because something told me I would *not* want to hang around after that.

"Whoa, Katie. This place is incredible. Pity your mum is such a bitch, or I'd seriously consider asking your parents to adopt me." Joel's eyes looked ready to pop out of his head.

Annie punched his shoulder and gave him a filthy look. "Seriously? You really needed to say that?"

Joel rubbed his arm and threw his other one around my shoulder. "Sorry, Katie, my bad. How ya holding up?"

I nudged Joel and smiled. "I'll survive. But another

crack like that, and *you* may not. Annie has a mean streak a mile wide."

We were almost at the door when it opened, and Dad stepped out. "Hey, sweetie. It's so good to see you. You have no idea how quiet this place has been without you." He pulled me into a bear hug, and I instantly found myself fighting back tears... again.

"Hey, Dad. Good to see you, too. This is Joel; he was Annie's buddy in the new scheme I told you about."

Joel stepped forward and held out his hand. I had to smile at the way he tried to hide the hero-worship in his eyes. "Pleased to meet you, Mr Simpson."

Dad smiled as he took Joel's hand. "You too, Joel. And please, call me Reece. Hey, Annie. Good to see you too, sweetheart. Well, come on in, everyone. Coffee's made, or there are cold drinks in the fridge."

I looked over at the four-car garage and noticed Mum's car was missing. "So, where's Mum?" I asked, dropping my bag in the entrance foyer and indicating to Annie and Joel to do the same. I tried to hide my relief at my mother's absence as we all moved toward the lounge room.

Dad's eyes clouded, his mouth tightening. But the smile was back before I'd even blinked. I wouldn't have noticed it if I hadn't been watching for his reaction. *How many more of those fleeting looks had I missed over the years?*

"Oh, yes. She... ummm... had a meeting she couldn't get out of. But she promised to be home in time for lunch. So... I thought we'd have a barbecue by the pool."

Yeah right. Couldn't get out of it, huh? More like she

organised it so she didn't have to spend too much time with her embarrassing daughter.

I smiled at Dad, wanting to erase the worried look in his eyes. How long had this tension been around, and I'd never even noticed? "Yeah, Dad, a barbecue sounds great. But first, did I hear the word coffee?"

Dad chuckled, all trace of his worry gone. "Well, I figured you'd be in need of a caffeine fix by the time you got here. Joel? Annie? You need a brew as well?"

Annie laughed and jumped up from the lounge. "You know it. How about I make them? I know where everything is and how everyone likes theirs. Come on, Joel, you can give me a hand." Annie grabbed Joel's shirt and dragged him toward the kitchen before anyone could speak.

I slipped off my shoes and relaxed into the soft lounge. It was good to be home and to spend some time alone with Dad.

"So, where's your buddy, sweetie? I thought he was coming too?" He tried to make it sound like a passing comment, but I knew he was watching me like a hawk. He always could read me like a book.

"Ummm... yeah... Riley had some stuff he had to deal with at home this weekend."

Well, at least it was the truth... according to Riley.

Damn it. Do. Not. Cry.

"Okay, these things happen, I guess. Are you okay, sweetie? You look exhausted. Maybe you shouldn't have pushed yourself—"

"No, Dad. I'm fine... honestly. It's just been a busy

week. Hey, did I tell you I got a part in the end-of-semester show?"

Dad's face lit up. "No, you didn't. That's wonderful Katie. What are you doing?"

"An excerpt from *Kiss Me Kate*. The show is a tribute to Cole Porter's music."

Oh yeah... and I have to kiss Riley... not as my boyfriend, or even my friend... but as my acquaintance.

"Well, I'm very proud of you. I'll look forward to the end of the semester for more than just the fact we'll have you home for a while."

"Make way... coffee incoming," Annie called as she came out of the kitchen. She looked flushed, her eyes sparkling as she crossed the room and placed the steaming cups on the coffee table. Joel bounced in behind her, a cheeky grin on his face.

Okaaay... what was going on? I couldn't wait to get Annie alone and find out what that was all about.

I was surprised by how quickly everyone relaxed, and we sat around talking and laughing about life at *Crescendo*. My heart ached at not having Riley there to be a part of it. I'd been so sure something special was developing between us. The conversation continued to flow around me, but I had no idea what they were saying. Cradling my coffee in my hands, my mind kept replaying our last kiss. There'd been no indication he'd had a change of heart. So, how could he have gone from *that* to running away? He'd been so caring and supportive when he'd heard about Mum's cruelty, and I'd hoped he'd fallen for me almost as badly as I had for him.

Wrong again, sucker.

"Katie? Honey? You okay?" The concern in Dad's voice pulled me from my thoughts.

I tried to paste a smile on my face. "Yeah, sorry. Just—" I jumped as the sound of the doorbell flooded the room.

Phew, saved by the bell... literally.

"Be back in a minute..." Dad said, his eyes promising this conversation wasn't over as he stood and went to answer the door. Damnit, I needed to come up with a good reason for acting like a wet blanket. The less Dad knew about the Riley situation, the better.

Dad cleared his voice, standing in the doorway to the lounge room and scratching his head. "Ummm... apparently, your buddy made it after all. Riley is outside, asking if he can speak to you alone for a minute. Is there something going on I should know about?"

I stared at Dad in a stunned stupor, wondering if I'd heard him right. I *thought* he'd said Riley was here. Annie's squeal as she jumped up and pulled me off the lounge snapped me out of my frozen state.

Wait... Riley was here?

Outside?

How...?

What...?

"*Katie!* Will you please get your butt out there and talk to him." Annie hissed, giving me an *if-not-I'll-kick-said-butt* look.

Hope slammed into me as the reality of the situation sunk in. After a less-than-gentle shove from Annie, I moved toward the front door as if wading through molasses.

Riley was here... that was a good sign... right?
Please let it be a good sign.

Riley

I STOOD outside the front door of the mansion that was Katie's home and fought down the nausea. *Holy shit.* This place was like something out of a Hollywood movie. I wiped my sweaty palms on my jeans and focused on a mental image of Katie's beautiful, smiling face.

It didn't matter where she lived or how much money she had. This house no more represented *who* she was than my own sad excuse for a home did me. The girl I loved more than life itself was inside, and I just needed to work up the guts to ring the damn doorbell and have her back where she belonged... in my arms.

Sucking in a deep breath and holding it, I pushed the button outside the front door. My knees threatened to give out as a tall, good-looking man with salt and pepper hair answered the door.

Oh shit...

This was Katie's dad...

Reece freakin' Simpson.

Feeling like my head might explode, I slowly released the breath I'd been holding and stuck out my hand. "Good morning. I'm Riley Stone, Katie's buddy from school. Sorry I'm late; I had some family business to deal with."

Reece scanned me from head to foot, a scowl crossing his face.

Yep, here we go.

He's judging me on my looks.

Reece finally nodded and took my hand, searching my eyes for... something. I held his gaze, hoping mine conveyed my honesty to the man studying me. Man, it felt like he could see through to my soul.

"Yes, well. Come in Riley. We're just having coffee—"

"Ummm, sorry, sir. But I wondered if I might speak to Katie alone for a minute? I can wait out here..."

Reece's eyebrows rose, curiosity oozing from every pore.

Please just get Katie and let me do this without an audience.

Whatever Reece saw in my eyes must have satisfied him because he finally nodded again and took a step back. "Sure... I'll get her..."

I sagged in relief and wiped away the sweat trickling down the side of my face. Holy shit... I was on the verge of becoming a blithering idiot. I turned to admire the ocean view across the road, trying to pull myself together.

C'mon man. You only have one shot at this.

"R-Riley? Where the hell have you been? And how did you even know where I lived? I thought..."

There she was—my Katie. Hovering between angry, and sad, and hurt, and... maybe a bit happy to see me? My hands itched to reach out and pull her into my arms, but I was terrified she'd push me away and tell me to leave.

"Hey." My voice came out shaken and raspy. Clearing

my throat, I stuffed my twitching hands into my pockets. *Talking first, Stone...* "Katie, I'm so sorry. I promise I can explain everything. Can you please just give me a chance before you tell me to take a hike?"

Katie put her hands on her hips and tilted her head, as if trying to decide whether she should listen. "Fine. You have my undivided attention for two minutes. Aaand... go."

"Okay... so... my mum has a mental illness. She was diagnosed with Manic Depression when I was ten. The night I left, I got a text from my brother, Sean. It said Mum had tried to OD. It wasn't the first time she'd tried to kill herself, but it was the first time I hadn't been there to stop her." I ran my hands through my hair and sucked in a breath, pacing like a caged tiger as the words spewed from my mouth. "I was in such a hurry to pack that I left my phone charger in my room at *Crescendo*. So, of course, my phone died, and I didn't even have anyone's number to call. I've been at the hospital pretty much every minute since I left. I'm so sorry, babe. I know what you must have been thinking. That I bailed under pressure. But I would never do that to you... I couldn't. Because... well... *damnit*... I love you, Katie."

The most beautiful smile I'd ever seen spread across Katie's face. "Well, *that's* a relief. 'Cos I love you too, Riley Stone."

My heart leapt as Katie threw herself into my arms, pressing her sweet lips against mine. All the heartache and tension of the last few days slipped away at the feel of Katie back in my arms. *She felt so good.* How could I *ever* have imagined I could walk away from the best thing that ever happened to me?

This *was home.*

Being with Katie.

Nothing else mattered.

When we finally came up for air, I leaned my forehead against hers. "I missed you so much, baby. You were all I could think about while—"

"Why didn't you just tell me? I'd have gone with you. I hate the thought of you going through all this alone. How... how is your mum? Was she okay with you coming—"

"She's in a coma. She doesn't even know I left. She's... the... the doctor says she won't be waking up." My voice broke, the tears I'd held back for days rolling down my face. Damnit... it wasn't supposed to be like this. I'd wanted our reunion to be happy. I wasn't supposed to break down and turn into a blubbering mess. But the love in Katie's eyes was such a relief... and talking about Mum...

Kate brushed the tears away, cradling my face in her hands. "Oh, baby. I'm so sorry. You should have let me be there for you."

"You have no idea how much I wished I'd..." The floodgates opened, huge ugly sobs wracking my chest. Katie just held me, rubbing small circles on my back and whispering comforting words. She sat down on the verandah and pulled me down beside her, holding my head against her chest, allowing me to release all the pain and fear I'd kept buried for so long.

"Have the doctors given you any idea how long your mum has left?" Katie asked softly against my ear.

I sucked in a couple of deep breaths and pulled myself together. I looked up into Katie's beautiful green eyes, humbled by the love pouring from them. "Yeah. A week... max."

"Oh no, Riley. I'm so sorry. What are you doing here then? You should be—"

I put a finger to her sweet lips, pressing a kiss against her forehead. "I'm right where I need to be. Sean is there with her. I kinda told him all about you, and he told me he'd kick my sorry arse if I didn't come fix things with you. I missed the ferry you were on by, like, five minutes."

"Wait... how did you even know where I lived?"

Rubbing the back of my neck, I gave her a sheepish grin. "You don't wanna know—"

"Riley Stone. What did you do?"

"I rang the Academy and spoke to Mark Barnes."

All the colour drained from Katie's face. "You what?" she hissed.

"Hang on. Before you go all *feral-Katie* on me. Mark was nothing like what I was expecting. He totally grilled me about *why* I needed your address. I had to tell him I was... *ahem*... in love with you, before he'd even think about giving it up. I think maybe Annie was right about him being sorry."

"Wait... wait... you told *Mark Barnes* you were *in love with me*?"

I chuckled, my face starting to burn. "Hey... I'd have shouted it to the world if it meant I could get to you. This was *not* a conversation I wanted to have over the phone." I shrugged, rubbing my thumb over her hand. "Besides, you needed me to be here... so here I am. Better late than never, right?"

Katie's eyes widened at my declaration, and she pulled me in for another soul-searing kiss. I wanted time to stop and for the world to disappear. Kissing my Katie had become my favourite thing in the whole world.

"Excuse me. What on earth is going on here? Get your hands off my daughter." The angry female voice was followed by the sound of a car door slamming. *Shit, shit, shit.* I hadn't even heard the car pull into the driveway. Katie froze in my arms, leaving no doubt in my mind that the perfectly dressed and coiffured woman marching toward us was Katie's Mum, Olivia Simpson.

Chapter Thirty-Three

Katie

Unbelievable!

My heart lurched, the sound of my mother's angry voice sending shivers down my spine. Great... so much for introducing Riley as my *buddy* from *Crescendo*. Now all the bullshit would start, and I'd—

But then the new, confident Katie—*Riley's Katie*—reminded me I didn't care what this woman thought any more. I bit back the words begging to leave my mouth, the ones that told my mother she no longer had the right to judge what I did. But I'd vowed to keep things amicable until tomorrow. Somehow, I just needed to pretend to play the game for another twenty-four hours.

I almost giggled as a soft growl erupted from Riley's chest. Maybe this confrontation wasn't going to wait after all. He stood up, reaching for my hand as we waited for my mother to reach us. With a huge smile on his face, he stuck out his hand toward my mother. "Hello, Mrs Simpson. I'm Riley, Katie's boyfriend. Pleased to meet you."

A giggle burst out at the shocked look on Mum's face. This was priceless. It was the first time in my entire life I'd seen my mother speechless. Shooting us a scathing look, she ignored Riley's hand and pushed past us through the door.

"We'll see about that," she muttered as she disappeared through the door.

I threw my arms around Riley's neck. "I can't believe you did that."

"Too much too soon?" His wicked smile was dimmed by the uncertainty in his baby-blue eyes.

"Perfect." I brushed a kiss across his lips. "But I think it might be time to enter the lion's den. You up for this?"

"Bring. It. On." Riley wrapped his arm around my waist, kissing the tip of my nose as we went in the door.

I could hear my mother's ranting voice before we even reached the lounge room. Riley's arm squeezed my waist, and we entered the lounge room both wearing goofy smiles.

"Well? Are you going to do something about this?" Mum's eyes were shooting daggers at my Dad. I swallowed and prepared for the onslaught.

I almost fell over when Dad stood and moved toward us, a relieved smile on his face. "I certainly am. Hello again, Riley. I'm guessing you're responsible for the beaming smile on my daughter's face? I'm so glad you made it. I was dreading spending the weekend with the miserable Katie who arrived earlier. Come and join us. Coffee?"

"Reece? Are you serious? We don't know anything about this boy. He could be—"

Dad shot her a murderous look. "In love with Katie? I think you may be right. What else could we possibly need to know about him?"

I almost choked as I watched my mother's face contort with rage. The woman was actually speechless for the second time in one day. *Wow. This weekend was looking better every minute.*

Dad threw me a loving smile. "Katie? Why don't you take the boys to the pool house and get them settled in? You and Annie can take your bags to the guest bedroom later."

Annie and Joel shot to their feet, looking so relieved to escape the tension I almost laughed. Throwing an arm around Dad's neck, I kissed him on the cheek, whispering a soft *thank you*. Riley kept a tight grip on my hand as we headed toward the foyer to grab the boys' bags, almost tripping over each other in our haste to be anywhere but here.

I SNUGGLED UP beside Riley on the lounge in the pool-house and let out a contented sigh. He was telling Annie and Joel everything that had happened since he received the text about his mum on Wednesday night. By the time he'd finished, both Annie and I had big, fat tears rolling down our faces.

Annie jumped up and wrapped Riley in a huge hug. "Oh, Riley, I'm *so* sorry." He just nodded and hugged her back.

Even Joel had tears in his eyes. "Man... that totally sucks. Why didn't you ever tell me you were going through that kind of shit?"

Riley shrugged and pulled me a little closer. "Maybe because I was a stupid jerk who thought people would judge me. Until someone amazing came into my life, and I realised it didn't matter." My heart fluttered as he kissed the top of my head.

Annie sighed and cleared her throat. "Okay. I can't hold it in any longer. I just have to say *I told you so* about Mark. Who'd have thought the douche from hell would help you two be together, eh?"

I bit my lip and nodded. "Yeah, I guess it wouldn't hurt to at least listen to what he has to say next time I see him."

Joel jumped to his feet and slapped his hands against his thighs. "Right. Enough of this maudlin shit. We are sitting in a freakin' pool-house, at a mansion, with a pool right outside the door. And I have no intention of wasting another minute. Who's up for a swim?"

Annie clapped her hands and jumped up beside him. "Lucky I decided to put my swimmers on under my clothes this morning. 'Cos the thought of going back inside to grab my bag..." She shuddered, and we all laughed.

Riley squeezed my hand and looked down into my eyes. "How about we meet you out there? I need a bit of alone time with my girl."

Annie put her hands on her hips, but her eyes were dancing with mischief. "Fine. You've got five minutes. *Please don't make me have to come get you.* Come on Kenny, that pool is looking pretty good about now." She winked as she turned and left, Joel scratching his head and muttering under his breath as he followed her out.

Riley grinned and pulled me into his lap. "You know what? I got the feeling your dad has had enough of your mum's bullshit as well. Looks like we might have an unexpected ally in our corner."

Katie's lips curled into a cheeky grin. "*You* know what? I couldn't care less what *anybody* thinks about us being together. As long as we *are* together. From now on, *your* problems are *my* problems, and vice-versa. No more secrets. We'll take on whatever the universe throws at us and hope for the best. I love you Riley Stone... and I *trust* you one hundred percent."

"I love you too, beautiful girl. Now, can you please stop talking and *Kiss me, Katie?*

Epilogue

Seven Weeks Later...

Riley

Standing in the foyer of the auditorium at the *Crescendo* Academy of Performing Arts, one arm wrapped firmly around Katie's waist, I smiled and thanked the parents, students, and staff congratulating us on our final performance in the end-of-semester show. To be honest, I was still reeling from the standing ovation we'd received. My life had turned so many corners in the past ten weeks, and I wouldn't have changed any of it.

Katie had stood between Sean and me at Mum's funeral, propping us up and supporting us through the grieving process. She was the most incredible person I'd ever met. She and Annie had insisted on organising the wake for the few people who'd attended, flitting around and playing the roles of hostesses like they'd been born to it.

Annie, in her usual *this-is-way-too-serious-and-you-need-to-cheer-up* way, had suggested she and Katie wear cute little maid's outfits. After we'd all cracked up laughing, I'd firmly declined her gracious offer. Although, I must admit, picturing Katie in one of those outfits as she moved around the room helped me survive the ordeal.

After everyone had left, Joel, Annie, Katie, Sean and I sat around the kitchen table, chatting and sharing a few drinks. I don't know how I'd have survived it without the love and support of the people at that table.

"There's my baby girl. I am *so* proud of you, honey." Reece Simpson's jovial voice jolted me out of my maudlin thoughts. He pulled Katie in for a hug and then turned to me. "And Riley, nice work son. Although that kiss may have been a bit... well, let's go with *long*." He winked as he shook my hand. Knowing how much I loved his daughter, and she loved me, he'd welcomed me into the family with open arms... so to speak.

So much had changed since that first awkward weekend at Katie's. Turns out Katie's Mum had been suffering from undiagnosed depression for years. Unbeknownst to Katie, Olivia had been pregnant and miscarried when Katie was just over a year old, and the doctors had told her she couldn't have any more children. Believing herself a failure, she'd made it her life's mission to never fail at anything again. She'd viewed Katie's weight problem as another one of her failures as a mother, and Katie had paid the price.

Anyway, long story short—Olivia was now on medication, and the relationship between Katie and her Mum was improving. In fact, Katie and I were spending the two-week break between semesters at their house. Of course, I was staying in the pool-house, but Katie had mastered the art of sneaking in and out of the house long ago.

Joel nudged my shoulder as he slunk up beside me. "So... this being a 'celebrity' thing has its rewards. I've never had so many hot girls interested in getting-to-know-me-better." But no matter what words were coming out of his mouth, he couldn't hide that he only had eyes for Annie. Who, I couldn't help noticing, was currently standing *very* close to Mikey Everett, looking up into his eyes and giggling at something he'd said. I almost cracked up laughing when, just as I was about to look away, I caught her sneaking a glance at Joel.

These two were absolutely hopeless.

A pair of arms slipped around my waist from behind, followed by a warm, sexy voice in my ear. "Ummm... you ready to get out of here? I believe there's a lounge in the Year-Eleven common room with our name on it."

I spun around and pulled her against me. "Hell yeah. But I think it might be best if we sneak away. I am *so* not waiting for all the long-winded goodbyes."

She giggled. "Well, Dad's already gone, so I think we might get away with it. Maybe if we leave separately? So it looks like we're just going to the bathroom?"

"Fine. I'll give you a two-minute head-start."

"Make it one minute." She winked, giggling as she turned and—*knowing I'd be watching her*—swung her sexy butt all the way to the stairs.

She was so gorgeous...

... and smart,

... and feisty
... and funny
and mine.

Stuff it; a minute was way too long to wait. I needed to wrap my girl in my arms and kiss her, long and slow, right *now!*

To use an old cliché... *I couldn't wait another minute...*

~The End~

About the Author

Thank you so much for reading Kiss Me Katie. I hope you enjoyed reading it as much as I did writing it. I hope to get the time to write and release a second book based at Crescendo Academy, picking up where we left off in the story of Annie and Joel.

I'd love you to visit my website and sign up for my newsletter so you're kept in the know about further updates and release dates at:

jenniferredmile.com

P.S. I'd be forever grateful if you'd consider leaving a review on Amazon.

www.ingramcontent.com/pod-product-compliance
Lightning Source LLC
Chambersburg PA
CBHW020649120726
47906CB00001B/191